"*Jillian vs Parasite Planet* is a thrilling middle-grade sci-fi novel, with a plucky and ingenious hero who never gives up, and an A.I. partner we all wish we could have."
—Samantha M. Clark, author of *The Boy, the Boat, and the Beast*

"Huzzah! Great space fun (with a lot of ick thrown in as well)."
—Jane Yolen, author of *Owl Moon* and *The Midnight Circus*

"*The Martian* for kids—a fun yet surprisingly gritty story of resourcefulness and survival in the wilds of outer space."
—Sophia McDougall, author of *Mars Evacuees*

"Action, science, and creepy crawly creatures. This is everything I ever wanted in an all-ages space adventure."
—Landry Walker, author of *Star Wars Adventures*

"With fantastic worldbuilding, a hero you can't help but root for, and the best sidekick this side of the galaxy, this engaging, inventive tale of survival will leave readers turning pages."
—Katie Slivensky, author of *The Countdown Conspiracy*

"Not many books have worms. This one does. It's a romp. It's a space romp. It's a romping story in which food is mentioned, and there are worms, and a neat kid who's realer than some kids you meet in books."
—Daniel Pinkwater, author of *Adventures of a Dwergish Girl*

"A fast-paced story of survival—in the face of alien worms and your own anxieties—with a hero kids will relate to and a robot sidekick they'll wish they could take to school!"
—Gareth Wronski, author of *Holly Farb and the Princess of the Galaxy*

Also by the Author

Archivist Wasp series
Archivist Wasp (2015)
Latchkey (2018)

Novels
Desideria (2008)
Firebreak (2021)

JILLIAN
VS
PARASITE PLANET

NICOLE
KORNHER-STACE

TACHYON
SAN FRANCISCO

Cover art and interior illustrations copyright © 2021 by Scott Brown
Interior design by Elizabeth Story
Author illustration by Elizabeth Story

Tachyon Publications LLC
1459 18th Street #139
San Francisco, CA 94107
415.285.5615
www.tachyonpublications.com
tachyon@tachyonpublications.com

Series Editor: Jacob Weisman
Editor: Jaymee Goh

Print ISBN: 978-1-61696-354-5
Digital ISBN: 978-1-61696-355-2
Printed in the United States by Versa Press, Inc.

First Edition: 2021
9 8 7 6 5 4 3 2 1

For Julian, my biggest and most unexpected adventure

CHAPTER 1

Jillian had no idea what she expected a space-exploration facility to look like, but whatever it was, it wasn't this. For one thing, the StellaTech building looked like any other office building in the city, all metal and glass, nothing interesting about it. For another thing, it smelled like a hospital. It *looked* like a hospital, too, on the inside: all squeaky clean and white like the teeth in a toothpaste commercial. But the smell was what hit her first.

On a normal day, this would have brought back memories of when she had her tonsils out three years ago, or when she fell out of that tree last summer pretending she was exploring the underwater skyscrapers of old San Francisco. It would have made her palms sweat, her heart race. And it would absolutely, positively have made her want to run straight to the car and tell it to drive her back home.

But today was not a normal day. Today was the furthest possible thing from a normal day. Today was the closest she was ever going to get, in her whole entire eleven years of life, to an actual adventure.

Most of her friends from school thought Take Your Kid to Work Day was going to be boring. And for them, maybe that was true. Tara's mom was a dentist, Scott's dad owned a smart-clothing store, and both of Kyle's moms worked in advertising together. Angelique had the worst luck—her dad was the assistant principal. Jillian felt kind of bad for her, having to sit in the main office and do paperwork or something in an empty school.

But Jillian's parents weren't dentists or clothing store owners or advertising people or assistant principals. They were materials acquisitions surveyors for StellaTech, and today they were going to space.

Without her.

At least I'm here, she reminded herself for the millionth time that morning. *At least I'm finally here.*

And she reminded herself, also, of the plan.

Step one: finally go with her parents to StellaTech and see where all that sweet, sweet space magic happened. (*Obviously not* actual *magic*, she corrected herself, *but* close enough.)

Step two: be on her absolute, positive, one-hundred-percent best behavior. Do whatever her parents and the other StellaTech people asked of her with zero complaints. Even volunteer for extra work. For a solid month she'd been practicing saying things like, "Would you like me to bring you some coffee?" and "Let me help you with that" and "No, please, after you; I'll hold the door." Basically, make herself useful in any and every way possible.

Step three: by accomplishing step two, make her parents and the other StellaTech people realize how responsible and helpful and un-leave-behindable she really was. Specifically: how useful she'd be on an actual mission. In actual space.

Step four: not today, and probably not next year either, but someday, some distant Take Your Kid to Work Day sometime in her future, when she was old enough to be allowed to go to space, the StellaTech people would look at Jillian and say to themselves: *Here is a person who is ready.*

Here, now, after weeks of planning, Step One was finally a reality. Step Two started the second she set foot in the StellaTech building.

The pressure was doing wonders for her nerves. Her palms were sweating. She wiped them on her jeans.

Don't you screw this up, she told herself. *Don't you dare.*

"Don't worry, kid," her mom said over one shoulder as they walked across the lobby. Even without looking, she always knew when Jillian's anxiety was spiking up. Though she sometimes misunderstood the cause. "You'll do great."

Her doctor had explained anxiety to Jillian like this: that her brain saw threats that didn't exist. That it went straight to fight-or-flight when there was nothing there to fight or flee from. It felt like an itch in her brain, impossible to reach.

But to say *why* her anxiety was spiking up now would be to give away the plan. The last thing Jillian wanted was for her parents to give her that *look*. The one that meant she was asking for something they'd love to give her, but was simply impossible. She'd gotten the *look* when she'd begged for a puppy last Christmas ("not allowed in the apartment"), and when she'd asked to be homeschooled ("logistically impossible"), and when she'd planned out a whole camping trip last fall, outside of the city and in the actual real-live wilderness upstate . . . and then her parents had been called into work last minute because the scheduled survey team had caught the flu.

She didn't need to hear about how she was too young to go to space. She knew that. But since when did that stop her planning something out way, way, *way* in advance? It was how she kept her mind calm, her thoughts in order. Not only that, but it was fun.

Up until the point where that fight-or-flight thing had swept in to ruin everything for her.

"Shut up," Jillian whispered at her brain, out loud this time, but not so loud that anyone else would hear. She'd never been in the StellaTech facility before. She'd seen it in the documentary from last year, of course, just like everybody else, but watching it on a screen wasn't remotely the same as being there herself. It looked bigger, shinier, more intimidating. People walked into this place and walked out onto other planets orbiting other stars in other solar systems. Her *parents* did that. It was their job. Plan or no, it didn't really hit her until she was looking up at those same high ceilings, her sneakers squeaking on that same floor.

Materials Acquisitions Surveyor sounded like somebody had spent a week trying to think up the most boring-sounding name possible for a job that didn't actually sound boring at all. It actually sounded awesome. Her dad said they were like scientist-explorers. Her mom said they were more like treasure hunters, looking for usable resources on other planets. Earth had all been explored long ago already, even to the bottom of the sea in the early 2040s. That had showed up on Jillian's science tests every year since fourth grade. It had all been explored, and way too much of it had been used up. They needed to look somewhere else.

So her parents went on lots of work trips. The StellaTech documentary had taught everyone that while there were thousands of people working in the facility, only about thirty actually went to space, in teams of two to four, on five-day expeditions. Jillian already knew all this, of course, because her parents were two of those thirty explorers.

Her friends had lost their entire minds when they saw that little two-second shot of Jillian's parents in the documentary, but really all their fancy job meant for Jillian was that for one school week out of every six, Jillian had to stay with her Aunt Alex, who let her stay up late and eat whatever she wanted but wouldn't let her play video games.

Today was going to end just like all those other days—Jillian at Aunt Alex's—but everything up until that point was within her control. She could sulk and not be invited back next year. Be stuck on Earth forever, or at least until she was an adult and did whatever her parents had to do to get this job in the first place. Or she could take matters into her own hands.

She pictured herself handing space suits to her parents. Walking around with a clipboard. Making coffee for mission control. Waving goodbye as her mom and dad rode the quadpod through the portal onto another planet without her. And then going to Aunt Alex's for a week like usual. She even had a worksheet from school to fill out on what she learned today, which didn't seem fair at all. Her teacher had seen the StellaTech documentary just like everybody else.

Jillian could feel the not-being-able-to-go-to-space disappointment rising up in her. So she shoved it into a big box in the back of her mind, slammed the lid down, and sat on it. This was her chance. Her one chance. She wasn't going to let it go that easy.

She followed her parents across the lobby, shiny and white and huge like an airport terminal. They passed some uncomfortable-looking chairs and tables with fake flowers in vases and a fountain decorated with StellaTech's starry logo.

They stopped at a desk. A long line had already formed there. Other parents. Other kids. Other workers without kids. One by one, they stepped up to the desk so the receptionist could scan the ID badges implanted in their temples. Some workers had implants that were yellow glass squares, some orange, some red. Jillian's parents were the only workers in the line whose badges were blue.

"Visitors just get wristbands," her dad reassured her, noticing Jillian staring. "Nothing permanent."

What she got first, though, was a scan. It turned out to be nothing scary at all, just a silver dot on the end of the receptionist's index finger that beeped when she pointed it at Jillian's eyes.

Then Jillian had to put her hand into the front of a box

and keep it there for the count of *three*. On three there was a faint whirring and a click, and when she pulled her hand back out, there was a shiny blue stripe of *something* on her wrist, like it had been printed straight onto her skin.

"Hold it out toward me," the receptionist said. When she pointed the scanner at the band, words appeared, projected on the air just above her wrist. The letters were tiny but neat enough to read. The receptionist just glanced at them and nodded, satisfied.

Jillian held her wrist up to the light. The letters were much more visible from certain angles. She made out her name, her birthdate, and today's date and time. 04/28/2113, 09:32 AM.

Under that it read CLEARANCE LEVEL: BLUE.

Blue made sense, Jillian realized, thinking of the color of her parents' badges. *Clearance* was a word she'd heard only in movies, but seemed to mean *being allowed to know things*. Having the same level clearance as her parents felt like a good sign for steps Two through Four of her plan.

Her dad caught her smiling. "You're doing great," he said. "Sorry about the long line."

"No problem," Jillian said in her best fellow-scientist-and-colleague voice. "It happens."

"Better than school, huh?" her mom asked, elbowing her playfully.

"No giant portals to space in school," Jillian said. "So that's a definite yes."

They led her out of the lobby and onto a moving floor that relayed them down a sparkling white hallway. On the walls were photos of landscapes like Jillian had seen at doctor's offices and hotels. Except these landscapes were all labeled with the planets they came from, and none of them were Earth.

Jillian squinted to read them as she walked past.

82 Eridani b.

Gliese 832 e.

Kepler 16 b.

Even at the names, dry and boring-sounding as they were, a shiver went down her spine. These pictures were taken in space. By people like her parents, or robots or smart cameras that had gone to space with them. For all she knew, her parents might have *taken* some of them.

The photo of Saturn's moon Enceladus brought her up short. It looked like the world's greatest snow day—white as far as the eye could see—up until the starry black horizon, with Saturn's rings in the background.

Jillian's parents noticed she wasn't following them anymore and doubled back to stand with her. "Pretty, huh?" her dad said.

Jillian could only nod. "Did you take any of these?" she asked when she got her words back.

"None of these ones," her mom said. "One of our shots from Proxima Centauri b made it into the documentary, but you've seen it. That's the one we have framed above the couch at home."

"Where are you going today?" Jillian asked, although standing here, looking at these photos, she knew it might only hurt more to know. She cleared her throat, removing any traces of whininess. Curious was good. Inquisitive. Studious. "On your mission?"

"80 UMa c," her mom said. "It orbits Alcor in the Big Dipper. Alcor and Mizar are a binary star system, which means—"

"Double," Jillian rushed to say. "They have a shared orbit."

"Of course you'd know that," her mom said. "Sorry."

"What's the UMa in the designation, then, smart guy?" her dad asked jokingly.

Jillian thought for a second, but only a second. "Ursa Major," she said. "The Big Dipper is part of it." She grinned. "Too easy. Give me a hard one."

"Oh, I like to think we have some challenges in store for you," her mom said. "Don't you fret. Now come on. Take Your Kid to Work Day Rule Number One: Get Your Kid to Work on Time."

At the end of the hall there was a bank of elevators. Jillian followed her parents into one. "Hold your wristband up," her dad said. "Let the elevator scan you."

"More scans?" Jillian asked, then immediately wished she hadn't, because she didn't know if it sounded like complaining. "I mean, it doesn't bother me," she added, holding her wrist up extra-still. "I just want to know everything about how this place works."

"We know you do," her dad said. "You've been waiting ages for this. We know you've been excited. Do you want to press the button?"

It took Jillian a second to realize he meant the button for the elevator. Part of her wanted to say that stopped being exciting when she was about five years old, but the rest of her refused to say that out loud. "Sure," she said. "Which floor?"

"First basement."

This struck her as weird. For some reason when she'd pictured her parents' lab, Jillian had expected something like in a movie, all glass and chrome and light-up panels, and an amazing view through full-wall windows on the fiftieth or whatever floor. What she hadn't pictured was a basement. But she pressed the button all the same.

"Those other kids we saw upstairs," she said as the doors shut and the elevator started to move. "Do *they* get to go to space?"

Both her parents shook their heads. "Only Materials Acquisitions people go to space," her mom said. "Those kids' parents are in other departments. I know at least one of them worked on that documentary you saw. Maybe her kid will learn about that today."

The elevator stopped, the doors whisking open. Where they were looked nothing like where they'd come from. It was a basement, all right. It looked like the basement of her school. Utility closets. A water fountain. A restroom. Where was the space stuff?

The hall funneled them through a security checkpoint, where Jillian's wristband and her parents' chips got scanned yet again—this time by a pair of armed guards. "Just an extra little check-in for the downstairs stuff," Jillian's mom told her as they continued down the hallway. "Like at the airport!"

Just when Jillian was beginning to think her whole day was going to be nothing but walking from one scanner to the next, her parents stopped at a door with a plaque beside it reading, ROOM 121: MATERIALS ACQUISITIONS.

In the doorway she paused, suddenly nervous again for no real reason except that this, all of this, was new. The fact that she'd wanted it—desperately—made no difference to her sweaty palms, her hammering pulse. She almost blurted out: *Is it dangerous in there?*, even though nobody had told her that it would be. But she didn't think space explorers would ask that kind of question, so she bit it back. What she heard herself say instead was, "So there's no other kids here?"

"Nope," her dad said. "Other departments."

"Which isn't to say you won't make new friends here," her mom said mysteriously. "You never know."

Room 121 was clean and white and smaller than Jillian had expected. Maybe the size of three or four classrooms stuck together. One whole side of it was a glass wall like a giant window, separating the main part of the room from a darkened area Jillian couldn't see into. In front of that were a bunch of chairs facing wide, flat screens. A man in a white coat like a doctor's coat was sitting in front of one. Things changed on the screen as he blinked at them.

From across the room Jillian couldn't see what was displayed on the screen. Columns of numbers scrolling past, it looked like. Some complicated-looking diagrams. A woman in an identical white coat came over and blinked at a few of the diagrams herself, nodded, and walked off. Then the diagrams vanished and were replaced by an image that looked like the framed landscape photos in the lobby upstairs.

A lot like Earth, but . . . not. The sky was too green, the dirt too orange. Spiky black rocks and strange plants like piles of purple feathers. Along the top edge of the image was a string of letters and numbers: 80 UMa c / 191.43 N / 27.88 W.

80 UMa c. That's where her parents were going.

And it wasn't a photo. It was a video. As Jillian watched, a breeze rustled one of the feather-plants, making it stretch out long violet fingers. They looked like they were reaching for something.

Jillian took a step forward to get a closer look. In an hour her parents might be standing in that frame. In a few years it might be her.

Her mom intercepted her. "Over here."

"Is that—"

"You'll see," her mom said, with the kind of voice she got when she had a really great surprise up her sleeve. "Come on."

Jillian gave the screen one more wistful glance. Then she followed her mom to a corner that looked weirdly like it had been stolen from some gym's locker room, shower stalls and all. Each stall was totally enclosed, with its own private changing area. Jillian's mom handed her a folded blue jumpsuit. She nodded toward the stall closest to the wall. "That one's you."

Jillian made a face. "I took a shower this morning."

"Not like this one. This one's for decontamination. We're covered in Earth microbes. Germs. You wouldn't believe the trouble they cause when they get off-world."

At *off-world*, Jillian's hope spiked, but settled back down when she realized this was just another safety precaution. For the same reason you had to cover your mouth when you sneezed, or wash your hands after using the bathroom, she had to take a fancy shower. Even if she wasn't the one going to space.

It didn't seem fair. Not even a little bit. But she'd promised herself she wouldn't complain. She'd take a hundred fancy showers if that was what real StellaTech materials acquisitions people did.

Jillian lifted one shoulder of the jumpsuit experimentally. The fabric felt slithery and oddly cold.

"Part of the StellaTech experience," her dad called out, emerging from one of the stalls in a blue jumpsuit of his own. "Start your workday clean."

"What do I do with my old clothes?"

"There's a vacuum-seal bag in the changing stall. Put them in there before you hit the shower. They're just as full of germs as you are. Don't worry, you can grab them after we get back."

Back? We?

She must have frozen. There it was again, that stupid hope, slamming her heart like a punching bag. He meant back from the *tour*. They'd promised her a tour of their lab. At the end of it they'd leave: Jillian to Aunt Alex's, her parents to space. From this moment until then was her one and only chance to make a good impression.

She looked at the showers. Then she looked back over her shoulder. More of the panels were lit up now, more people in white coats sitting in those chairs, and someone had turned on power to whatever was in that glassed-in area beyond. The lights were still out beyond the glass, but something back there was humming rather loudly. It didn't sound like any kind of machine she knew. It sounded more like a swarm of bees. A really, really big swarm of bees. She was terrified of bees.

Jillian narrowed her eyes at it. "What's making that—"

"Shower first," her mom said. "Questions after. I don't mean to rush you, but we're kind of on the clock here."

Responsible, Jillian reminded herself. *Like a space explorer.* She decided not to let that bee sound make her nervous. They wouldn't let actual bees into a space lab. It had to be something else. She'd find out in a minute. But first she had to get clean. Responsible space explorers didn't bring germs to other planets. Rule number two.

Turned out her mom was right. It was nothing like the shower at home. Even calling it a shower seemed like a bit of a stretch. For one thing, there was no soap or shampoo. For another thing, there was no water. Jillian stood under what she thought was a showerhead until it started misting her with something chemical-smelling and invisible. She counted to ten, then opened her mouth to ask when she was supposed to come out, but before she got the words out, the mist stopped.

Even getting dressed was weirder than back home. The jumpsuit fit her all wrong. Too tight, too loose, too short, too long. "It's the wrong size," she yelled through the curtain.

"Touch the sensor," her mom called back from outside the stall.

"The what?"

"Button thing at the front of the neckline."

Jillian located it. It looked like no button she'd ever seen. It was more like a patch of silver fabric sewn onto the blue. She poked it with a fingertip. With a whispery sound, the jumpsuit began reshaping itself to fit her. The sleeves shortened, the pant legs widened, the torso elongated.

"Mom, the suit is *moving*."

"Yeah, they do that. Cool, huh?"

Jillian had seen smart clothes before, of course, but she'd never *worn* any. "*Really* cool," she said, watching the fabric finish tailoring itself. "I want my next jacket to be made out of this stuff."

"Sure, right after we win the lottery. That suit probably cost more than our car, so enjoy it while you can. Anyway, when you're done, come on out. We haven't even gotten to the good part."

When it was done resizing itself, the jumpsuit felt like a comfortable pair of pajamas. Jillian stretched out her arms and legs for inspection. "Huh," she said.

But something else was catching her attention. Without the spray noise of the shower, the beehive sound was—

louder? Closer? Both? Whatever it was, it was puzzling. Jillian liked puzzles. She stood there for a second, trying to decide if it sounded more like bees or like machinery. At last she settled on *neither*.

But she had no idea what it *did* sound like. She gave herself a second, like it was a riddle she was trying to figure out on her own. But her parents were waiting for her, the whole mission was waiting for her, and making them late was, like, the exact opposite of being responsible.

She pushed the curtain open and froze.

The area behind the glass wall was lit up now, and in it she could see the silver ring of the portal. It hadn't been turned on yet, so it just sat there, twice her height, shining and still. Like it would open any second and fix on her, some sleeping monster's eye.

Waiting in front of it was the quadpod, shiny and new, as if it had fallen out of the documentary to land there. Part spacecraft, part habitation, part storage container, part research lab, just big enough to fit her parents and enough gear to see them through a week off-world—and whatever they'd found on that world worth bringing back.

It sat there like a bright orange egg ten feet across. Lights played across its surface, responding to the blinks and midair gesturing of another white-coated worker. It flashed blue in one place, swirled red in another, then began to glow gently as some unseen mechanism inside it spun up. The worker nodded, spoke briefly into her wrist implant, and moved on to inspect the portal, which Jillian noticed was now set with tiny red lights, softly blinking on and off.

But it was nothing beside the thing that was hovering at eye level not five long steps away, almost invisible but not quite.

A shape on the air like a shifting, floating glob of water. The million-bees sound was coming from it.

Whatever it was, it was absolutely the weirdest thing Jillian had ever seen. She couldn't tell whether it was actually bees or some kind of machine that somehow looked like bees, but she *knew*, suddenly, certainly, that whatever it was, this thing was *watching* her. Like it was waiting to see what she would do.

"That isn't really bees. Is it? Please tell me it's not really bees."

The next thing she knew, her mom was beside her, one arm around her shoulders, grinning like she'd just single-handedly pulled off the greatest surprise party in the history of the known universe.

"That," her mom said, "is the good part."

As if in response, the hovering thing turned iridescent, rainbowy and slick as an oil spill. Then it broke into five pieces. Each piece changed color and somehow shaped itself into a ball, and the balls began to juggle themselves—red, blue, green, yellow, orange—faster and faster until they blurred into a ring. Then the ring flipped over on its side and slowly stopped spinning. When it came to rest, it was a rainbowy pancake, and it was purring—*purring?*—like the world's weirdest cat.

"I've been waiting a long time to be able to say this," her mom said. "Jillian, I'd like you to meet SABRINA."

CHAPTER 2

J illian blinked hard, like that would help her eyes see something different. Something that didn't hurt her brain to look at. It was like the nastiest optical illusion ever invented, and her vision went swimmy trying to bring the thing into focus and keep it there. It wouldn't stay still long enough for her mind to land on it properly. It was going from pancake to ring to snake to spikes to cloud to star faster than her eyes could even track. The thing's purring was so low-pitched that Jillian didn't so much hear it as *feel* it, itching in her spine and teeth, her belly, and the backs of her hands. "But—"

"Semi-Autonomous Bio-Reconnoitering Intelligent Nanobot Array," her dad said helpfully. Like the name of the thing was the problem. "SABRINA."

"No. *That?* It—" Jillian's mouth had forgotten how to make sentences.

"Like on the t-shirt we got you," her mom said. "Remember?"

But that was exactly the problem. Jillian did remember. SABRINA was practically the StellaTech mascot. It was in their ads, their merchandising, wearing the company logo on its side like a tattoo. But *that* SABRINA looked harmless. Cuddly. A little bit adorably dumb. Like what alien kids might keep as pets instead of puppies. You could picture that SABRINA chasing a ball or curling up with you on the couch while you watched cartoons. Stealing your snacks. *This* thing looked like it fell out of the kind of scary movie Aunt Alex wouldn't let Jillian see.

"I didn't know all the letters stood for something," she said at last. "I thought it was just, like, a name."

"That's called an acronym," her dad said.

"I know," Jillian replied distantly. Too many conflicting emotions were barreling through her, all at once, and if someone had asked her right this second if she was okay, she wasn't sure what the answer would be.

SABRINA—the real one, not the mascot in the logo— was classified technology. Nobody but StellaTech people got to see it. It wasn't even in the documentary. And here it was in front of her. It was beyond a doubt the absolute coolest thing Jillian had ever set eyes on. It *was* like something out of a movie, in the strangest and best possible way.

Compared to the SABRINA on her t-shirt, though, or the plush SABRINA that used to protect her from nightmares when she was little, the real one was a lot to get used to.

"SABRINA's extremely cutting-edge," Jillian's mom said. "We know how much you wanted to learn all about this place, and it's one of the coolest toys we have here. You're the first nonemployee to get a personal introduction."

"Not to mention the first kid," her dad said.

"Ever?" Jillian asked.

"Ever."

Her mom's arms were still around her shoulders, but Jillian wasn't quite ready to step away. She stayed where she was, examining SABRINA. It had settled into a kind of nonthreatening blobby shape, like a water balloon that had just rolled down a hill and come to rest. It was very, very still. It looked like the thing was listening to her speak.

"It stopped moving."

"It's trying not to freak you out. It knows it can be a bit much to take in. Say hi if you want. It's okay."

Jillian opened her mouth, but nothing came out. Because all at once, too fast to track, SABRINA had changed again. Now it looked *exactly* like it did as toys and plushies. In the ads. Printed on the t-shirt Jillian had slept in just last night. This version of SABRINA was pudgy and round, with a little swish of a tail and pointy ears like a fox. It was flame-colored, shading from blue through white-yellow to orange and red. Even there, on its side, in silvery white, the company logo: sixteen stars in a circle with an arrow shooting through.

SABRINA stood on six fat little legs for exactly three seconds, then plopped back on its butt and tilted its head at her like a dog waiting for a treat. Even its face was the same.

The same huge, cartoony eyes, the same contented smile.

It was completely adorable. But Jillian wasn't quite ready to trust it just yet. She remembered the bee-swarm shape too clearly. Which one was its true form, the puppy or the swarm? Or something else she hadn't seen yet? Did it even *have* a true form?

"Is it ... alive?" she asked. "Or a machine, or ... ?"

"Neither, exactly," her mom said. "And also a bit of both. Think of, like, a swarm of very tiny robots, each one smaller than a grain of sand. But they all share a mind. SABRINA's patterned off of hive minds in the animal kingdom here on Earth. Ant colonies. Bee colonies. Flocks of birds. Schools of fish. That sort of thing. Except unlike with bees or ants, there's no part of SABRINA that corresponds to a queen. No one part gives the commands. No centralized brain. The mind is dispersed through the array. Like if every part of you could think, from the ends of your hair to the soles of your feet. And every part had the same thoughts at the same time."

Looking at SABRINA, Jillian could easily believe that. The way it changed shape effortlessly, gathering and scattering, made her think of a gag she'd seen in clips from retro cartoons. Where an angry swarm of bees, chasing a character, would communicate by making shapes. A question mark for *where'd he go?* An arrow for *that way!* and maybe an exclamation point for good measure.

SABRINA was all that and much more. Watching it, even in a stable shape like it was now, was mesmerizing. Like staring into a fire.

"—back, please," one of the workers in white coats was saying.

Jillian pried her attention off SABRINA and drew the worker into focus. "Wha—?"

The woman smiled tightly. "Step back, please."

Jillian looked down. Somehow she had taken several steps away from her mom and toward SABRINA without knowing, and was reaching one hand out like she wanted to touch it.

She jumped back like she'd seen a snake in her path. "Sorry," she muttered, embarrassed.

"This is Dr. Park," her mom said, putting her hand on the woman's shoulder. "She's SABRINA's handler. We asked her to take a few minutes out of her day to give you a personal demonstration of what SABRINA could do. We'll be right over there going over some last-minute paperwork while you hang out here with her. That okay?"

Jillian swallowed. She glanced at SABRINA, then at Dr. Park. Weird as SABRINA clearly was, it had made no move to hurt her.

"Sure," she said. She smiled at Dr. Park. "Nice to meet you."

Dr. Park handed Jillian a pair of safety goggles. "Put these on, please."

Jillian was about to protest that she didn't need them, she understood now to stay back and not touch any classified technology, but then she glanced at SABRINA, which was now apparently entertaining itself by fountaining what looked like actual fire out of its tail. She put the goggles on.

"Very good," Dr. Park said, pulling a thermometer from her pocket and swiping it on. The readout flickered on in midair above her hand. She gave it to Jillian. "Read this, please."

Jillian tilted it so the hologram display faced her. "Seventy-two degrees."

"Very good. Room temperature." Dr. Park turned to the flame-colored not-a-dog that sat wagging its tail on the tiles. "SABRINA, warm this, please. Ten-point-two degrees will be sufficient."

"Request acknowledged," SABRINA said. "On it."

Jillian's mouth fell open. "It can *talk*?"

"Oh yes," said Dr. Park, in a tone that said *sometimes we wish it couldn't*. "Say hello, SABRINA."

"Hello, SABRINA," said SABRINA.

"We just love its sense of humor," Dr. Park said.

Jillian just stared.

"Ten-point-two degrees," SABRINA said. "Easy peasy."

There was something so distractingly weird about the words *easy peasy* coming out of this thing that Jillian only now noticed that SABRINA had reached out one stubby leg and taken hold of the thermometer. She hadn't even seen it move. It now sat, five stubby legs and one unsettlingly stretched-out one. Where was its voice coming from? Not its mouth. It sounded like it was talking from every part of itself all at once, like every crumb of it had a mouth of its own, but they all spoke in one voice.

"Read it again, please," Dr. Park told Jillian.

Jillian leaned in. "Eighty-two-point-two degrees."

"Thank you, Jillian. Thank you, SABRINA. Now cool it down, please. Twenty-six-point-four degrees."

"Sure thing," SABRINA said.

The readout dropped accordingly.

"Note the exactitude."

"I'm noting it," Jillian said. "It's very, um, nice."

Dr. Park took a bottle of water and a glass from the nearest desk. "Hand these to SABRINA, please."

Jillian paused, unsure what to do. "It doesn't have any hands—ahh!"

She very nearly dropped the bottle. Standing before her was a scarily accurate replica of herself, right down to the bitten fingernails and the silver patch on its jumpsuit. It reached out and took the glass and bottle neatly. "Thaaank *you.*"

Then, with an inhuman smoothness, part of SABRINA was holding the bottle, another part of SABRINA was holding the glass, and what was being poured back and forth between them was . . . SABRINA. It had turned the poured part of itself neon green for some reason. With what looked like gold glitter in it. Then it poured itself back into person shape and handed the glass and bottle to Jillian.

Dr. Park took the bottle back from her, but not the glass.

"Drop that, please," Dr. Park said.

"On the floor?"

"On the floor."

Jillian, by now having learned there was no point in questioning this, held the glass out over the tile floor, then let go.

Instead of shattering, it came to rest around knee level

in midair, and SABRINA was gone. The glass floated, suspended, as if in a cloud of clear jelly. Which then grew a pair of cartoony eyes and winked at Jillian.

Next SABRINA shot out a pair of long, thin spikes and used them as knitting needles to make a washcloth-sized square, also of its own material. ("Observe the tensile strength of the fabric," Dr. Park suggested.)

Then it made needle-tipped darts and fired them into a clipboard Dr. Park held up, each dart splitting the last at the dead center of the bull's-eye. ("Lucky shot," SABRINA said each time, with what sounded like way more humble-bragging irony than needed.) Then the darts dissolved and floated back to SABRINA as iridescent mist.

Then it folded bits of itself into paper airplanes and flew them into every wastepaper basket in the room, turned part of itself into a screen and played a few seconds of a movie, and took a light bulb out of a ceiling panel and lit it up, brighter and brighter, until it exploded with a flash and a spray of glass. SABRINA caught every splinter.

"Oh no," SABRINA said, sounding amused. "Oopsy daisy."

"Doesn't really talk like a robot," Jillian said.

"Well," Dr. Park said, "SABRINA's not like other robots. Even the modern robots you're probably thinking of—the teachers and medbots and so forth, all top of the line in their own right—are very simple machines compared to it."

"Oh stop," SABRINA said. "You'll make me blush."

Jillian studied SABRINA. "Does it know it's a robot?"

"Do you know you're not?" SABRINA replied. "And if so"—it paused dramatically—"how, exactly?"

"Manners," Dr. Park told it. "No asking our new guest existential questions on her first day."

"My only day," Jillian corrected, trying to keep the disappointment from her voice. Being able to see everything she'd be missing out on was just making it harder to think about being sent home. SABRINA was about to go to 80 UMa c with her parents. Jillian, as much as she loved Aunt Alex, couldn't help but be just a *little* jealous.

Dr. Park didn't seem to hear her, anyway. "As you've probably gathered," she said, "SABRINA is fully sentient. It learns from the world much like a child does. Its personality has some set parameters—our field crews wouldn't get too far if SABRINA wasn't helpful and innovative, for instance—but it's also constantly informed by input from its surroundings and upbringing and the company it keeps, same as yours and mine. So, you know"—Dr. Park smiled briefly—"try to set a good example."

Jillian glanced around the lab. Very serious-looking men and women, dressed in white coats like Dr. Park, were up to their eyeballs in work. She got the impression they tended to stay that way, at least while they were in this room. "Where'd it learn its, um, sense of humor?"

"Oh." Dr. Park made a face. "SABRINA watches a lot of TV." Then she lifted her chin toward SABRINA. "Look."

The shards of light bulb that SABRINA had caught were beginning to *sink*, like SABRINA was made of quicksand. Dr. Park handed it the plastic bottle from before.

"Much obliged," SABRINA said. Now it had shape-shifted into an octopus for some reason, hanging from the ceiling by two arms while two lifted the bottle daintily and three more tied themselves into intricate knots, seemingly for fun. The last arm was busy spitting the glass shards out from its tip and into the bottle, one by one, with delicate little *ptoo* sounds and a faint musical tinkling as they hit bottom. After those came the light bulb's base and housing, which wouldn't fit into the bottle opening. So SABRINA made a blade and sliced off the entire top of the bottle, then put those things inside and reassembled the bottle around them, melting the halves back together with heat it produced from somewhere.

SABRINA gave a tiny burp from somewhere ("Excuse me."), handed the bottle to Jillian, and transformed back into the flame-colored dog. Jillian noted that it had kept two of the octopus arms this time, and it was now jumping rope with them, humming a little tune to itself.

Dr. Park reached into a pocket and produced a rock the size of an orange.

"Time for the grand finale," she said. "Your parents requested this demonstration specifically, just for you. Kind of a souvenir of your tour."

Jillian knew what that meant. She'd have to leave soon. She felt like she'd just gotten here, but like her mom said, they were on the clock. Getting to space on time was more important than Jillian's tour. She forced a smile.

"Stand here," Dr. Park said, pointing to an X made on the floor with tape.

Jillian stood on it.

"Take this." Dr. Park passed the rock to her.

Jillian took it.

"Throw it at SABRINA," Dr. Park said. "As hard as you can."

Jillian raised an eyebrow. Dr. Park nodded encouragingly.

"Bring it on," said SABRINA. "I can catch bullets. See?"

SABRINA stretched and flattened into another screen, then tilted down to present Jillian its surface as it played a video for her. There was SABRINA, absorbing machine-gun fire and regurgitating it at a series of paper targets in the distance. The next shot in the video was, of course, the obliterated bull's-eyes. Closer up, the targets weren't paper. They were steel-armored reinforced concrete, thicker than Jillian's whole body. Each had a hole in the back where its bullet had punched straight through.

"No big deal," SABRINA said coolly, lifting its shoulder in what weirdly did actually look like a shrug.

"Way too dangerous to do that one in here," Jillian's dad called out from the sidelines. "There's another one with a flamethrower that we can't do either. But trust me. It's cool."

"But if it can catch bullets," Jillian asked, hefting the rock, "why bother with this?"

"SABRINA won't be catching it," Dr. Park said. "Go on."

"Okay," Jillian said. Dramatically, she wound up the pitch and let it fly.

Maybe a bit too dramatically. The rock sailed out of her

hand and fully over her head, toward the expensive-looking, fragile-looking machinery in the room behind her. Reflexively, she shut her eyes, waiting for the crash and the yelling and the getting kicked out of the lab and sent back to school.

None of that came. She turned.

Behind her was what looked like a tornado made of lemon-yellow cotton candy. Behind *that* was a satiny-looking cushion on the tile floor, also lemon yellow, but with ruby-red fringe and purple tassels. There was something on it. Several somethings. Jillian had to take a few steps toward the stuff on the cushion before she recognized what it was.

The rock she'd thrown. Somehow, in the split second when she hadn't been looking, SABRINA had sliced it into hundreds of paper-thin shards. Each with a beautiful sky-blue center and a hole in the middle like a doughnut.

"Oh cool," she whispered. "A geode."

Then she realized what she was *really* looking at. She'd cracked geodes with a hammer before. It had taken forever and come out a total mess. These looked like they'd been cut by a laser. Even at that see-through thinness, not one looked to have broken. The whole process hadn't made a sound.

The yellow tornado dissipated into a fine sparkling mist and spread across the room. It was like being in a snow globe full of glitter.

Dr. Park, meanwhile, brought the pillow over to a desk and scraped off the geode slices into an envelope. "These are yours to keep," she told Jillian. Then she tossed the pillow up into the air, where it also vaporized and began to spread smokily across the ceiling.

"As you can see," she said, "SABRINA is not a toy. It is an exquisitely calibrated piece of technology. Think of it as part equipment, part teammate. You want to get to know your teammates before you work with them, right? All new surveyors have to meet with it like this, familiarize them-selves with what it can do, before they're in a position to rely on it in the field."

"Maybe someday," Jillian said wistfully.

"Well, you're here, aren't you? Take Your Kid to Work Day, right?"

"Right," Jillian said, trying to hide the disappointment in her voice. Pretending like SABRINA was going to be *her* teammate in the field just made her sad.

She thought of the logo on her T-shirt. She thought of the machine guns, the bullet holes. "What is it really, though? Some kind of weapon?"

"No," Dr. Park said. "Think of SABRINA as a very advanced probe. We send it through before the field teams to make sure everything at the destination is safe for hu-man exposure. That alone has saved lives. And then once they're through—*if* SABRINA's determined the environ-ment is suitable—it serves as part of their equipment. It's very useful."

"Understatement of the year," Jillian's dad said. "SABRI-NA's saved our butts a million times. You wouldn't believe how easy it is to stay under weight capacity, bringing it in-stead of trying to stuff a mountain of gear into the pod."

"So it's, like, a multitool," Jillian said, thinking of the one in her hiking backpack that she never really got to use. Hers had a screwdriver and a little knife and a compass and some tweezers and whatnot. SABRINA was a multitool times ten thousand.

"Exactly," her mom said. "A multitool that's mission safe. We tend not to travel with sharp things. What you really *don't* want, in space, is a punctured suit."

"I thought SABRINA's job is to make sure a planet is safe for humans," Jillian said. "With air and an atmosphere and whatever."

"It is," her dad said. "And it does. You're right: we don't usually go to planets where we need the suits. We wear them through the portal anyway. Just like they make the pod about ninety-eight percent out of plastic, in case we encounter an atmosphere that corrodes metal. We're extremely careful. Wait'll you see the suits. They're very old-school."

Jillian had a hard time imagining anything in this place being *old-school*. But as she was finding, it was pretty hard to get excited about suits when you had a cloud of talking, shape-shifting, microscopic smart robots standing—or hovering—right there in front of you.

"So it just, like, does whatever you say?" She pointed up at the ceiling, where the cloud was now spiraling, like SABRINA was thinking of cooking up another tornado. "You didn't tell it to do that."

"SABRINA is semi-autonomous," Dr. Park said. "That means it takes directives from its handlers—that would be me in the lab, and the teams in the field—but in between it pretty much does what it wants."

In demonstration, SABRINA turned itself in midair into a velociraptor and dropped down onto Dr. Park's head, safely tucking its clawed hind legs underneath it and fluffing its feathers. Then it lay down and curled up like an oversized cat.

Dr. Park lifted it gently down. It squawked in protest but allowed itself to be lowered. "Within reason."

SABRINA was weaving between Jillian's legs now, booping its velociraptor head against her knees and making ridiculously adorable little *meep*ing noises. She had to resist a bizarre urge to scritch it behind where its ears would be. "Would it listen to me?"

"Not without one of these," Dr. Park said, tapping the blue square at her temple. "SABRINA's not keyed to you. But it might do what you ask if it likes you. And you ask nicely."

SABRINA snapped its head up to stare at Jillian. Its eyes glittered with intelligence.

"That's fine," Jillian blurted, suddenly nervous. "I was just curious. I'm good just watching it from here."

"Give it a try," her mom coaxed.

Her dad joined in. "You never know what you like until you try!" Then he turned to Dr. Park. "She does have the wristband," he told her. "It might work."

"It should," Dr. Park agreed. "Anyone with lab clearance should be able to assign directives."

The stares of three adults and one robot were now fixed on Jillian.

"Um," she said. Wristband or no, the idea of asking SABRINA to perform tricks felt *wrong* somehow. If SABRINA was a dog, Jillian could give it treats. But she had nothing a machine would want, and she hated being told what to do for no good reason.

"No, really, it's okay," she said airily. Then, half out of interest and half just to change the subject, she pointed across the room. "Hey, what's over there behind the glass anyway? Is that the portal? Can I see?"

"That is indeed what's next on the list for your tour," Dr. Park said. "Come on over."

She led Jillian and her parents over to the dividing wall. The glass was thicker than Jillian had expected it to be, reinforced with steel plates. The heads of the bolts were bigger across than the palm of her hand. There was wire mesh embedded into the glass, floor to ceiling.

Those walls hadn't been in the documentary. In the documentary it had just been the bare metal ring of the portal itself, and the bright orange egg of the quadpod. Figures in suits had climbed into the pod, and the pod had glided forward on its runners into the portal and disappeared.

Jillian reached out a fist and knocked on the glass. The thickness and density of the wall absorbed the sound entirely.

A door was tucked into the far side of the wall, also glass, but with some kind of unseen scanner that beeped at their approach and slid softly open.

Several workers entered, and Jillian's parents, but SABRINA stood by, holding the door open for Jillian, goofily bowing like she was somebody important. "After you," it said in its beehive voice.

Jillian raised one foot to step forward, then put it down. That close, the portal was huge. It could have gulped a dozen of her whole. "I don't know," she said.

What are you saying? she asked herself. *This is what you wanted! This is where they go to space! You've waited forever to see this!*

"It's cool, new kid," SABRINA told her. "Trust me."

Jillian had no idea why this was so reassuring. Maybe because SABRINA had turned itself back into the mascot, and it was hard to think of a six-legged cuddly dog lying to you. Maybe she'd just seen enough movies to know that robots weren't supposed to lie to humans, period. Or maybe she just knew, deep down, that the scarier a thing seemed to start with, the cooler it ended up being. Like learning to swim, or riding a hoverbike.

Maybe this room being extra scary just meant that it would end up extra cool.

She swallowed, and braced herself, and went through the door.

CHAPTER 3

The sound of the door shutting behind her was louder than Jillian had expected. It sounded like she was being shut into a tomb. What really didn't help the effect were the steel bars that slid smoothly out of the back wall and horizontally across the door. Or the fact that another white-coated worker was holding something out to Jillian that looked impossibly like—

"What is that? Is that a space suit? Why are you handing me a space suit?"

"Technically," her dad said, "it's not a space suit. It's a podsuit."

"But—"

"Well," her mom said, smiling a little, "it's like you said earlier. We thought that to really do Take Your Kid to Work Day the *right* way, we'd . . . you know . . . take our kid to work."

For two seconds Jillian thought she must have heard

wrong. Then a strong, unidentifiable feeling rushed up and swamped her heart, making it hard to breathe. It felt like waking up on your birthday morning, except times a million.

"Wait," she said anyway, because there *had* to have been a mistake; she'd been asking for this exact thing for years, and the answer had always been: *You're too young. You're not ready. It's not safe without the proper training.* "You mean I'm—"

"Going to space with us," her mom said, grinning. "Yeah."

Jillian blinked a few times. The idea of it was too big. It wasn't sinking in. She realized they were waiting for her to say something. "Oh," she said.

Her dad nudged her shoulder. "That's it? 'Oh?' I was expecting more of a reaction. Isn't this what you've always wanted?"

"Well, *yeah*, but . . ." Jillian trailed off. But what? She didn't *want* to be having second thoughts out of nowhere. So why was she?

"Maybe we shouldn't have surprised her with it," her dad was telling her mom. "We should have told her this morning."

"We just need to give her a second to *be* surprised," her mom said. "It was scary our first time through the portal too. And you don't have to go if you don't want to," she told Jillian. "It's your choice, one hundred percent."

"Entirely," her dad said. "Nobody's forcing you to do anything."

Jillian's brain felt like it had been locked up in a box, and she couldn't hear it think. She felt like she should be jumping up and down and shrieking with how excited she was. It honestly did feel like a million birthdays all rolled into one.

And yet—the portal was staring at her with its huge silver eye, like it was judging her. Looking deep into her heart and seeing the anxiety she was trying desperately to hide.

What if they were right before? Too young, not ready, not safe to go without training? She'd always thought of space as this distant goal, like a treasure it would take her years to find. That was the whole *point* of the plan. To be ready when the time came. She had a supply list tacked on her wall with all the stuff she would pack when this day finally arrived. And none of that stuff was here.

It was dizzying, literally dizzying. There was nowhere to sit down. She set one hand on the pod for support.

"You said it was too dangerous to bring kids to space," she said. "Just this morning you said that."

"It wouldn't have even been an option to bring you if the mission was remotely dangerous," her mom replied. "This is an easy one, which is why it's okay. We've gone to 80 UMa c plenty of times before."

"There's nothing at the site that can hurt you," her dad added. "Like your mom says, we've been there before, and you'll see how careful we are regardless. We'll be there, SABRINA will be there, and even if there was anything there that *could* hurt you—which there isn't—we'd all be there to protect you."

"So here's what's happening now," her mom said. "I know big new things make you nervous, so I'll give you the run-down while you think it over. They've got all the calculations ready for the portal projection. They'll open this side, run more diagnostics, send SABRINA in for—wait for it— even more diagnostics. A truly ridiculous pile of diagnostics. Then we go through, find what they want us to find, and rendezvous with the portal when they re-project it for us next week."

Jillian was grateful for this. Grateful her parents understood that lists like this helped keep her from getting overwhelmed, and took the time to spell them out. When it came to terrifying new experiences, she needed a clear, calm, step-by-step outline to follow, or else her brain would start *what-now*ing and *what-if*ing, and then there was no shutting it up.

Still, whether she was grateful or not, the last part of the list snagged at Jillian's attention like a thorn on a sleeve. "Next week?"

In the following silence, her brain supplied the answer. *Of course next week. It's Friday today, and their trips are five days long. It's not like they can just zap you a new portal when you get bored of 80 UMa whatsit and want to go home.*

Bored, her brain added helpfully, *or terrified.*

"We were hoping," her dad said at length, "you might want to spend part of your spring break trying something new."

"Without *asking* me?"

Her parents exchanged a confused look. In her mind, Jillian was pretty much giving herself a confused look of her own. She had no idea where this sudden anger was coming from. This was what she'd *wanted*. What she'd wanted *forever*. Why should it matter that it was happening out of nowhere? Just this morning she'd happily have gone into space via catapult. She wished the *what-if* part of her brain would just shut up and leave her alone.

"Honey," her mom said carefully, "we thought you'd love this. We assumed you'd be, like, *beside* yourself with excitement here."

"I thought if anything, you'd be running around the room right now, and we'd have to stop you from knocking over the equipment," her dad added.

I do love it, Jillian wanted to say. *I'm super excited, I swear. I don't know why I'm like this. Why my brain can't let me just like things without overthinking them. I'm sorry.*

Her face gave one horrible twist, like she was about to start crying in front of her parents and SABRINA and the portal and all these strangers in white coats.

"You can say no if you want to," her mom said. "As long as you're absolutely sure that's what you want. Aunt Alex can be here in fifteen minutes. It's entirely up to you."

Jillian opened her mouth. Then she closed it. She *liked* trying new things. She *loved* collecting new information. She even—sometimes—was super into surprises.

And going to *space*? She'd wished on all the stars and all her birthday candles and every dandelion she picked for just that exact same thing since she was little.

And it wasn't only *going to space*. It was going on a space *expedition*. Out in uninhabited wilderness. Just like those hiking and camping trips her parents were always too busy to take her on, except *in actual freakin' space.*

In the thinking part of her brain she knew all this. But seeing everything up close—the portal, the quadpod, the giant cage of this room—not to mention SABRINA, which had switched back into its near-invisible jelly state, maybe having (wrongly) decided that Jillian was more likely to trust what she couldn't clearly see—it was a whole bunch of weird to take in.

But if she said no and walked away from this kind of adventure, she'd regret it. Intensely. Forever. All week at Aunt Alex's, she'd be kicking herself in the butt for taking the easy way. For turning down *space.* And the next Take Your Kid to Work Day was a whole year from now.

On the one hand, she might be braver by then. On the other hand, there might not *be* another Take Your Kid to Work Day, and even if there was, they probably wouldn't invite back some scared kid who just ran away when things got challenging. She might not get a second chance.

"We need to load the pod," a man in a white coat told Jillian's mom. "We were told three surveyors. Gear for three surveyors. It's right here on the manifest. I have no idea what favors you people called in above my head to even go off-script like this, but you can't just change the manifest at the last minute. *Especially* not after we completely re-rigged the pod interior to stay under capacity while adding random children to the crew."

By the end of this little speech, the man was up in Jillian's mom's face, waving a handheld screen at her. She gazed back at him evenly. In the end she leaned in and muttered something in his ear that made him back off fast. Then she turned to Jillian.

"It's up to you," she said again. "It does complicate things if you don't want to go. The pod team worked overtime to fit you in, and we'd of course love for you to come, and I honestly think you'd have the most amazing time ever if you just gave it a chance—*but* we did kind of spring this on you last second, and I realize it's a big decision."

It was a moment before Jillian found her voice. "Will you get in trouble if I don't go?"

"Nah," her mom said. "They might be mad at us for a few minutes, but hey." She cupped one hand to her mouth to whisper conspiratorially. "Betcha ten bucks they forget all about it by the time we get back."

Jillian took a deep breath and exhaled slowly. "What would I be doing?" She gestured at the great maw of the portal with her eyes, then averted them quickly. "Through there."

"Help us set up base camp," her dad said. "That's the first thing. Then you help us with the expedition. Finding and carrying. Then back to camp and sleep. Next morning, rinse, repeat."

"Finding what? Carrying what?"

"Look," the white-coat man said. "We're on the clock here. We'll redo the manifest. Just you two. Call your babysitter, suit up, and get in."

"Algae," Jillian's mom said, ignoring him. "Or something that looks and behaves a lot like Earth algae. They use it to make fuel cells. Just like we make here on Earth with Earth algae, but better. More efficient. And on 80 UMa c, there's a *lot* of it. And we happen to work for the only company in the world with the technology to go get it."

"Truly clean energy in abundance," her dad said. "In time, on a large enough scale, it'd mean no more electricity rationing. No more water tickets. No more blackouts. Real world-saving stuff. Not to brag, but, you know, me and your mom, we're basically superheroes."

Jillian considered this. "You said you've been to this Uma planet before?"

"Yup," her dad said. "Field crews have been going to 80 UMa c for about eight months now. Your mom and I have been there four times already. It's totally safe. We wouldn't even consider bringing you along if it wasn't. You could breathe the air without a suit if you wanted to. You can eat the fruit off the trees. It tastes a little weird, and too much of it will give you the runs, but I mean, that's what food bars are for. They'll stop you *right* up again—"

"There's fruit? Real fruit?"

"All you can eat. No produce rationing there. And it's not the fake stuff. You pick it right off the trees."

Jillian paused. "What about . . ." She had been about to say *aliens*. "Life? Um, intelligent life?"

Her dad grinned. "Aliens?"

"I guess."

"Not like you're probably thinking. There're a few complex life-forms, but nothing really big or remotely scary. There're some things kind of like birds, but not, and some things kind of like salamanders, but really not, and something maybe the *tiniest* little bit like a deer? And another thing like a fat green earthworm. About the size of a big slug."

"Let me guess," she said. "They have acid for blood."

"Acid for saliva, actually."

"Ha, ha."

"No, really. Well, the worm things do. But they don't bite. They live underground, and the soil is much lower in nutrients than most soil on Earth, so the acid helps them process tasty microorganisms out of the dirt. Anyway, they pretty much keep to themselves. We've never seen any in the field. We only know about them because another team captured a few for study a few months ago."

"That's *seriously* the worst of it? You *promise?*"

"Come on," her dad said jokingly. "You really think they'd let us bring you if it was dangerous? Losing kids on space missions would *really* not look good for the company."

Jillian's mom held out one hand dramatically, like she was safe atop a cliff and Jillian was dangling off it. "So what do you say? Want to go on an adventure?"

Jillian opened her mouth to answer, but for a moment she was truly unsure what she'd say. She'd never really gone on an adventure before. Read about adventures in books, yes. Watched other people have adventures in movies, sure. Saved the world about a million times in video games. But *go on a real-life adventure herself?* The closest she'd come to that was—she didn't know. Camping, maybe? Or that time she'd gotten lost on the field trip to the biome conservatory and pretended she was an explorer on her own in open wilderness . . .

What she was being offered today was a once-in-a-life-time chance to do a thing she'd always dreamed of. *You always regret it when you talk yourself into not trying new things*, she told herself. *Always.*

"Yeah," she said at last. "I think I do."

Her first look at the interior of the quadpod seemed non-scary enough. It was like being inside an egg, rounded all over but slightly pointed on one end. The pointed end, the one facing the portal, was full of collapsible containers of food, water, medical supplies, and so on, all labeled neatly. Most of the containers were already collapsed, empty. *For what we bring back*, she realized. *The algae stuff.*

All the storage stuff took up the whole narrower half of the pod. The other, wider half contained the bunks. They were stacked on top of one another, one two three, with doors on the front that looked tricky to crawl into. There were more supply containers packed into either side of the stack.

The bunk doors were open, so Jillian peeked inside. It was an empty tube with no pillow or blanket, just a touchscreen panel on the inside wall.

Jillian and her parents had suited up before opening the quadpod. The podsuits were smart like the jumpsuits, and auto-fit to Jillian's shape and size, but the material was much thicker and hard to move around in. It felt huge and bulky on her, like she was wearing a suit of armor. She eyed that narrow tube skeptically.

"We had to leave out a few crates," the man from before said. "To fit the third bunk. You're each going to have to stow some loose supplies in your bunk with you."

"That sounds comfortable," Jillian's dad said with cheery sarcasm.

"Oh, it won't be," the man replied. "But you didn't leave us with a whole lot of options."

"It'll be fine," Jillian's mom reassured her. "We won't be in there for long. Come on. You want the top bunk?"

Jillian didn't want *any* bunk. She would rather have rattled around loose in the quadpod than jam herself in there. She *hated* tight spaces. She wanted to scream just looking at it.

Still, she'd read enough books about the history of space travel to know that this little annoyance was nothing. At least she wasn't being frozen alive and shipped to Mars for six months with no food.

She'd made up her mind to do this, and she was going to do it. She could take a few minutes of discomfort on the way.

She took a deep breath. "Sure," she said. "Top bunk sounds great."

Climbing in the suit was annoyingly hard, but there were rungs mounted on the right side of each of the round doors and grippy stuff on the gloves of the suit. She scrambled headfirst into the top bunk, worming her way into the tube.

She'd guessed right. It was the absolute most uncomfortable thing ever. Her arms were wedged under her body, layers of podsuit fabric and jumpsuit fabric were tangled around her legs, she was overheating, and there was nowhere to put her head.

And then it got worse.

"Wrong way around," the man called up impatiently. "Feet first. Get out and do it again."

Frustration seized her, and Jillian wanted to kick her way out through the wall of the tube. Instead, she took a deep breath, worked her arms free, put her palms on the rear wall of the tube, and shoved. Her legs oozed out, then her hips, and then she was free and dropping boots-first to the pod floor. With a lot of pushing and clambering and accidental kicking, her parents helped her get in the right way around. She was really glad the suit helmet hid the embarrassed look on her face.

Right way around was marginally more comfortable. The touchscreen panel was beside her face now instead of beside her ankles, for one thing. Her mom showed her how it wasn't a touchscreen at all, but voice-activated. She could tell it to warm or cool her bunk, dispensing with the need for a blanket, and raise or lower the section of tube under her head, replacing a pillow. But it was still absolutely nothing like a bed.

She twisted her neck around to try and see the portal from there, but her view ended at the inner egg-curve of the quadpod. Through gaps between supply containers she could make out glints of orange pod wall. "I wish we could see the portal from here," she said.

In response, a second tech leaned halfway through the

pod doorway, reached out toward the front wall of the pod, and made a motion with her hand like she was grabbing a curtain and pulling it aside.

Five feet away, the front wall of the pod became transparent.

"Window," the tech said curtly, and ducked back out.

So Jillian craned her neck even more to look. Instead of orange between the stacks of stuff, now there was the toothpaste-ad white that she immediately recognized as a wall of the lab. Way over on the edge she could make out a bit of silver rim. She was looking into the dead eye of the portal. She suppressed a shiver that was half nervousness, half excitement.

This was it. Uncomfortable or not, in a few minutes she was going through that portal and onto another planet. No more planning, no more wishing, no more *someday when I'm older*. She was going to space *right now*.

Her parents climbed into their bunks after her, and one of the techs closed them in. First, though, as expected, they each had to wedge some loose packages of supplies in around them. Jillian couldn't see what her parents got, but someone reached up and handed her some vacuum-packed bags with labels like MULTIVITAMIN/ELECTRO-LYTE TABS and WATER PURIFICATION TABS and INSTANT SPLIT PEA SOUP and HIGH-CALORIE FOOD BAR: EMERGENCY USE ONLY. She rolled over onto her back and tucked them in as best she could between her sides and the walls.

It got even more tight and uncomfortable, but nothing

she couldn't handle. She decided to focus on the fun parts. Camping in space. Exploring in space. Even having space picnics with this weird-looking food sounded, honestly, pretty great.

She wondered if SABRINA needed to eat, or what its fuel was. She decided it was probably solar-powered, like a space telescope. But then, what did you call *solar-powered* when the star you were closest to wasn't the Sun anymore?

This stumped her for a few moments, which was a nice distraction. Then she realized she hadn't seen SABRINA get into the quadpod. It might have made her pretty nervous to start with, but she realized she was disappointed to realize it might not be coming with them.

"Where's SABRINA?" she asked into the voice intake on her suit.

"Present," SABRINA chirped through Jillian's earpiece from who knew where.

Jillian glanced down curiously at the packages wedged between her and the tube. If SABRINA was hiding among them, camouflaged, would she know? "It's in the pod?"

"Nah," came her mom's voice from the next bunk down. "SABRINA's still out in the lab, waiting just like us. This is just a normal Friday for it. We'll see it on the other side."

From Jillian's earpiece came the sound of SABRINA's swarm-voice humming "Twinkle, Twinkle, Little Star."

"Okay," Jillian's mom continued, "we're going to be waiting here for a few minutes, so let me walk you through what happens next. Comfy?"

Jillian shifted irritably. "Um."

"Me neither. Don't worry, nobody likes this part. All you can really do is put up with it, and you're way ahead of me. There's an itch on my back that's killing me, and I can't reach it at all."

"Same," Jillian said. Mentioning it only made it worse, so she decided to change the subject. "What's going on out there?"

"Well, not a whole lot at the moment. The techs will have all cleared out of the enclosure. It's just the quadpod in here, and SABRINA."

"I'm on the roof!" SABRINA cut in merrily, followed by knocking sounds from above. Like SABRINA was knocking with many fists together. Musically. It sounded more like a short drum solo than anything. A short, elaborate drum solo.

"SABRINA's always liked it up there," Jillian's dad said. "It's like a cat. A big, weird, shape-shifting, talking cat."

"The portal's not fired up yet," Jillian's mom continued. "Right now they'll be, like, quintuple-checking their calculations before initiating the actual endpoint projection—"

"The enclosure being the big cage thing?" Jillian asked. "Cleared out why?"

"Standard operating procedure," her mom said.

At the same time her dad said, "Safety precaution."

Then Jillian remembered something she'd noticed earlier. "That cage thing wasn't even in the documentary."

"There was a miscalculation," her mom said. "Once. October 7, 2109. The containment system—the enclosure—is us learning from our mistakes."

"What happened?"

"Eleven casualties," SABRINA said. It was still humming "Twinkle, Twinkle, Little Star" in the background with another part of its voice as it spoke. "The environment on 82 Eridani b was"—it paused delicately, still humming—"incompatible with human life. At least during the flood season. Turns out."

"Needless to say," her dad said, "we don't go there anymore." He nodded toward something in the direction of the portal. "StellaTech doesn't talk about it, and the official story is it never happened, but here in the lab we remember. No matter what they say."

Jillian squinted toward whatever he was nodding at.

There, beside the portal, was a single sheet of paper tacked to the wall. A list of names. Someone had written them lovingly, with big, bold, fancy lettering, in what looked like glitter pen. Beneath it, on a little shelf, was a single flower in a tiny vase.

She couldn't read the names from here, but they were written one per line, and she could count them easily enough. "You said eleven casualties. There are twelve names on that paper."

Jillian's mom sighed. "We lost one surveyor. Back in the early days of the program."

"What do you mean you *lost*—" Jillian cut herself off. "Lost how?"

"She never rendezvoused with her portal," her mom explained. "Nobody knows what happened to her. But she never came home."

Jillian looked at the list again. "That only happened one time?"

"That's right."

She chewed this over for a moment. Something else was bothering her, deep in the back of her mind. She didn't know what it was yet, only that it was there, like something uncomfortably stuck between your teeth.

In a moment she put it together.

"Flood season."

"Very violent ones on 82 Eridani b," her mom said. "Not like Earth. Think like a cross between a flash flood and a tsunami."

"And all this water poured through the portal and into the facility?"

"*All* is a bit dramatic," SABRINA said. "Only until they closed the portal. Which they were *very quick to do*. I have never seen humans move so fast. It was quite a sight to behold. They were like little—"

"But that won't happen today," her mom said. "Remember, surveyor crews have been going to 80 UMa c for eight months now. You can sleep directly on the ground there. Lick a rock if you wanted to. It's fine."

"Breathe the air, eat the fruit, get the runs," her dad added. "Remember? Besides, the pod itself will protect us in pretty much all scenarios."

"Like what?"

"On 80 UMa c? I don't even know. No floods, that's for sure. There's not a whole ton of water. A few ponds, some streams. Nothing that's going to try to drown a building.

They're always extra careful about germs, though."

"Like the showers we had to take."

"That's right. We do that all over again when we get back, except this time the pod gets cleaned too. Then the entire enclosure gets hosed down with about a dozen different kinds of neutralizers and disinfectants while we fill out paperwork about whether anybody on the mission so much as sneezed. Boring, yes. Dangerous, no."

For a long moment Jillian thought this over. In the silence SABRINA's humming came through loud and clear.

"There was only one accident?" she asked finally. "One accident and one missing person, and everything's been safe ever since? That's all of it? No more secrets?"

"That's all of it," her mom said solemnly. "No more secrets. We didn't want to worry you about things that had a zero-percent chance of happening today. That accident happened before we had the enclosure, or the containment doors, or today's diagnostics, or a book of emergency protocol two inches thick. And it was before we had SABRINA. If it'd been there on 82 Eridani b, they'd never have made that mistake. It would have seen the flood coming from a mile off. Literally."

"*Lit*erally," SABRINA echoed.

"But it just said it *watched*—"

"The surveillance feed," her dad said. "SABRINA'S watched the whole archive, like, fifty times by now. They're like action movies to it. It loves them. Sometimes it even makes popcorn." He paused. "It can't *digest* it, exactly, but . . . "

"Well," Jillian said, and then stopped cold. Something was humming, and this time it wasn't SABRINA. There was no beehive sound to this, no mistaking it for anything but pure machine. It could only be one thing.

The portal.

Jillian strained to see out the washing-machine door of her bunk. Where before she'd seen a blank wall, now she . . . still saw a blank wall. Except now there was a kind of flickering, the way the air got wavy over a fire. The wavering slowly intensified until it was hard to look at without getting dizzy. The humming sound got stronger too. It buzzed deep in Jillian's ears and vibrated in her teeth. It got worse and worse and *worse* and then—it was gone.

Jillian opened her eyes. She hadn't realized she'd closed them.

Out the transparent front wall of the quadpod, her view was no longer toothpaste-commercial white. And it wasn't flickering. She caught glimpses of pale purple something, black something else. Something orange, not as bright as the pod. It looked familiar, but she couldn't place from where.

"That's my stop," SABRINA said. "Later, gators."

Then, humming some kind of parade-type marching music, SABRINA floated through the portal. Jillian could only see a little of its current form, which seemed a little like a jellyfish, a tendril-y umbrella shape. It drifted through into that other place like it was going through a door. If Jillian squinted hard at the biggest gap between supply stacks, she could just see bits of SABRINA lift off the main body and go drifting away in all directions like tiny drones.

"Hold for clearance," came a new voice through Jillian's earpiece. She recognized it as the man who had argued with her mom outside the pod. All the nastiness was gone from his voice, though. Now it was all business.

"Field crew holding," her dad replied.

"What does that mean?" Jillian asked.

"It means," her dad said, "we wait."

Jillian tried to wait. It was hard. The bunk wasn't exactly getting more comfortable. "What's SABRINA looking for out there?"

"It's making sure there were no errors in the preliminary diagnostics," her mom said. "At the same time there are about a zillion sensors in the enclosure and on the outside skin of the pod that are double-checking the same things. Okay temperature. Breathable air. Everything we already know, but check anyway. We do this every time."

"Nothing *incompatible with human life*," Jillian deadpanned.

"No indeedy," her dad said.

"Why isn't it talking anymore?"

"SABRINA? It can't hear us from there. And we can't hear it from here."

"But it's right there. I can see it."

"Looks close, right? There's nothing *right there* about it. SABRINA's eighty-three light-years away," her mom said. "Total comms blackout. When the portal closes after us, that goes for us too. We're on our own for a week until they send us a new portal. Just us and SABRINA. Like camping!" Jillian could almost hear her mom beaming. "But okay, so. SABRINA just fired off a bunch of recon probes. Those things you saw hover off of it like tiny helicopters? Little blobs of light?"

Jillian nodded. Then she remembered her mom couldn't see her. "Yeah," she said. "I saw."

"Right now they're panning over an area of six square miles. Our harvesting site. They're constantly reporting back to SABRINA's main body." Her mom paused. "Actually, *reporting back* isn't entirely accurate. SABRINA can receive data from each of them simultaneously."

"Yeah, but what if those parts find something dangerous? What happens then?"

"What happens then is that if even *one* of them finds something even *slightly* dangerous, SABRINA abandons the probes. It drops them from its network, and only the main body returns."

This made Jillian think of salamanders abandoning their tails to predators. "Can it grow them back?"

"With some help from the guys in the lab," her mom said. "So SABRINA comes back, they close the portal, and we sit here through two solid hours of decontamination protocol. SABRINA'S still out there, which is promising. Usually if it's coming back, it's back by now."

As if on cue, SABRINA's main body sprouted an arm, raised it in the air, and flashed a thumbs-up back through the portal. This struck Jillian as a shockingly casual way to determine whether or not they were about to be murdered in cold blood by a hostile planet.

They've been going here for eight months, she reminded

herself. *They'd know if it wasn't safe.*

Instead she focused on what she could see through the portal. Orange dirt that looked a bit like Mars. She pictured hiking her way across it, looking for ponds, gathering this special algae that might help save the world.

Camping in the pod. Cooking rations over a fire. Looking out at the stars. But she'd be on a planet orbiting a star in the Big Dipper. She'd see different stars from there, she realized, or the same stars from different angles. She wondered if she'd recognize any of them.

She opened her mouth to say as much to her parents when the man's voice broke back in. "All checks clear," he said. "Base is go for launch."

"Field crew is go for launch," Jillian's mom said.

Something under the pod began to whir softly.

"Launch is go," he replied. "Initiate on my mark."

"That's it?" Jillian hissed. In old space travel movies there was always a much longer series of checks. This was almost as outrageous as the thumbs-up.

"Well, we're not being strapped to a giant rocket and shot through five layers of atmosphere while doing our best not to explode," her mom whispered back. "We're just going through a door."

"Easy peasy," Jillian said, her mind still on SABRINA.

"Exactly."

"Launch in ten. Nine. Eight."

It's really happening, Jillian said to herself. *This is really, actually, finally happening.*

"Seven. Six. Five."

"Better than school, right?" her dad said.

"Four. Three. Two."

"You're going to love it," her mom said. "We're so proud of you."

This confused her. "But I didn't do anything yet!"

"You're here, aren't you? You were scared, but you said yes, anyway. That's—"

"One. Good luck out there, field crew. We'll keep the home fires burning."

And just like that, the pod shot forward on its runners, and the entire Earth disappeared.

CHAPTER 4

Jillian opened her eyes.

It felt like she'd been asleep for a few seconds. Like she'd dozed off during a boring movie, then snapped awake. Except she hadn't. She was in the bunk. In the pod. There were food bars digging into her ribs. Her head hurt. Why did her head hurt? They'd gone through the portal and—

"Mom? Is it okay to come out of the bunk now?"

Faint static through the earpiece, but no reply.

"Mom? Dad?"

Nothing.

"Mom!"

Silence. Her scalp prickled. Something wasn't right.

"I'm coming out."

Jillian got her feet braced on some packages and pushed the door open. The mechanism was still functional, and it swung open at her touch. That was the good news.

The bad news was: it didn't swing *out*. It swung *up*.

Easy enough to picture the quadpod's interior. Jillian was standing upright, so the pod must have landed on its end somehow, everybody's feet pointing toward the ground. But she didn't remember the pod rolling backward. She didn't remember it arriving. It was like someone had reached into her memory and deleted everything between *portal* and *now*.

She jumped for the opening, grabbed at the edge, missed, and fell back. She did this twice more, then paused, gasping for breath. Her head was one big storm of worry. What was wrong with the pod? Where was SABRINA? Why weren't her parents answering her? Why weren't they helping her get out?

It didn't matter. They were probably busy doing something important and would get to her in a minute. Maybe they were preparing another surprise. Getting ready for their first family hike on 80 UMa c. Setting out stuff to make space s'mores.

Jillian waited for a few seconds before realizing she didn't want to sit around waiting to be helped. Just like giving her the choice to come here in the first place, maybe her parents were waiting to see what she would do in this situation for herself. How independently and responsibly she could solve this little problem on her own.

Well, she wouldn't be much of a space explorer if she couldn't figure out how to get out of a bunk.

The tube was too narrow for her to easily maneuver inside, but she managed to work all the packages to the bottom, where her feet were. She kicked them into a sort of pile with her clunky boots. When she stepped up onto it, the pile sank a little under her weight, but still raised her up a few inches.

It was enough. This time when she jumped, she caught the edge, and the grippy gloves helped her hold on. Maybe gravity was lower on 80 UMa c, or maybe Jillian had a good dose of the same adrenaline that was supposed to let you lift a car off an injured person, but she thrashed and scrambled and eventually got her elbows locked around the rim. Bit by bit, she hauled herself up.

There her weight made the bunk top-heavy. It teetered and tipped over, rolling her out into the mud.

Mud?

Jillian stood up, breathing hard, ears ringing. She didn't want to believe what she was seeing. Her bunk was no longer in the pod. It was lying on its side in several inches of gloppy orange mud at the edge of some kind of swamp, gray water overgrown with lumpy blackish muck that was probably the alien algae they were here to collect. From here it didn't look like algae at all. Just alien.

In front of her was a low hill. In fact, the face of the hill seemed to be on all sides of her. It was like she was sitting in a soup bowl made of dull yellow-orange dirt, and the swamp was the soup. Some kind of crater?

The pod—and her parents—were nowhere to be seen.

"Mom!" she yelled. *"Dad!"*

"Up here," came the reply. It didn't sound like her parents. "SABRINA?"

"Hurry."

All the goofy sarcasm was gone from its voice, replaced with smooth urgency. This brought Jillian's *what-ifs* up on full alert. "Where are you?"

"I said—" There came a kind of blue firework from high on Jillian's left. It rose and glittered and solidified into the shape of an arrow, blinking on and off, pointing to the top of the ridge. "*Up* here."

Jillian had sort of expected SABRINA to come fetch her. At least make a rope to throw down to her. Something. But she was on her own.

"Okay," she said. She started clambering up the hill as fast as she could. The ground was drier here away from the swamp, at least, and the crater wall wasn't too steep on this side.

When she got to the top, at first she wasn't sure exactly what she was looking at. The ground looked *crumpled*, like a giant hand had grabbed it and squeezed. Green stuff showed through the cracks, like it had boiled up from underground.

The pod must have landed right on the peak of the buckling ground and slid off, because it was lying on its side next to it, in a patch of more of that green stuff, fully twenty feet to the right of the portal. It had *split* somehow, like something had torn its belly open, spilling supplies. Her bunk must have shot right out of the rupture and over the ridge.

But that wasn't the worst part.

The worst part was that Jillian realized—immediately, horribly—why SABRINA hadn't helped her.

It looked like SABRINA was already pretty busy just keeping her parents alive.

"Mom!" Jillian yelled, tearing across the rocky ridgetop as fast as the suit would allow. "Dad!"

What exactly was going on over there? She couldn't really tell. Her parents' bunks were empty. She could see the open doors through the rupture in the pod. There was something up on top of a wide, flat boulder. She could only see one end of it, but it looked like a giant cocoon. No. Two giant cocoons. Made out of something that could only have been SABRINA.

Looking at them drove all the air from her lungs.

No, she thought. *No, no, no*—

"This way," something said near her face. Jillian was so freaked out that she swatted at the thing reflexively. It dissolved to let her hand pass through, then reformed.

"Hey," it said. "Quit that."

"SABRINA? Where are my—"

"Shush." It was just a tiny fragment of SABRINA, vaguely mothlike, hovering at her shoulder. "Follow me," it told her. "Eyes forward. If I've analyzed your personality correctly, which I have, I'm at least ninety-nine-point-eight percent sure you don't want to look to your left."

So Jillian looked to the left. Toward the pod.

The hole in its side looked bigger than it had even a moment ago. That green stuff was not just under it now but inside it. And it wasn't one green something but a lot of green somethings, the way SABRINA was a lot of little somethings moving together, except that these somethings were much, much bigger than SABRINA's nanobots. They were like fat green worms. If worms swarmed like bees. Which Jillian was quite certain they did not.

There was something oozing out of the pod now, bright orange against the green stuff it had landed in. Then she realized it *was* the pod. The outer skin of the pod. Their home for a week. Where all their supplies were stored. Their food. Their water. Everything.

It was *melting*.

"I told you not to look!"

"What *is* that? What happened to my parents? Are they okay? Is that them over there on that big rock?"

"Less talk, more follow," said SABRINA. "Your parents are in stable condition. And it's me who's keeping them there, so I can't carry you. You're going to have to climb."

All Jillian knew of *stable condition* was that it happened on the newsfeeds a lot, after things like really bad traffic accidents. You ended up in a hospital, with tubes coming out of your body, or all wrapped up in bandages. *Or in a cocoon*, she thought, and broke into a sprint.

It wasn't far to the boulder. The next thing she knew, she was standing at the foot of it.

"Up you go," SABRINA said.

Jillian had to tilt her head way back just to see the top edge of the boulder. There were no handholds or footholds, and the rock face was sheer. But her parents were up there, and almost all of SABRINA was taken up with helping them, so she had to try. She thought for a second, then ran around to the back of the boulder. There were some smaller rocks piled up next to it, which she was able to climb. That put her about halfway up the main boulder. From there, the adrenaline was driving again. Her parents could be dying up there, for all she knew. She jumped and grabbed the edge and somehow pulled herself up.

She fell to her knees beside her parents. She couldn't really get a good look at them because they were mostly covered by SABRINA. It had split in half to enclose each of her parents individually, like sleeping bags. Only their heads poked out. Their helmets were off, and there was more SABRINA wrapped around her mom's forehead like the kind of bandage you wrap around a sprained ankle. But the only actual wound Jillian could see was just below her dad's eye, a kind of burned-looking patch of skin, almost perfectly circular, which there had apparently not been quite enough SABRINA to cover.

"I got her," SABRINA was saying to them. "She's here. They didn't get her. She's all in one piece." Tiny moth eyes squinted at her. "You *are* in one piece, aren't you?"

Jillian didn't know what to do. Or say. Or anything. She collapsed across them, hugging them both at once. She knew it probably hurt them, but she couldn't stop.

They couldn't hug her back, because SABRINA was pinning their arms, but they kept saying things over and over again like *Jillian* and *You're okay* and *Are you hurt?* and *We didn't know where you were.*

"I'm okay," she told them. "I'm not hurt, I'm fine, I'm okay. I think my bunk fell down the hill when the pod broke."

The pod. A little ways away, that mass of green things was still in there, squirming.

"What happened to you guys?" Jillian said. "What are those things in the pod?" Then she saw the look on her mom's face. "Mom?"

But when her mom spoke, it wasn't to her. It was to SABRINA. Her voice sounded weird, thick, like she had something stuck in her throat. It took Jillian a second to realize she sounded like that because she was trying not to cry. Her blood ran cold. Whatever this was, it was really, really bad.

Her mom fastened her *Do What I Say Now or Else* stare on SABRINA. "Get her out of here."

Jillian's heart slammed up against her ribs so hard it hurt. "Mom?"

"You got it, boss," SABRINA said. The sleeping-bag shapes dissolved and re-formed, and now SABRINA was a floating pancake again, just like it'd been in the lab. It even made Jillian a helpful little stepladder. "Hop on."

Jillian scrambled to her feet, took a step back. "No."

Now that SABRINA wasn't covering her parents, Jillian could see there was something very wrong with their suits. There were *holes* in them, lots of almost perfectly round holes, with burned skin underneath. Just like what was on her dad's face. It looked painful in the extreme. They needed a hospital. All that was here was the supplies. Which were in the pod. Which was dissolving right before her eyes.

They didn't get her, SABRINA had told her parents. *They who?* The worms? But the worms didn't bite people. None of this made any sense.

"Jillian, listen to me very carefully. The portal will only remain open for another two minutes."

"One minute, fifty-eight seconds," SABRINA corrected. It projected a countdown clock in midair. "One minute, fifty-seven."

"SABRINA's going to take you home. The site is compromised."

"What *are those things*?"

"Local fauna, behaving *very* abnormally. I don't know why. What I do know is it's not safe for you to be here. You have to go. Don't take off your helmet or touch the ground between here and the portal."

"SABRINA can carry you," her dad said. "Like a flying carpet. It'll be cool."

Jillian looked at the portal. Then she looked at her parents. "What about you?" she said in a tiny voice. Though she already knew the answer.

Silence.

"No," she said. Then she said it louder. *"No."*

"Jillian—"

"Why are you pretending like it's okay that I just *go without you*?"

"We can't walk," her dad said gently. "And SABRINA can't carry us all."

"But it can take you," her mom said. "Just you. And only if you go *right now*."

"So tell them to keep the portal open!" Jillian shouted. "Or send somebody in to help you, or—"

"Honey, they can't," her mom said. "We can't talk to them from here, and we won't make it to the portal without SABRINA."

Jillian's mind raced. "So SABRINA can go through and tell them!"

"SABRINA is getting you out of here. That's the priority now. Once you're through, they can figure out the rest. Get on it, and we'll try to distract those things long enough for you to get away."

Jillian had seen enough movies to know what that meant. "No way. I'm staying here with you."

"It's the only way. There's no time. We love you so, so much, and we're so—"

"I'm not going without you!"

"SABRINA. Get her home safe. That's an order. We're going down to clear a path."

"Acknowledged," said SABRINA. "It's been nice working with you."

"No!" Jillian yelled. She punched at SABRINA. It split and swarmed around her fist, untouched. She swung again. "I *said* I'm staying *here*, and—"

Something grabbed Jillian's shoulders from behind, not quite hard enough to hurt. Startled, she tried to turn. SABRINA had hold of her with its octopus arms, strong as steel cables, with a grip like glue. "Buckle up," it said.

She could feel herself being lifted very slightly off the ground.

"Put me down," she shouted. "Put me *down*!"

"Sorry, new kid," said SABRINA. "Orders are orders.

68

This is going to go a lot more smoothly if you cooperate."

SABRINA began drifting toward the edge of the boulder. Jillian's feet kicked at empty air. Like she was in a nightmare, she watched helplessly as her parents started to climb down the boulder. Back toward the pod. To give themselves to those *things*. To clear a path. To save her. While SABRINA *let* them, just because they'd *told* it to—

Jillian froze.

Because they'd told it to.

She reached over and pulled off her left glove. She pushed up the suit sleeve, the jumpsuit sleeve underneath. It wouldn't go up much, but it didn't need to.

Then she shoved the wristband up and in the direction of SABRINA's face.

"I have clearance," she said. Her voice shook. She ignored it. "Security clearance blue. Just like them. Orders are orders. Like you said."

SABRINA paused, hovering.

"And I *order* you to put me down."

The tip of one arm tapped Jillian's shoulder pensively. "Interesting. This *is* a dilemma."

"No, it isn't!" Jillian's dad yelled at SABRINA from the edge of the boulder. "You get her through there *now*. I *order you to*—"

"And *I* order you not to. I will go over there, and I will pull out their security chips, and I will throw them in that swamp before I let you *leave them here to die*."

"Ew," said SABRINA admiringly. "Gross. Hardcore, but gross."

It lowered Jillian to the boulder and plopped down next to her, a friendly fire-colored dog with six legs and a crown of stars on the side of its butt.

Jillian crumpled, both ears ringing. Her mind felt like lightning. It was looping one thought, over and over: *it listened to me it listened to me it listened to me.*

Her parents were beside her on the boulder. They were both yelling. At SABRINA? At her? Jillian didn't care. Let them be mad. It didn't matter. *She* was mad. She was furious. Or terrified. Or relieved. She didn't know what she was. She thought she might have to throw up. Or cry. Or pass out. She—

A sound came from behind Jillian. Or rather, a sound disappeared. It had been so quiet, so much a part of the background, that she hadn't really noticed it until it was gone. She turned to look, although deep down she already knew what it was.

The portal had vanished.

"Okay," SABRINA said. "Now what?"

CHAPTER 5

I don't know, Jillian thought. *I honestly have literally no idea.*

About nine-tenths of her wanted to yell it out loud, then curl up into a little ball and wait for her parents to fix this mess and get them all home.

But one-tenth of her knew she couldn't do either of those things. She didn't know SABRINA very well, but she remembered how it had watched her in the lab, like it was grading her on some secret test she didn't even know she was taking. Even now she could feel it watching her. If Jillian wanted it to keep following her orders, she'd better keep sounding like somebody with order-giving authority. Somebody like her parents.

But her parents had gone weirdly quiet. Weirdly still. Their faces were pale and sweaty, even though the air on 80 UMa c was cool as an October morning. Her dad's eyes were shut, but her mom was staring blankly into the too-green sky. They lay there and said nothing, just taking fast, shallow, tiny sips of air.

Jillian's heart punched up in her chest like a fist. Everything she knew about badly injured people came from movies. Shock? Were they going into shock? Was that right?

She swallowed her fear and stood up as straight as she could. SABRINA gazed up at her, head cocked, wagging the flame of its tail.

"SABRINA. I order you to go back to, um, being bandages. The field crew requires medical attention."

"No prob," SABRINA said. Within two seconds it had split in half and re-cocooned her parents. They didn't protest. They didn't do much of anything. She wanted them to wake up and yell at her some more for refusing to leave when they'd told her to go. This was infinitely worse.

All that was left behind of SABRINA was the moth-thing. It landed on Jillian's shoulder. "I am not equipped for advanced medical care," it told her. "All I can do is keep them stable, and I can't do that forever."

"Okay," Jillian said, shoving down a rising panic. *Nobody else is here to save them*, she told herself. *It has to be you.* She pointed at the bandages. "What exactly are you doing under there?"

"I neutralized and cleaned the chemical burns. I applied a self-cleaning layer of coverage, which will help prevent infection and introduction of debris into the wounds. But I'm not a medbot."

Jillian glanced at the pod. "Do we have one?" she asked doubtfully.

"No."

"Will they be okay until the portal comes back if we *don't* have one?"

"No. They need days in an intensive care burn unit re-growing the damaged skin. All I can do is try to keep them alive as best I can until the portal returns. After that . . ." SABRINA went quiet, consulting some unseen diagnostic. "I give them fair to middling odds. Let's say sixty-forty."

Jillian decided not to ask which outcome was the sixty and which the forty.

"But you—" she said, gesturing at the cocoons.

"Like I said, I'm not a medbot. This isn't my field."

"No," Jillian said, suddenly angry. The thinking part of her brain knew that what had happened to her parents had been an accident. Knew that when her anxiety spiked up, it made her irritable. But holding on to her terror felt like squeezing a balloon. She might be able to squash it down in one place, but it'd just pop back up somewhere else. And SABRINA was the only thing here. "Your field is making sure this place is safe for us to begin with. But it isn't, and now we're stuck here."

SABRINA just watched her blankly. *Of course you can't hurt its feelings*, Jillian told herself. *It's a machine. It doesn't have any.* Still, she took a deep breath and managed to say the next part more calmly. "So we figure out how to get down there and get the medical supplies while we still can. I know we brought some. I saw them in the pod."

"I thought we weren't going down there," SABRINA said. "I thought we were very specifically not doing that very specific thing."

"Believe me," Jillian said, "I don't want to."

But she went to the edge of the boulder and looked out at the pod. It wasn't too far. Maybe the length of a hallway at school. She could sprint that in a minute, easy. Not that the distance was even a measurable fraction of the problem.

Fat green worms had burrowed into the pod like maggots into a peach, turning everything they touched into frothy goop. The medical supplies. The food. The pod itself, which was supposed to be Jillian's family's shelter for a week. Even the bunks were dissolving.

"SABRINA, tell me what those worm things are, and how we get past them." As Jillian watched, a water tank tumbled out of the pod's storage bay and through the hole. Green worms clung to it, covering it almost entirely. The thick plastic walls of the tank began to look foamy.

Suddenly she knew exactly what she was looking at.

Something her dad had told her back in the facility. About life-forms on 80 UMa c.

A thing like a fat green earthworm. About the size of a big slug.

Acid for saliva.

But if they'd never attacked a field crew before—why today?

Jillian pushed the question away. It was a huge one, and took some serious shoving. But their supplies were literally melting away while she stood there doing nothing.

"Actually, forget the first part. We need to get our stuff out of there *now*."

"Sounds good," said SABRINA. "Kinda busy here, though." It spoke from the cocoons, not the moth on Jillian's shoulder, so she'd get the point loud and clear. "Or are you ordering me to reallocate?"

Jillian wasn't a hundred percent sure what *reallocate* meant, but she figured she got the basic idea. There wasn't enough SABRINA to go around—to be bandages *and* moth *and* whatever went down with Jillian to the pod.

"They'll be okay for a few minutes without you while we go down there and grab medical supplies," she said. "I mean, probably? Right? Can you just real quick fly down there and do, like"—Jillian rooted through more movie-based vocabulary—"do some recon? Maybe pick some stuff up and fly it back? Like you were going to fly me down to the portal a few minutes ago? Can you do that?"

Even as she asked, it felt like a long shot. A one-way trip to the portal carrying Jillian was one thing, but going back and forth with hundreds of pounds of supplies was another. And SABRINA had barely been able to raise her off the ground.

"I am *shatteringly* awesome," SABRINA admitted, "but I was not designed for heavy lifting. If I could carry that much stuff, I could carry three humans no problem, and we'd be back in the lab right now sitting through decontamination protocol, and I would be telling you jokes. I know twelve hundred and nineteen jokes, all of which are excellent. Don't listen to Dr. Park. They're excellent."

Jillian wasn't really listening to SABRINA's chatter. A new idea was coming to her. The longer she looked at her parents, cocooned in the SABRINA bandage, the more solid that idea got.

"The worm things. The acid. Does it . . . hurt you? Damage you, I mean?"

SABRINA seemed to consider this. "I don't know." Then it perked up. "Do you want me to find out? I love learning new things about myself. I could go annoy one of them. See what it does. Oh! I could poke it with a stick. Isn't that a thing you humans do?"

Jillian tilted her head at it. "Not . . . really? Okay, when you were getting my parents out of the pod, did the worm things attack you at all?"

"They did not. They were very busy attacking your parents. Would you like to see?"

No, Jillian thought. But she had to know as much as she could about those worms, and quickly. Going down there knowing nothing was only going to get her hurt.

She nodded.

SABRINA began a replay video for Jillian, just like the one of it catching bullets in the lab. Except this one played on the side of her dad's cocoon. There wasn't enough extra SABRINA to make a screen.

So Jillian watched as the quadpod shot through the portal, toward a patch of normal-looking yellow-orange dirt. It landed and slid forward—and the ground shoved up beneath it, cracking and heaving and vomiting up thousands of fat green worms.

It happened so fast. Like the weight of the pod had pressed some unseen button labeled *worm volcano*. Why hadn't SABRINA triggered it when it'd come through first?

Oh, Jillian realized, remembering the floating jellyfish form SABRINA had taken. *It never touched the ground.*

The pod tumbled sideways off the violently buckled ground, rocking backward hard. As it did, the foot end of Jillian's bunk ruptured the soft skin of the pod, fell out backward, and slid out of view.

Jillian could hear someone screaming in the replay. Then she realized it was her.

"Skip forward," she said.

SABRINA obeyed. Next there were her parents yelling her name even as SABRINA provided cover for their escape toward the boulder, shielding them from the onrushing wave of worms. They were *fast*, faster than any worms she'd ever seen before. They moved more like startled snakes, whispery-silent and whip-quick.

Jillian's mom helped boost her dad up, and he reached back to help her climb. SABRINA hovered up behind them.

Too slow. Fat green worms suckered onto them like leeches. Their suits began to bubble. Then their skin. They ripped the worms off themselves and each other and threw them off the boulder, back into that seething green sea.

SABRINA helped, going octopus again and growing extra arms for the purpose. But the worms never bit SABRINA. Never even tried.

"Okay, here's your next order," Jillian said. "I want you to get off of my mom and dad. Leave just enough of—um, of yourself?—there to keep the worst of their wounds covered.

The rest of you is coming with me."

Immediately SABRINA was a floating pancake again. It waited in silence for Jillian to climb aboard. But she shook her head.

"You don't want me to carry you?"

"I have an even better idea," Jillian said. "Your handler told me you watch a lot of TV."

"Yeeeesss," SABRINA replied warily. "I suppose you're about to order me to read a book or somethi—"

"Then I guess you already know what a mech suit is."

SABRINA brightened. "Please tell me you're thinking what I think you're thinking."

"How fast can you make—*whoa*."

All at once, SABRINA swarmed her, just like the bees shape it had made back in the lab. Except this time there was nothing scary about it. Jillian couldn't even feel it through the podsuit. Then, before she could even get another word out, SABRINA was done.

Jillian looked down at herself. "Wow," she breathed.

Mech-SABRINA was candy-apple red and shiny. The twin suns of 80 UMa c gleamed off its glossy shell. Her hands looked suspiciously like rocket gloves. One of them was holding a sword. A really big, really awesome sword. It looked like red glass with a razor edge. Like it could cut through anything.

"Fast enough for you?" came a voice at her ear. Jillian reached up and felt a helmet that definitely didn't feel like the podsuit helmet. For starters, it had a shark fin.

"Maybe not the rocket gloves," she said. "Or the sword."

"Go big or go home, right?" SABRINA said. "And we can't go home, so . . ."

"SABRINA, I need my hands to climb. If there's extra of you, make it into more armor, or send it back to my parents."

"Aw," it said. SABRINA sounded genuinely disappointed, which made no sense.

"You can put the sword back on when I get off these rocks," Jillian compromised. "After all, I might need it to fight the worms."

"You think so? *I* thought so."

"Yeah," Jillian said. "I do. Now let's go rescue our stuff."

What Jillian really wanted was to jump down off the boulder, come crashing down like a meteor, land in a cool action-movie-ninja stance, and take off running so fast she left scorch marks. But she remembered the replay of the landing SABRINA had shown her. The way the ground had looked utterly normal until the pod put its weight on it. She climbed down the boulder the way she'd come up, from rock to rock, and made *very* sure to touch down lightly.

Inside the jumpsuit, the podsuit, and the outer armor of mech-SABRINA, Jillian expected to feel like the solid center of a nesting doll. Or like some kind of walking, talking, armored, weaponized, giant turducken. But it really wasn't that weird at all.

SABRINA was smart. Really smart. And apparently super adaptable. It moved when she moved. Gave her extra grippies on her gloves when she climbed down the rocks. Sent part of itself to the soles of her boots to absorb the noise and vibration of her footsteps. It did all this without being asked.

And it gave her back the sword. She felt about a hundred times safer with it. Like something out of a movie. Something invincible.

But she knew better.

Jillian paused at the base of the boulder, getting her bearings. It was almost a straight shot to the pod, rocky but doable. The pod, however, was leaning to one side like a scoop of ice cream on a hot day, slowly dissolving into a green pond of worm things maybe fifty feet across. From the edge of that puddle to the pod there was no clear path at all.

"Okay," Jillian said under her breath. She bounced on her toes a little, trying to work up the nerve. This was easily, hands down, no contest, the scariest thing she'd ever done. "Okay."

"I don't think the *worm things*, as you insist on calling them, are using visual guidance to track you," SABRINA said, "but I'm gonna go ahead and make you invisible anyway. Partly because I thought it might reassure you. Mostly because it'll be cool."

There was no sound, no noticeable change. But when Jillian looked down at her body, it was gone. She had turned into a vague person-shape made of the now-transparent jelly of SABRINA.

She was as ready as she was going to get. Which was not very. "All right," she said, as much for herself as for

SABRINA. "Let's do this."

Quick and light, they tiptoed their way across to the edge of the worm-pond. Jillian squinted, peering into the dim interior of the quadpod. All the crates and containers of supplies were labeled clearly, but a lot of the labels—along with the things they were stenciled on, and the stuff *inside* the things they were stenciled on—had already dissolved.

Her stomach twisted. Her eyes prickled. *I'm too late*, she thought, and then shook her head fiercely. *Won't know until we try.*

"Send in one of your little probe things," she told SABRINA. "Find out where the medical supplies are."

"Your wish is my command," SABRINA said, and a speck of Jillian's invisible mech suit detached and zipped through the air into the darkness of the pod, blinking on-off like a firefly. "Found it," the suit part of SABRINA said into Jillian's ear. "Follow the beacon."

The SABRINA firefly blinked faster now. Somehow it was already visibly farther off than before. If Jillian stood there hesitating for one more second, she was going to lose it entirely, so before she could change her mind, she charged in, worms squelching under her boots.

This seemed to get their attention. Green worms boiled out of the pod and toward the vibrations of her footsteps. Jillian froze.

"They didn't want to bite *me*," SABRINA chose this moment to clarify, "but chances are fair to excellent that they can easily smell *you*. If you can move just a *teeny* bit faster, now would be an optimal time to do that."

Worms were scrambling over one another, barreling at Jillian in a wave.

Panic seized her. Panic and anger combined. It ran up through the soles of her feet, along her spine, out the top of her skull. It blasted out of her mouth in a huge, wordless yell.

Jillian hefted the sword and charged.

Together she and SABRINA went through the mass of worms like a chain saw. She kicked and stomped and slashed her way to the pod, scattering and splattering.

She tried not to think of how her parents would have made a path through the worms to get her to the portal safely. She thought of it anyway and started slashing harder.

Acid saliva or no, they were just worms, and she felt almost—*almost*—bad for them by the time her mucky boots hit the floor of the pod. Then she realized how few supplies were left intact, and all her pity shriveled up and died.

One crate of medical supplies, half turned to sludge.

One intact five-gallon container of water.

A few orange tarps, made out of the same stuff as the pod exterior, partially melted but maybe salvageable if she cut the damage away.

A couple of sealed packages that had no stenciled labels, which she wasn't about to hang around and identify.

That was all. Most of the containers were ruined, their contents turned to slop. Even the bunks that remained in the pod had been chewed through, and anything left in there was long gone.

She slapped worms off the least damaged-looking crates and grabbed what she could while SABRINA flicked more worms off her legs and shoulders. They just kept coming, up and up from underground.

"Persistent," SABRINA said. "You have to give them that."

Suddenly, the sword was gone. SABRINA had absorbed it. Within about half a second that material had been repurposed to cover Jillian with long, sharp quills, like a porcupine. It bought her a few moments, but the worms seemed disturbingly unconcerned with their own safety. They were trying to wriggle down through the quills, *impaling* themselves on the quills and still trying to bite their way toward Jillian.

Like in a zombie movie, she thought. And just like that, she hit her limit. It was all she could do not to escape back up that rock to safety. But she needed those supplies. She dug her feet in and bit her lip so hard she drew blood.

"Get them off me!" she yelled at SABRINA. Even though she could see that SABRINA was busily doing exactly that already. "Make some hands and *grab something*."

"*Something* as in worms, or *something* as in supplies?"

"As in I don't care! As in both! As in we need to get out of here!"

"Specificity," SABRINA said primly, "is the essence of efficient communication."

"I order you to shut up and help me."

Then she remembered. It might watch cartoons and tell jokes and design excellent mech suits, but it was still a robot.

It needed orders. Orders that she, with her blue clearance wristband, had to give.

She struggled through the panic and made herself think. The worms—so far—weren't biting through the SABRINA armor. She had time. More than the supplies did, anyway. Most of them were already lost.

"Help me get this stuff out of here before it all melts. I can't carry it all."

"Roger that, Boss." With that, SABRINA shot out tendrils of material and wrapped them securely around Jillian and her oversized armload of stuff. "Like that?"

"That's great." Jillian shambled forward, weighed down by the pile of supplies. She made it three steps and stopped. "Wait. I forgot the water. I couldn't carry—"

"No worries, new kid I got it." Another tendril shot out, hardened into a hook, scooped the water container up by the handle, and slung it out the pod door.

Jillian held her breath as that one remaining container of water sailed up over the sea of worms in a mathematically perfect arc—toward the edge of the green and past it into the safe zone of worm-free yellow-orange—and came crashing down in the dirt, breaking open instantly.

Water glugged out, cup by precious cup.

"Hmm," SABRINA said. "That should have worked. There must have been a weakness in the container. Come to think of it, that makes total sense. What with the acid and all."

Jillian stared at the container for a moment, stunned into speechlessness. Then she found her voice. "SABRINA, get over there and plug that up *quick*."

A grapefruit-sized chunk of SABRINA peeled off and skimmed away toward the container. Jillian, arms full, hurled herself after, squishing worms as she went.

By the time she reached the safe zone, SABRINA had the hole patched and the container set upright, but she couldn't stop to pick it up with her arms pinned in front of her. So she kept running, certain there was a tidal wave of green worms right on her heels, and didn't stop until she reached the boulder.

There she dumped her armload of stuff and scrambled up, rock by rock by rock, pushing the half-ruined crate of medical supplies before her. The SABRINA suit dissolved as Jillian climbed, which freed the worms impaled on the spikes, and they rained down around her, plopping onto the dirt below. Meanwhile, SABRINA remade itself into a shield guarding her back as she climbed. She'd have to come back for the other things, the tarps and whatnot. That was fine.

But SABRINA hovered up beside her as she paused on top of the boulder to catch her breath. Now it was a kind of floating net, carrying the tarps and mystery packages on its surface.

"The good news is, these are light enough for me to carry," it said. "The bad news is . . . well. Hmm. Pretty much the same thing, really, come to think of it."

"It's not too heavy because we couldn't save much stuff," Jillian panted. "I get it. Can you bring the water?"

"Sure. See, the good news, is the water container is now

light enough for me to carry," SABRINA said, levitating it easily. "And the bad news—"

"Let me guess. It's light enough because we lost most of the water."

"Right!" SABRINA set the crate on the boulder. "I didn't mean to break it."

"I know."

"It was an accident. My trajectory calculations failed to take into account that the acid might have undermined—"

"SABRINA. It's okay. We'll figure it out. Let me take a look at this other stuff first."

Jillian knelt beside the medical supply crate and pulled open what was left of the lid. Inside was treasure—or would have been, if half of it hadn't been ruined. Worse, the foamy meltiness was slowly spreading from the damaged stuff to the undamaged stuff. The texture of the plastic looked like whipped cream that had sat in hot chocolate for a while. Jillian wasn't one hundred percent sure what would happen to her hands if she touched it, but she had a pretty good guess. She thought for a second, then turned the whole crate over and dumped it out onto the rock. The undamaged stuff went into one pile and the damaged stuff went into another pile, which then got kicked off the side of the boulder onto the ground. She could still hear it fizzing from ten feet below.

What was left was . . . not much. A couple little bundles of smart bandages in two different sizes. A tiny tube of antibiotic cream, its lid eaten away but mostly intact. A broken little case of single-use insta-stitches, mostly corroded, with maybe two or three salvageable doses. One tissue-thin self-heating blanket. A pair of tweezers. A roll of industrial-strength duct tape with a chunk eaten out of one side so it formed a letter C. A blister pack of pills in perfect condition, but unlabeled, and she'd already kicked the dissolving box over the side, so Jillian had no idea what they were for.

She ripped open the two mystery packages. *Food*, she thought. *Please be food.*

One was a spare set of the slithery blue jumpsuits, vacuum-packed into a brick. The other was . . . bathroom stuff. Toothbrushes. Soap. Toilet paper. Dry shampoo. A little collapsible cup. She almost threw it off the boulder in frustration.

Instead, Jillian looked at her sad little pile. Then she looked at her parents. With the full-body SABRINA bandages off, they somehow looked worse. She couldn't see the acid burns the worms had given them, but she *could* see all the holes in their podsuits, and knew it would be hard to keep them warm when the suns went down. She could see all the whitish dots and patches of stuff on their bodies, where SABRINA had covered the worst of the wounds as instructed, and knew there weren't anywhere near enough smart bandages in her pile to fix them.

The water container was half full at best. There was no food at all. The pod—their home for a week—was lost. And she had two dozen smart bandages for easily eight dozen wounds. And, as SABRINA had so helpfully pointed out, no medbot. No portal. No way to get home for five days.

SABRINA wasn't a medbot. And Jillian definitely wasn't. But her parents were hurt. Badly hurt. And nobody was here to save them except her.

Not that she had the first idea how. Even looking at the wounds was making her a little queasy. Her parents were more helpless than she'd ever seen them. What if she messed up?

She must have thought this last part out loud, because SABRINA answered.

"Oh, you probably will," it said. "But they're going to be a lot worse off if you don't try."

Jillian thought about this for a moment. Then she took a deep breath, counted to ten, exhaled slowly. Then she peeled off her gloves and stowed them carefully in her podsuit pocket. *First thing a doctor does*, she remembered, *is wash their hands.*

"Okay," she said to SABRINA, or to herself. "Let's do this."

CHƎPTER 6

Two agonizing hours later (by SABRINA's very accurate and very irrelevant tracking of Earth time), Jillian sat on the edge of the boulder, kicking her legs over the drop. Glaring out at the place where in four days, twenty-one hours, nineteen minutes, and twelve seconds, a portal would zap into existence and bring them all home.

Her parents were patched up to the best of Jillian's ability, with a bunch of SABRINA's help. *Not a medbot* was right. She remembered meeting the medbots who took out her tonsils and fixed her broken arm, and SABRINA was definitely not anything like them. A medbot would have had laser cauterizers. Injectors of a half-dozen kinds of antibiotic built into its fingers. Speedheal patches, which she could stick on her parents' necks for a slow feed of steroids and nutrients into their systems. Intravenous hydration packs. But SABRINA—and Jillian—had none of these things.

What she'd had was a spray tube of no-rinse foam soap and a busted container of water. Nowhere near enough antibiotic cream. A quarter as many smart bandages as she really needed. The insta-stitches—one of the least-ruined things in the crate—had been pretty much useless for the specific kind of wounds her parents had. She'd done her best, but there was no way to tell whether it was good enough. Only time would give her that answer. Watching and waiting, not knowing what to expect. Basically the exact opposite of what she was good at.

The best find had also posed the hardest decision—the blister pack of mystery pills. All the useful labeling and dosage information must have been on the box, because there was nothing on the pack itself except a string of numbers.

In the end she'd taken one pill out and examined it, hoping it would look familiar. That hadn't gotten her anywhere, but then SABRINA had plucked the pill out of her hand and held it for three seconds without looking at it before announcing: "Painkiller and sedative. Dosage: one pill per person every twelve hours."

Painkiller sounded like a great idea, but *sedative* was scary. Her parents were already pretty out of it. Jillian racked her brain for more movie vocabulary. Was this what a concussion looked like? Was she even supposed to *let* them go to sleep? How much longer could she hold this whole mess together without them?

The countdown clock shone down helpfully: *four days, twenty-one hours, seventeen minutes, three seconds.*

But those burns looked really painful, and every time she'd been sick, her mom had told her to sleep so she'd heal faster. She'd opened a second pill, then handed both to SABRINA and nodded.

Her parents now lay asleep, sandwiched between the two damaged tarps, dressed in two of the spare jumpsuits, breathing more steadily than before. The self-heating blanket was too small to cover them both, so she put it under them. The boulder was getting cold, and probably wasn't too comfortable to lie on directly anyway.

SABRINA was fussing over them, making pillows for their heads, lovingly dripping water into their mouths through funnels it had apparently just designed for the purpose. "There, there," it was saying to them, over and over, in a singsongy tone it probably thought was reassuring but mostly came off as mildly creepy. "There, there."

At the same time, in a lower register, it was muttering to itself. Jillian wasn't really listening, but bits of this monologue reached her anyway. It seemed to be about fifty percent concern for SABRINA's patients, fifty percent trash-talking medbots and their general inability to morph into fluffy pillows at will.

Just a few days, Jillian thought, double-checking the new countdown clock SABRINA had projected into the sky for her, as if staring at it would make it go faster. *We just have to last that long, and then we'll all be okay. I last longer than that at Aunt Alex's house all the time.*

But she was already thirsty. She was getting hungry too, but she'd found literally not a crumb of edible food in the pod. It had all gone to the worms. And she was very, very reluctant to use up what little water they had. She'd already gone through some of it to clean her parents' wounds. There was maybe a gallon left in the container. SABRINA wouldn't need to drink any, of course, but three other people would have to figure out how to live off it for days yet.

Even worse, it was getting colder. She'd pulled the third spare jumpsuit over the one she had on already, then zipped the podsuit back on over both. It helped, but just a little. One of 80 UMa c's two suns was still fairly high in the sky, but the larger one was setting, darkening the greenish sky to purple all along the horizon. In other circumstances, it would have been really pretty. She would have been itching to draw it, or take a picture, so she had some memory of this place to bring home and keep forever. But now Jillian looked at that spreading darkness and saw nothing but doom.

What was left of the pod looked like a giant foot had stomped on it. It was a shapeless mass now, barely recognizable as the shiny orange egg from the facility just that morning. She didn't like to think what would happen when the worms finally ate everything in the pod and went looking for dessert.

Had the sea of worms grown at all? She couldn't tell for sure. It certainly hadn't gotten any smaller. She squinted in the purpling light, looking for landmarks. There was the path she'd made, and there was the puddle where the water container had broken, and—

Jillian squinted. Something looked *wrong*. Even more

wrong than the rest of it, which was saying something. "SABRINA."

"You rang?"

"Come take a look at this. Tell me what you see."

SABRINA aimed and deployed a shimmering gold paper airplane of itself. It glided to rest on Jillian's shoulder. "Worms," it said. "Some more worms. Oh—Wait—I think I see—no. Just worms."

Was it being deliberately obnoxious or just extremely literal-minded? Jillian wasn't sure.

"Look there." Patiently, Jillian pointed at the puddle. Dead worms floated on its surface. Not ones that she'd squashed. They looked whole. And more worms were crowding into the puddle even as she watched.

At first she thought they were drinking her spilled water. Then she realized they were shoving their heads down into the water and keeping them there. She didn't know a whole lot about alien worm anatomy, but it looked exactly like they were trying to drown themselves.

"*Dead* worms," SABRINA declared. Then it changed into a bubble gum-pink praying mantis and flew back to Jillian's parents.

But my bunk landed in mud, Jillian was thinking. *Right by the water. And there were no worms down there. Not even dead ones. I think I would have noticed if there—*

Wait.

Her bunk.

Her bunk, crammed with food bars and water purification tabs and soup mix. The worms had gotten to her parents' bunks already, but they might not have found hers.

She was halfway off the boulder before she even noticed she'd gotten up.

"Afternoon stroll?" SABRINA tilted the triangle of its mantis-head at the two suns. "Or is it evening?"

"It's both," Jillian said. "Come on. We're losing the light."

SABRINA flew up and alighted on Jillian's shoulder. The weight of it there was like nothing at all.

Jillian's bunk was exactly as she'd left it: lying on its side at the edge of the swamp. She could see it clearly from the top of the ridge. Getting down to it safely was another matter. She couldn't remember where she'd found that less-steep part of the crater. From here it looked like sprained ankle city the whole way down. And those rocks were *sharp*. Tearing her suit wouldn't deprive her of oxygen—pretty much the one thing 80 UMa c had going for it so far was that the atmosphere wouldn't kill her—but she was all out of smart bandages and fresh jumpsuits, and the night was going to be cold.

SABRINA seemed to sense her hesitation. It spoke from behind her. "Want a lift?"

Jillian turned. Part of SABRINA had stayed behind to keep an eye on her parents, but it must have borrowed some material from their fluffy pillows, because there next to Jillian was something that looked exactly like a sled, except that it was hovering three inches off the ground. SABRINA apparently couldn't decide whether to decorate it with racing stripes, lightning bolts, or flames. So it had gone with all three.

"It's beautiful," Jillian said, and meant it. "Thanks, SA-BRINA."

She climbed on. The edges of the sled cupped up around her and got cushiony. The front edge sprouted handles. "Hold on to your butt," it suggested, and launched itself down the slope. It was a smooth ride, and fast, and exhilarating, and for a few seconds Jillian almost forgot the depth of the trouble she was in. She was just a kid on a hoversled, breathless, grinning, speeding toward a purple sunset with alien wind in her hair.

The next thing she knew they were skidding to a halt at the edge of the swamp, parking themselves neatly in midair an inch above the mud.

When Jillian stepped out, this was no longer the case. Gray-orange muck was sticky around her ankles. She pulled her boots out one by one and waddled to the bunk, fingers crossed that the worms hadn't gotten there before her.

They had—probably drawn by the weight of her bunk in the same way they were drawn to the pod—but the mud seemed to be confusing them. They were periodically sticking their heads in, pulling them back out, and looping in confused little circles, making their way toward the swamp.

They're looking for deeper water, Jillian realized with a chill. *They're trying to die.*

First the ones up on the ridge, drowning themselves in the puddle, and now this. Why would they drown themselves on purpose? It made no sense.

But she didn't have time to figure it out now. Already it was darker in the crater than up on the ridge, and noticeably colder. Jillian hustled to the open door of the pod, crouched down, and flicked on the podsuit headlamp. Thanks to the stored solar charge of two suns, the beam was strong.

She was able to crawl in and haul the packages out from the foot of the bunk, no problem. Nothing heavy, not like the water container or the medical supply crate, so she just tossed each package over a shoulder for SABRINA to catch and lower gently to the ground.

It was all intact. Eight small packages in all. It didn't look like it would feed three people until the portal came back, but it was a whole lot better than nothing. Whatever fruit her dad had told her about back at the lab, it certainly wasn't growing anywhere she could see. Maybe she could go look for it when this stuff ran out.

That still left the water problem, though. She wasn't too sure how the little packet of water purification tabs was going to stand up to alien planet swamp water, but there weren't exactly a whole lot of other drinks on the menu. Was this mystery fruit full of water, like a melon, or more starchy, like a banana? She wished she could wake her dad up and ask. And where to find it, for that matter. Not that she was in a huge rush to go walking out into the worm-infested dark in search of it.

Last package in hand, she straightened, playing the beam of her headlamp over the gray endlessness of the swamp.

And nearly dropped the brick of food bars she was holding.

The lumpy black glop on the surface wasn't algae, like she'd thought earlier. Or alien water flowers. Or any kind of plant matter at all.

It was bodies.

Hundreds and hundreds of drowned bodies, rotting and overgrown with scum. Worms, yes. But other, larger things as well.

Her dad's voice echoed in her memory. *There're some things kind of like birds, but not. Some things kind of like salamanders, but really not. Something the* tiniest *little bit like a deer.*

"SABRINA?" Jillian whispered. Her voice shook. She needed her parents. She needed the portal. She needed to be off this planet. She wanted to turn and run, but that meant putting her back to the swamp. Just thinking about it made her skin crawl.

Something thrashed in the distance, weakly, and sank out of view.

SABRINA hovered up. "How may I be of serv— Eww." It paused a beat. "I am suddenly *really glad* that drinking water is not a requirement of my continued existence."

"They all drowned," Jillian murmured, like saying it out loud would force it to make sense. "All of them."

"Yep," SABRINA said. "Look, there goes one now." It pointed at one of the circling worms, which seemed to have sensed its nearness to the deeper water and put on a burst of speed. It was racing forward like the swamp was full of birthday presents instead of certain death. This struck Jillian as so *wrong* that she was sure she was about to puke.

Meanwhile, SABRINA was staring at the worm in fascination. After a moment it gasped and sent up a literal cartoon light bulb over what passed for its head. "I'm going to poke it."

SABRINA extended a kind of too-long finger with too many joints and poked the worm. The worm recoiled, paused, then continued toward the swamp. SABRINA picked it up and turned it back toward safety. It nosed blindly in the mud for a second, got itself turned back around, and kept going.

"Fine," SABRINA told it. "Suit yourself."

"No," Jillian heard herself say. Sure, these things had attacked her parents, and it was just a worm, and she'd killed plenty of them herself while trying to rescue the supplies, but she couldn't stand here and watch anything *try to die*. "We can't just let it drown."

"Whatever you say," said SABRINA. The poky finger turned into a slotted soup spoon, and SABRINA scooped up the patch of water into which the worm was now diving headfirst. The water drained through and the worm remained, and the spoon turned into a cage to hold it. SABRINA held it out to Jillian. "Happy birthday. Don't say I never gave you anything."

But Jillian was staring at SABRINA. Something else had just hit her. "I thought you checked out this whole area. Before we came through the portal. You didn't notice *this*?"

"There was nothing to indicate contamination," SABRINA said. "All my readouts were in the green. Temperature. Atmosphere. No adverse biological agents in the water."

"There are *hundreds of dead animals in the water*. They went in there and *drowned themselves on purpose*."

"Exactly. The water didn't poison them. It didn't dissolve them. It didn't boil them alive. It's just water. Seventy-nine degrees Fahrenheit, by my reckoning. Quite pleasant. You could take a swim right now if you wanted to."

Jillian's mouth opened to tell SABRINA exactly what she thought of that idea, but then she shut it. "*Extremely* literal-minded," she muttered instead.

"Hmm?"

"Nothing."

SABRINA sighed melodically: a little five-note trill in three separate registers, in perfect harmony. "It's unusual, I'll grant you that. Organic life is *so* unpredictable."

"But *why*—"

"I don't think it even knows." SABRINA lifted the caged worm, which was still trying to force its way out, wedging its head between the bars and bobbing it toward the swamp pitifully. "My chemical receptors indicate that this stupid little creature is signaling confusion."

"Chemical receptors?"

"Sure. I can pick up on even trace amounts of serotonin, melatonin, adrenaline, oxytocin, endorphins—"

"Okay, okay. And in the worm you're picking up on, um, what exactly?"

SABRINA shook the cage at Jillian a little. "It *really* wants to get in that water!"

"Yeah," Jillian said, swallowing hard. "I see that."

"But also it doesn't." SABRINA paused, hefting the

cage up and down. "It wants to, but it doesn't want to. Or it doesn't know *why* it wants to."

Jillian stared at the worm. Then she shook her head once, hard, as if the weirdness of this place could be dislodged from her mind. It didn't work.

"Come on," she said, changing the subject. "Let's get this stuff back up the ridge before dark."

One time Jillian had seen a roadkill raccoon. It had made her a little sad and a little sick to look at, but she'd had a hard time looking away. This swamp had the same effect on her, except multiplied by a million. She had to give herself another shake before gathering the packages in both arms and trudging back up the hill.

It was the hardest thing in the world not to keep that swamp where she could see it. SABRINA must have noticed that Jillian kept glancing back over her shoulder, because after a moment Jillian felt it landing and settling itself on her head. Whatever shape it had taken, it felt like it had a lot of legs and was taking a few seconds to arrange them.

"Don't you fret, partner," came SABRINA's voice from above. One leg gave a languid little wave at the edge of Jillian's field of vision. "I got your six. Anything back there so much as looks at you funny, I'll light it up." A series of cartoony *pew pew pew* sounds followed. Despite everything, Jillian found that she was grinning.

She kept her eyes forward and climbed.

CHAPTER 7

Back up on the boulder, Jillian took inventory of her find.

INSTANT SPLIT PEA SOUP, one thin, notebook-sized pouch.

INSTANT NOODLES AND SAUCE, same.

INSTANT BLUEBERRY CRUMBLE, same.

POWDERED SOY PROTEIN BEVERAGE, one brick-sized package.

HIGH-CALORIE FOOD BAR: EMERGENCY USE ONLY, two brick-sized packages.

WATER PURIFICATION TABS, one tiny packet.

MULTIVITAMIN/ELECTROLYTE TABS, one even tinier packet.

Jillian had been way too excited to eat much breakfast before coming to the facility that morning, and she was starting to regret it. Now that the worms seemed to be staying down by the pod, and she and her parents were safely up on the boulder with at least a fighting chance of making it through the night, what she really wanted was to tear open the bag labeled INSTANT BLUEBERRY CRUMBLE and pour it directly into her mouth.

Instead, she spread everything out before her, then sat back on her heels and considered her strategy. Each food pouch said it contained four servings. Each brick of food bars said it contained enough calories for one person for two days. The brick of powdered soy milk would probably see them through another day or two if they were a) careful, and b) really hungry by the end of it. And there were the vitamin tabs to supplement it.

She did the math in her head. They'd be hungry, but they weren't going to literally starve. All they had to do was stay put and wait for the portal, somewhere away from the worms and hopefully out of sight of that swamp. They wouldn't need a ton of food for that. And they'd order a stack of pizzas as tall as Jillian the minute they got home.

But her parents were out cold, SABRINA curled up in its cuddly dog-shape beside them. Thanks to those painkiller pills, they might not wake up for a while. There'd been two dozen pills, which would see them both through six days at most. And that was if she didn't waste any by waking her parents partway through their healing sleep. They weren't going to be chewing any noodles or blueberry crumble or food bars anytime soon.

So she took those out of the pile and set them aside. Then she took out the water purification tabs, because while they were super important, they weren't food. That left the powdered soy milk, the soup mix, and the multivitamin/electrolyte tabs.

And one very large burning question. Everything—the soup, the noodles, everything but the food bars—was freeze-dried. The soup was a bunch of shriveled peas and seasoning granules. The noodles were a dry nest in a pouch of powdered sauce. Each package had a big orange label on it reading, JUST ADD WATER. She skimmed the directions. One cup of water per serving. Four cups of water per package.

That was a whole lot of cups of water she didn't have.

Jillian's stomach growled. By now she was kicking herself pretty hard for not eating a huge breakfast before leaving for the facility. A tower of blueberry pancakes instead of the one lousy piece of toast she'd managed to get down. She thought back on all the food there'd been in her kitchen back home to choose from. It was all still there, however many light-years away, and here she was, stuck on a rock in outer space with freeze-dried peas.

Which was, she had to admit, a whole lot better than being stuck on a rock in outer space with *nothing*. She knew from her hiking and camping books that she wouldn't starve to death in five days.

But she might die of dehydration.

Which meant she had to let herself use the water they'd rescued from the pod. That was a big one. A big, scary, paralyzing dilemma that looked equally bad whichever way she cut it. When that water ran out, she didn't know what would happen. She'd have to drink that drowned-animal swamp-water. But how? Even if she dumped the whole packet of water purification tabs into it first, she'd still almost rather drink her own pee than that water. Real life, movies, video games, whatever—that swamp was the creepiest thing she'd ever seen in any of them.

But . . . she needed water. Her parents needed water. Death by dehydration was a definite if they didn't drink *something*.

People *did* drink their own pee in the wilderness, when they were lost and desperate. She'd seen that in some real-life survival video. But did they do something to it first? She couldn't remember. *Absolute last resort*, she told herself. *Other options first.*

She glanced over her shoulder toward the swamp. All that water, taunting her. In this light, the bottom of the crater was in full shadow. A bowl of darkness. Anything could crawl out of it, and she'd never know until it had made its way up the ridge, onto her boulder, and—

Not helping, she told herself.

She opened the soy milk package decisively. Air hissed out of the vacuum seal, turning it from a brick into a resealable pouch. Jillian ripped off the rest of the seal, careful not to spill any of the powder. Trying not to wonder if the jagged tearing sound of the perforated plastic would sound like a dinner bell to the worms, who'd already eaten all the *other* plastic—and everything else—in the pod.

Jillian dared a peek toward the pod, half-expecting a green wave to be making its way up the boulder—but no. The worms stayed put. For now.

"SABRINA," she said. "You know how you made that funnel thing earlier? And you were using it to feed water to my mom and dad?"

"I remember everything that has ever happened to me," SABRINA replied, but without its usual peppiness. It sounded almost depressed. "If I couldn't remember what I was doing"—here the barest eyeblink of a pause—"seventy-four minutes and sixteen seconds ago, you'd probably stand a better chance of survival out here if you'd brought a calculator and a Swiss Army knife instead."

Jillian held out the soy-milk powder. "I want to mix some of this in." She picked up the multivitamin tabs in the other hand. "Actually, I want to dissolve one of these in water *with* the powder and feed them that. Can you help me? I don't have a container."

"Can do," SABRINA said dully. It stood up on five stubby legs, holding the sixth one out toward Jillian. The next second, SABRINA's dog body was a little less chubby, and there was a container like a lemonade pitcher balanced on top of that sixth leg, which SABRINA had flattened out into a little platform.

"Thanks." Jillian shook some soy-milk powder into the pitcher, paused, then added a little more. Then she dropped in two vitamin tabs. Last, as carefully as she knew how, she hefted the broken water container and poured in enough to cover the powder, then added the tiniest bit more.

That done, she stuck her hand into the pitcher and stirred the mixture with her pointer finger. When she pulled it out, she went to wipe her hand on her suit leg, then stopped and licked her finger clean instead. She couldn't let even a tiny bit of nutrition go to waste.

Jillian nodded, satisfied with her work, and the pitcher floated back to her parents. There a chunk of SABRINA turned itself into a pedestal for the pitcher. Elaborately curly straws appeared from the sides of the pitcher, which it fed into Jillian's parents' mouths.

"How can they drink that?" she asked SABRINA. "If they're asleep."

"I'm just dripping it in," SABRINA said. "It's slow, but it's better than nothing." SABRINA seemed to realize Jillian was still standing there, arms folded, brow furrowed, watching her parents. "I got this, new kid. Eat something. You won't starve to death before the portal gets back, but you might pass out, and another of my faults, along with breaking water containers and not knowing about killer worms before giving my field crew access to a site, is that I can't carry water very far."

"Um," Jillian said. "Right. Okay. I'll get some food."

She opened up the instant noodles, broke off a portion, shook out some powdered sauce, and mixed it with a precious half-cup of water in a bowl SABRINA made and floated over to her. Jillian swirled the water into the powder, which kinda, sorta made a sauce, but the noodles didn't cook. They just sat there. So SABRINA heated Jillian's bowl and made a lid for it, holding in the steam as the noodles cooked and softened.

It didn't say anything the entire time. Everything was so quiet that Jillian could hear the night noises of 80 UMa c.

Breeze, some kind of crickety bug noise, a small distant animal rummaging around in the dirt. It sounded almost peaceful.

Still, something was obviously bothering SABRINA, and that was worrying. If there was some new problem, if things were worse than Jillian had thought, bad enough for SABRINA to have gone quiet, did she really want to know?

But not knowing was worse. Not knowing was how the *what-ifs* got in, and that was always, always worse.

"Hey," she said lightly. "What's the matter? Do you have, like, a low battery or something?"

"Low battery? Do I look like a phone to you?"

"If you were," she tried to joke, "we could call back home. *Hello, I'd like to place an order? One portal, please.*"

SABRINA made a moody little *mm* sound. Then Jillian remembered what it had said a minute ago.

"Look," she said. "The thing with the water container was an accident. There's got to be more water around here. You mapped this place, right? You probably know exactly where it is. So tonight we rest up, and tomorrow we go out and find it."

Silence.

Jillian had no idea if she sounded convincing. At first she didn't feel very convincing. But a weird thing was happening. The more she tried to make SABRINA feel better, the more she started feeling better herself. More determined. More ready to face whatever 80 UMa c had left to throw at them.

"And hey," she continued. "Whatever's happening with the worms, it's obviously new. My parents would never have brought me here if there was danger. And I bet their bosses would never have let them go either. Whatever's going on, it's weird and scary, and we'll figure it out together. You've already helped us out tons. We would have been worm food if it wasn't for you."

She swiped the last of her noodle sauce and licked her finger. She could have devoured the rest of the package of noodles easily, but that was tomorrow's food, and maybe the next day's too. Instead, reluctantly, she gave the bowl one last swipe and held it out in the general direction of SABRINA's main body. It evaporated in midair and floated off to rejoin her parents' pillows. "I don't care what you say, you're the coolest medbot I've ever seen."

"I'm not a—" SABRINA began, but broke off as something in Jillian's face or voice—or, more likely, Jillian realized as she remembered the worm by the swamp, the chemicals it could taste her skin exuding—made it realize she was teasing it. "Well," it said instead. "You're the most statistically nonstandard materials acquisitions surveyor *I've* ever seen, so I guess that makes us even."

It paused, giving her a moment to say, *I'm not a materials acquisitions surveyor*, but Jillian had clamped down on that reflex already.

SABRINA pointed a twisty straw at her. "Gotcha."

Jillian grinned. "I didn't say it."

"You thought it."

Jillian opened her mouth, then closed it. Friendly banter

was one thing, but if she admitted defeat at friendly banter, SABRINA would never let her hear the end of it. Instead she made a show of zipping her podsuit the last inch up to her neck, making sure the cuffs at her wrists and ankles were tight enough to keep out the cold.

And it *was* getting cold. And dark. 80 UMa c's larger sun was long gone below the horizon, and the smaller one was well on its way to joining it. *Good*, she thought at the sky. *Get out of here. One day down. Just four to go.*

Then she made the mistake of glancing up at SABRINA's projected countdown clock and groaned. Four days, fifteen hours, eight minutes, twenty-one seconds. Somehow, dark though it was, stars out and everything, only a few hours had passed since the portal had disappeared. Everything that had happened since had only taken the length of time of a handful of movies. It felt unreal.

Jillian already knew that a day was twenty-four hours on Earth just because it rotated at a certain speed. A day on another planet could look very, very different. A Mars day was only slightly longer than an Earth day, but a day on Venus was the same as more than half a year on Earth.

And how did you measure a day on a planet with two suns? Now that one sun had been down for a while and the other one was just setting, did that make it early evening or the middle of the night? None of her space books or videos or simulator games had really covered that.

She had to admit it was kind of pretty. The second sunset was blue, that smaller sun balanced on the horizon like a sapphire. The rest of the sky was already turning to full night. It was a color she didn't even have a name for, full of stars she didn't recognize.

Unbelievably full of stars. It looked like somebody had spilled a whole jar of glitter across a piece of velvet that was so dark purple-green it was almost black. What kind of constellations could be made from stars like those? She found one that kind of looked like a dog, and another that kind of looked like a hoverbike, and one that could have been a person running and waving their arms in the air.

A few of the glittery dots were bigger, more like sequins. It took her a moment to realize they were moons. Smaller or farther away than Earth's moon, but whatever they were, there were four of them. Or *were* they stars? Bigger, closer stars than what she'd seen from Earth? She couldn't tell, but now she was curious. Her parents might know, but that wasn't an option. SABRINA would almost definitely know, but she didn't want to distract it from taking care of her parents. She decided to look up the stars of the Big Dipper when she got home and find out for herself.

The sky made her think about how lost explorers in movies would use the North Star to guide them. If she had something like that here, and somewhere to go, that would almost make her feel better. Being able to *do* something to solve this problem besides waiting for rescue. She'd almost rather take her chances with frostbite or alien bears or whatever, like those movie explorers, and feel like she was progressing toward *something*. One foot in front of the other. Instead of sitting still.

She yawned, but stifled it. She couldn't sleep yet. She

knew SABRINA was keeping watch, but she still wanted to stay awake for her parents. If they woke up screaming in pain—or worse, if *Jillian* woke up to find them covered with a fresh layer of worms, already half dissolved, like the stuff in the pod—

Something brushed her back, and she startled hard. But it wasn't worms, wasn't anything scary. It felt soft and cozy. She glanced up, almost blind in the darkness. A blanket was draping itself over her shoulders. *Mom?* she thought. But she knew better. "Hey, SABRINA."

"Hey, yourself." There was a pause, which might have been SABRINA determining and following Jillian's line of sight. "Stars, huh?" Another pause. "I'm not very good at small talk." Yet another pause, while the fabric on Jillian's shoulders got noticeably cozier. "I *am* good at blankets."

"You're excellent at blankets," Jillian agreed. "How're my mom and dad doing? Don't you need this, um, blanket stuff for them?"

"Nah," SABRINA said. "They're good. If we keep them still, and keep them fed and watered, they should pull through A-okay."

Watered.

Well, that was a problem for tomorrow. For now, "A-okay" had gotten Jillian's hopes up. "So you *did* figure out how to heal them?"

"Let's not get ahead of ourselves. They'll be spending a lot of time around doctors when they get back, but at least they'll get back, instead of trying to hold off the worms so you could go through the portal without them. It's a good thing you decided not to do that. It really wouldn't have gone well for them." It paused. "At all." Another pause. "I ran the calculations, and their chances of survival would have been roughly four-point-five percent."

Jillian shivered. She rubbed the wristband beneath the podsuit cuff. Still there. "I'm glad you decided not to do that too." Then something occurred to her. "Will you get in trouble for not following orders? I mean, if you can even get in trouble. Can you?"

"I'm not sure. We'll have to find out together. Every day an adventure, I always say!"

"There's no way you can contact the lab back home?" Jillian asked, feeling like she'd asked already, or been told already. In any case, she knew. But she had to ask all the same. "High-tech thing like you can't turn into a, I don't know, a transmitter or something?"

"The human brain is the most complex computing system that exists," SABRINA replied. "You first."

Jillian yawned. Shorter days or not, she was exhausted. "Point taken."

"Get some sleep," SABRINA told her. "Growing kids on alien planets need their rest."

That was going to be hard. Or maybe not hard enough. She wanted to stay awake—*had* to stay awake—but her body had other ideas.

Jillian darted a look back toward her parents, then down in the direction of the pod. "No sign of the worms?"

"Oh, plenty," SABRINA said. "Down there." An appendage reached up from the blanket at Jillian's shoulder and pointed at the pitch-dark ridge. "See?"

The appendage lit up, a thin beam SABRINA aimed toward the ruin of the pod.

No—not toward the pod. They'd finally abandoned that. They'd moved on, drawn toward the puddle of water from the broken container. The worms had long since overflowed the puddle, but they were still wriggling toward it from all directions, trying to shove their heads down past the crowded mass of worms to the dregs of mud below. Worms piled onto that wet spot until they made a hill taller than Jillian.

"Yes," Jillian said weakly. "I see."

The already-slim chances of her getting any sleep at all were rapidly going down the toilet. But SABRINA was right. She had to try. She'd be useless tomorrow if she was too tired to think.

At least the worms were making no move to approach the boulder. She wasn't sure why, after they'd so thoroughly annihilated the pod, but whatever the reason, she'd take it.

"Sleep," SABRINA said, seconding Jillian's thoughts. "The substitute medbot insists. I'll keep watch."

True to its word, part of SABRINA detached and made a kind of telescope on a tripod, stationed at her parents' feet. Except that at the end of the telescope, instead of a lens, there was an eye. The telescope panned around in a full circle, then gave a soft click and panned back the other way, tracking the landscape relentlessly with that one unblinking eye. The soft click—and the whirring, humming noise it made as it spun its slow circle, back and forth—

wasn't necessary. SABRINA wasn't that kind of machine. It took Jillian a moment to realize SABRINA was doing that for her benefit. To give her something to listen to that wasn't the night noise of a lonely distant planet, and the quiet rustling of the worms.

So Jillian took her SABRINA blanket and squeezed in between her parents. The high point of her whole day ended up being that when she finally fell asleep, she didn't dream.

CHAPTER 8

A t first when Jillian woke up, she didn't know where she was. She lay there, eyes shut, sunlight shining through her eyelids. *Mom and Dad left on a work trip yesterday*, she thought blearily. *I'm at Aunt Alex's. The mattress in her guest bed is harder than I remember. The light is weird.*

Then it all came crashing back. She shot upright.

That was a mistake. Dizziness made her vision go all swirly, and her head was pounding. Had she ever been this hungry? She wasn't sure. Her mouth felt like she'd brushed her teeth with sand, and used more sand as mouthwash.

Something nudged her knee. She looked down, and there was a six-legged dog sitting in front of her, tongue hanging out.

"Morning, sunshine!"

Jillian stretched. She wanted water. No. She wanted orange juice. Just a few days left. She could do this. "Morning, SABRINA." She knuckled sleep out of her eyes and inspected her parents. They were still out cold. Her mom was mumbling something in her sleep like she was arguing with someone in a dream, and her dad was lightly snoring.

"They woke up a few hours ago," SABRINA said. "A while after you finally fell asleep. They didn't want to wake you. I gave them another dose of the medicine. They were still quite..." SABRINA paused carefully. "Uncomfortable."

"Uncomfortable," Jillian echoed. It'd probably been a whole lot worse than that. Whatever pain they'd had, they hadn't made enough noise to wake her. Jillian remembered all those burns and imagined how difficult that must have been for them. The thought rooted her to the spot for several seconds in which she could do nothing.

Feel sorry for them later, she scolded herself. *Do something to help them now.*

"Hang on," she said, leaping to her feet. "I'll mix up some more stuff with water for them."

SABRINA produced another bowl, and Jillian set about making breakfast for her parents. It was just watery soy milk with vitamin/electrolyte tabs, but it brought back memories of making her mom breakfast in bed for her birthday, and for a second Jillian didn't know whether she was more likely to laugh or cry.

But she didn't end up doing either, just nodded at the bowl when she was done, and it grew another pair of twisty straws. "Breakfast is served," SABRINA sang out, feeding the straws into its patients' mouths.

Jillian watched, arms folded like she was hugging herself to stay warm on a cold day. Then she shook it off and mixed herself up some blueberry crumble. It was the most breakfasty-looking thing there was in her pile. It wasn't half bad either.

As with dinner last night, she was still bottomlessly hungry after her carefully measured ration was gone. But she couldn't let herself eat another, no matter how much she wanted to. She still had days to go.

"When that packaged stuff runs out," SABRINA chose that moment to inform her, "you'll have to eat the worms." Then, misunderstanding the look of horror on Jillian's face, it added: "Don't worry. I can cook them. They're very nutritious."

"I'll eat my shoes first," Jillian declared. "I'll eat my podsuit. Just, I don't know, just boil it up and eat it with some imaginary ketchup."

"You would need at least two quarts of water to boil the podsuit," SABRINA said.

Do I even have that much? Jillian didn't ask. She wasn't sure what she would do if SABRINA said no. Instead she went to investigate the situation herself.

The container was noticeably emptier than yesterday. She ran this over in her head. SABRINA had given her parents some water, then two meals of soy-milk/vitamin mix. Jillian had mixed up two meals for herself. She hadn't even let herself drink any plain water on top of that, but she couldn't keep that up forever.

She lifted the container up and weighed it between her hands. It was scarily light. Maybe the weight of a jug of orange juice was left. What was that, half a gallon? That *was* two quarts. Some must have evaporated overnight. Or maybe they'd really just gone through it that quickly.

She made herself lift it to her mouth and take a tiny sip. Then another. It didn't even begin to take the edge off her thirst. It felt like the water was just running off her, like rain off a raincoat, never being absorbed.

She wanted to drink that whole container down and put a good dent in another. Instead she set it carefully back on

the boulder. Stared into the broken top corner. She could see her face down there, shakily reflected in the disturbed water. It was biting its lip with worry.

There was no way around it. They needed more water, and they needed it now. But from where? The swamp? It was so close. It was right down the ridge. *It's just water*, SABRINA had said. But it wasn't. It was water full of dead things. Things that had *chosen to die* in that water.

What if drinking that swamp-water was what made the worms get so confused? *Local fauna, behaving* very *abnormally*, her mom had said. Understatement of the year. But

what if Jillian drank that water and went *wrong* the way the worms had? What if all she had to do was *touch* the swamp for it to happen?

"Hey, SABRINA, question."

"Oooh. I *love* questions."

"When you came through the portal. Before the pod. You sent off some little bits of yourself to check out the area nearby. Little flying probe thingies?"

"Like this?" A swarming burst of little *somethings* lifted off the tip of the dog-SABRINA's tail. They were almost but not quite like the firefly it had made yesterday to lead Jillian to the supplies in the pod. They hovered a few inches in midair, drifting like dandelion fluff, before poofing back out of existence. "Yeah, that's a thing I can do. Ask me another. Oh! I know four hundred and thirteen different card tricks. Want to see?" A deck of cards appeared in front of Jillian, fanning itself out. "Pick one. Any one."

"Maybe later," Jillian said.

"Oh. Well. Sure. Okay." The cards vanished. SABRINA circled three times and lay down, curled into a comma with its flamy tail over its nose.

"Right now I kind of urgently need a water source. One that isn't"—Jillian pointed violently in the direction of the swamp—"*that*. But I don't want to get lost out there just kinda vaguely wandering around until I find one. I've seen enough movies to know that's . . . not the best idea."

"You said it," SABRINA said solemnly. "Next thing you know, you'd be trapped in a cave somewhere eating your own frostbitten toes for nourishment."

"I, um, I don't think I saw that movie."

"Me neither," SABRINA said, shrugging its first two legs. "But I *would* see that movie."

"You mapped this place. Tell me about other water sources." Then, remembering the very key feature of *this* water source that had somehow utterly escaped SABRINA's notice, Jillian was quick to specify: "Water sources that are not full of dead animals or anything else besides just plain regular water, please."

"Take your pick."

The whole side of SABRINA's dog body lit up like a screen, displaying little thumbnail pictures of various landscapes. Jillian squinted. "I just touch one to blow it up, or . . . ?"

"Go for it."

Jillian poked one that looked like a pond. *Please be clean water*, she thought at the picture as it blew up and rendered into focus. *Please, please, please.*

It was the swamp. SABRINA must have taken that photo from very high up in the air. Apart from the water in the bottom of it, it looked like the craters on the moon. Jillian knew what that meant. Craters on planets were caused by impacts. Meteors, asteroids, space debris. Something had slammed into 80 UMa c like a fist punching a pillow, and then the swamp had formed in the hole.

Even the blown-up picture wasn't close enough to give her much detail on what was *in* the swamp, which was a relief. Just clumps and clots of darkness on the gray water. That was plenty. She shrank that picture in a hurry.

"It didn't used to be there, you know," SABRINA said.

"What didn't? The swamp?"

"The swamp. The crater. That impact is recent. It wasn't there when they were running preliminary diagnostics on this site six weeks ago. See?"

A new picture appeared on SABRINA's side. This one was an empty field of orange dirt. Some scraggly purple plants grew on it. A few spiky black rocks. Jillian recognized the image from the lab. She'd seen it on a screen there. The image was time-stamped: 03/14/2113 11:39 AM.

Then that vanished, replaced by the picture of the crater. That one was time-stamped to yesterday. One of SABRINA's little probes must have taken it while Jillian and her parents had waited in the pod.

"So between six weeks ago and yesterday, something hit the planet. A meteor or something. Right?"

SABRINA gave another shrug. "Whatever it is, it either vaporized on impact, or it's sitting at the bottom of everybody's favorite swamp right now. If you'd like to dive for it, I'd be happy to outfit you with a breathing tube."

"I'm good, SABRINA, thanks."

After another minute or two of skimming through the thumbnails, Jillian found one that looked promising. She blew the picture up, and her breath caught. It was a waterfall, spilling from a high black rock. It was absolutely beautiful. It was the kind of place she would have loved to hike back on Earth, if her parents had ever gotten a chance to take her.

Well, she could take herself now. That was running water,

clean and clear. *Running* water meant nothing was lying in it, bloating and rotting, on-purpose-drowned.

"That. There. Where is that?"

SABRINA went still, like it was thinking. It didn't take long, less than a second before one stubby leg had lifted and pointed into the distance to Jillian's left. Away from the swamp, thankfully. "One-point-nine-seven miles north-northeast."

Less than two miles. That was nothing. She could do that, no problem. It was something she could get up off this rock and go out there and get *done*.

"What do you say?" she asked SABRINA. "Want to go with me on a field trip?"

But Jillian couldn't just march off the rock and down the ridge into alien wilderness. She had to be smart. She had to prepare. Lucky for her, she loved preparing. How many hikes and camping trips had she made careful checklists of supplies for, carefully packed extra layers and voice-activated headlamps and energy bars for, only to have the trip canceled by her parents' busy schedules? She could do this in her sleep.

At least, if today's hike were on Earth, she could. Where there were marked trails and rescue services in case she got lost. Where there weren't thousands of worms, hidden just underground, waiting for her to make a wrong move.

Suddenly she wasn't so sure.

She thought back on every survival movie she'd ever

seen. All the checklists in her hiking book. What did a person usually need to bring if she was going off into unknown wilderness? It was strangely satisfying to think about. *Just going for a hike*, she told herself. *In space. You got this.* She made a list in her head: *Food. Water. Matches. Tent. Flashlight. Compass. Knife. Phone or radio or something. Rope?*

Well, she had pretty much none of those things to hand.

What she did have, which those movie explorers did not, was SABRINA.

Jillian made a separate little pile of supplies. She'd only be gone a few hours, so she wouldn't need to take much.

The day was warming up, so she shucked off the extra jumpsuit and put it in that pile. She could layer it back on later, but she didn't want to get all sweaty while she walked.

The smart bandages were used up, so she took the broken roll of industrial-strength duct tape. She could use it to tape her toes if they started to blister in the podsuit boots.

All the food needed to be cooked before eating, so she almost didn't bring any. Taking food on a two-mile walk seemed like overkill anyway. But if those survival movies had taught her anything, it was that there was no such thing as being overprepared.

She picked up the food bars, hesitating only slightly over the label: EMERGENCY USE ONLY. "This is all an emergency," she told it, and dropped them on the pile.

That left the water. Once they got to the waterfall, she'd need something to carry some back in, and it would be too heavy for SABRINA, and use up too much of its material besides. She'd have to bring the container. But first she had to find a new home for the water that was already in it.

Jillian picked through the various packages and empty wrappers on the rock and came up with the empty pouch that had held the spare jumpsuits. It didn't have a resealable opening, but it looked sturdy.

Would it hold water, though? She couldn't exactly use any up to test. She thought for a second, then closed up most of the opening in one fist and blew air into the remaining hole, inflating the bag like a balloon. When she twisted the opening shut, the air stayed in.

If it held air, it should hold water. She sat down and propped the bag open, holding it steady between her feet. As carefully as she knew how, she poured the water in, folded down the top as many times as it would go, and closed it with a few strips of tape from the broken roll.

In the bag, their remaining water supply looked very, very small. Jillian locked the image of that waterfall in her mind and held it there. All that clean, fresh water. Hers for the taking.

She dried the outside of the empty water container on her podsuit sleeve. Then she did it again. The last thing she needed was to leave a trail of water drops for the worms to follow.

Next she stuffed the jumpsuit, tape, and food bars into the now-empty water container. Lastly she dropped the insta-stitches in there too, just in case. You couldn't be too careful in the wilderness. She bet that was extra true in space.

She inspected her little collection of supplies. It would help her in a general survival sense, but it wouldn't protect her from the worms.

SABRINA could. It had before. But that was when there'd been more of it to spare. This time was going to be trickier.

As if it was reading Jillian's thoughts, a fog of SABRINA particles was already gathering around Jillian. "I was thinking blue this time for the suit," it was saying. "And maybe lose the fin and do wings instead? They wouldn't work, but they'd look pretty cool. And keep the sword, obviously."

"No," Jillian said slowly. Because as safe and protected— and *awesome*—as she'd felt in the SABRINA mech suit, there was only so much of SABRINA to go around, and a lot of it needed to be here, keeping an eye on her parents. Jillian didn't like to think what would happen if SABRINA and she got back late for some reason and nobody had been here to give her parents their pain pills on time. "No wings. Maybe not even a suit, *exactly*? Just the parts I need most. And lose the sword."

SABRINA gave a little squawk of disbelief. "Who goes on an adventure without a *sword*?"

Jillian laughed. "Everybody, unfortunately. I'm pretty sure that stopped in the Middle Ages or something."

"Well." SABRINA sniffed. "Somebody should bring it back into style. I volunteer us."

"I'd love to," Jillian said. "Later. Right now we lose the sword *because* most of you will need to stay here and take care of my mom and dad. Last time you just left them for a few minutes while we got the stuff from the pod. This time we'll be gone longer." She looked at her parents and then looked away, blinking hard. "I can't help them," she admitted. "You can. And, I mean, look at you. You're doing an amazing job."

"I know." Immediately the telescope sentry was back, though smaller this time, its construction more streamlined. The height was the same, but the legs were spindlier, the telescope narrower as SABRINA conserved its material. "Like this?"

"Exactly like that. That's perfect. We should be back before they need their next dose of pain pills, but if we're not—"

"I'm on it." Dog-SABRINA appeared next to the telescope, lifting one paw in a weird little salute.

"But part of you has to come with me. I can carry the water but not find it. You can find the water but not carry it. We have to work together."

"Copy that, partner," SABRINA said.

"This time, just do the boots. To make my footsteps quiet so the worms don't find me."

Before she'd even finished talking, the boots were on Jillian's feet, the particles condensing into solid form without her even noticing. She lifted one foot to inspect it and broke into a smile. The boots were blue, and they had wings.

She knelt beside her parents and just looked at them for a moment, not saying anything. It was amazing how even grown-ups looked peaceful as little babies in their sleep.

She reached out and brushed their hair back from their faces, wiped a smudge of orange alien dirt away from the side of her mom's nose. She felt suddenly very small. Very helpless. Very alone.

Jillian was used to being away from her parents for days—but that was when she stayed with Aunt Alex, with all those wonderful Earth things she'd always taken for granted. Things like food and beds and drinkable water. Her worst enemy at Aunt Alex's was boredom. Now it was a whole planet. And she wasn't a hundred percent sure she was going to make it back alive.

"I don't know if you guys can hear me," she said, "but I'm going to go find water. SABRINA showed me a place where there's clean water just a little ways away. So if you wake up and I'm gone, that's where I am. I'll be back real soon." She paused, eyes prickling with tears. "I miss you guys. But I'm not sorry I didn't do what you said before. I couldn't just leave you here. And I'm not going to now either. I'm going to get you home."

She gave the whole makeshift camp one last once-over, seeing if there was anything she'd forgotten. SABRINA was pillows for her parents and the sentry guarding their sleep. They still had their blankets and tarps, and SABRINA had just finished dripping their breakfast into their mouths. The remaining water was secure in the pouch, and the food and supplies were all safely piled off to one side where her parents couldn't accidentally kick anything important off the boulder if they woke up again feeling *uncomfortable*.

After all this and the boots, just enough was left of

SABRINA to trot along beside Jillian. It looked like a ferret now, except it was apple-green and had eight eyes like a spider. It still somehow managed to be cute.

Jillian nodded at her parents, because if she said anything else, she knew the fear of what was out there would catch up with her and glue her to this boulder, and that would be the end. Instead she got to her feet, picked up the water container, and set off down the ridge.

CHAPTER 9

Descending the far side of the ridge looked much easier than the scramble down to the swamp. It was a gentler slope, and not so rocky. That was just fine by Jillian, because even empty the water container was big and awkward and hard to carry.

At least the SABRINA boots kept the worms from following. They still massed and clustered around the remains of the water spill, but the worm-pile was noticeably smaller than it had been last time Jillian checked. Where had the others gone? Back underground? Down to the swamp? She didn't know. They were paying approximately zero attention to the boulder, and that was good enough for her. She walked past that worm-pile in a careful wide circle, keeping one eye on it at all times. Weren't people mostly made of water? Was that why they'd attacked her parents?

Hush, she told herself.

When they reached the far edge of the ridge, Jillian

paused and looked down over the landscape. The worms were paying attention to the puddle here, but she didn't see any water down there. Nothing to keep the worms from noticing her instead. Before she took even one step into that wilderness, she had to know exactly where she was going and exactly how she'd get there. Point A to Point B, straight shot, no surprises.

From here it looked simple enough. Bare orange dirt down to the foot of the ridge and a little ways past it, and then from there it was overgrown with plant matter—short, sparse grass at first, then distant trees. A forest. It looked dark and mysterious and strangely inviting. She wished it were safe to explore and her parents were okay and they could all do a nice long hike in there together and end the day with a campfire and some space s'mores.

Instead she adjusted her grip on the water container and pointed out toward the trees. "The waterfall is in there?"

"No." The SABRINA ferret appeared on Jillian's outstretched arm. One green paw reached and nudged her pointer finger a fraction of an inch to the right. "It's in there."

"That's what I just said."

"It is *not*. You were a full two degrees off. You could have walked right into a bottomless abyss."

"There's a bottomless abyss?"

"No," SABRINA said patiently. "But you didn't know that."

"You lead, then," Jillian said. "I'll follow." In her mind she was laying out her worm-escaping strategy. After the footage SABRINA had shown her of the pod crash, she didn't want to be caught out over open ground. She scanned the space between her outstretched finger and those distant trees. *There's a big rock I could probably get up onto*, she noted. *And another. Three together in a group over there.* It was like plotting out a course for a game of The Floor Is Lava, except across what looked like miles.

Could the worms climb trees? She had no idea. But they hadn't climbed the boulder. They hadn't even tried.

Besides, on her to-do list for the morning, navigating that distant forest was step, like, three. Step one, of course, being: she had to *get* there.

"Ready when you are," she told SABRINA. "If you see anything suspicious, don't let me walk right into it this time, okay? Not like with the pod?"

She wasn't trying to sound mean, and she regretted it as soon as it was out of her mouth, but SABRINA just shrugged. "Sure," it said. It didn't sound even a little annoyed.

Of course it doesn't, Jillian chided herself. *It's a machine, remember? It doesn't have feelings. You just thought it was sad earlier because it talks like a person. But it—*

Mid-step, Jillian toppled over into powdery-soft orange dirt. It didn't hurt at all, but it was totally unexpected. She'd tripped on a rock? She hadn't thought there were any nearby.

No. The blue SABRINA-boots had adhered themselves to the ground, and Jillian's momentum had carried her forward with nowhere to go.

"Just testing," SABRINA said airily.

"Hey!" Jillian yelled, but she found that she was laughing. "Who taught you how to prank people?"

SABRINA twitched its ferret nose. "Natural talent, I guess."

"It's cartoons, isn't it."

"It . . . may be slightly that to some extent possibly yes."

Jillian picked herself up, which the boots allowed. "Teach me sometime?"

"Yeah?"

"Yeah."

From there they went down the rest of the ridge in silence. Either the shock-absorbing padding SABRINA had added to the blue boots was definitely working, or there were no worms on this side of the ridge anyway, because the whole way down, none appeared.

Jillian wanted to ask SABRINA about her parents but decided against it. *You've been gone five minutes*, she told herself. *Focus. They need water. They need to be able to rely on you to get it. If the worms were coming up onto the boulder, SABRINA would know. SABRINA would do something.*

The flip side of that reassuring thought, though, was: most of SABRINA had stayed on the boulder. Where it could do nothing to help Jillian if she ran into trouble.

Suddenly Jillian wished she had a weapon of some kind, not that she knew how to use any. Something. Even a stick would be better than nothing. But there were no trees here. There was a lot of walking yet between here and trees. She picked up one of the spiky black rocks and weighed it in her hand. It was small—not any bigger than her fist—but sharp. Holding it made her feel just the tiniest bit safer.

At the foot of the ridge, Jillian's boots spoke to her. "Back in a sec," they said. "Need to run a tiny errand real quick." But they stayed on her feet. Then she realized the spider-eyed SABRINA ferret was no longer beside her.

"What the—?" she said, glancing around. She wouldn't put it past SABRINA to turn itself into a rock and hide itself in plain sight in the landscape as a joke.

"Come on," she said, feeling slightly silly as she directed her voice down toward her boots. "I didn't mean teach me pranks *now*, I meant after we—*ahh!*"

The spider-eyed ferret was back, except now it was smaller. It had repurposed some material to make itself a set of bat wings, and was using them to hover inches from her face. And it had used more material to make a thing on its forehead like an anglerfish lure, dangling out in front of its nose. Except at the end of it was another little cage, just like the one SABRINA had made earlier.

In the cage was another one of the green worms. It writhed and squirmed and bit at the bars without obvious results. "Quiet, you," SABRINA advised it, shaking the cage a little. "Settle down."

Jillian scrambled back from the worm so fast she almost tripped again. "Keep that away from me!" Then an idea struck her. "Is that to help us find water?"

"I'm keeping myself occupied during the trip," SABRINA said innocently. "So I don't get bored. You don't want me to get bored. You know how a bored dog starts chewing on the furniture?"

Jillian nodded warily.

"It's like that. Except a whole lot worse. And I'm all out of furniture." It stared at her for a second and then winked half of its spider-eyes at her. "No, you're right. It's to help us find water."

"What about the waterfall? I thought you knew where that was."

"I do. But just like with the swamp, the landscape elsewhere might have changed too. There might be other water sources that my mapping missed, or that have appeared since. This little guy might help us shorten our trip."

"But your probe things. Couldn't you just send one on ahead?"

"Already done. But I don't want to rule anything out, and there could be underground water sources I wouldn't be able to see."

"But the worm might smell them," Jillian realized.

"Bingo."

"Huh," Jillian said. "Good thinking."

SABRINA did a weird little curtsy. "I try."

"Well," Jillian said, "let's get walking, then."

She took a few careful steps, then a few more. Even off the ridge, the SABRINA boots seemed to dull her footsteps enough that the worms didn't notice. She started walking faster. The SABRINA spider-ferret floated in front of her, kicking its goofy little legs like it was swimming in midair.

Jillian followed it for a while in silence. She counted her steps. One hundred, two hundred. When she got to three hundred, she paused and looked back over her shoulder at the ridge. It didn't look as far off as she'd hoped. Her arms were getting tired from holding the container. At least her feet were super comfy in the SABRINA boots. It felt like walking on a really soft mattress. She set her shoulders and kept walking.

At step five hundred and four, SABRINA sighed. "I'm bored. Why do you humans like hiking? It's *slow*."

"It's supposed to be slow," Jillian said. "So you can see what's around you. You don't really get a chance to see it most of the time. You're too busy doing other things. That's the whole point of hiking. To put that other stuff on pause and just, like, explore."

"I can explore *much* faster than this," SABRINA said. "When we get home, I'm going to have a nice long talk with Dr. Park about making me stronger so I can carry heavy things. I could have had that water back by now."

"Oh, it's not that bad," Jillian said, and realized she meant it. Out here walking meant doing something. Not just waiting. Actively trying to fix a problem. She was headed out into open alien wilderness, but she was about twenty times calmer than she'd been sitting on a rock thinking about worst-case scenarios. Compared to that, this wasn't that bad at all. She felt downright cheerful. "My mom and dad used to play I Spy with me on long car trips."

"We can do that!" SABRINA made a show of glancing around. One wing curled in to tap its chin thoughtfully. "I spy with my little eye . . . something that begins with . . ."

"Rule number one," Jillian said. "Things I can't see with my *human* eye don't count."

SABRINA groaned.

There was something very satisfying about getting ahead of its line of thinking. It wasn't even all that hard, now that Jillian was beginning to understand SABRINA a little better. "You're predictable, you know that?"

"*You're* predictable," SABRINA declared. "So predictable I knew you were going to say that."

There was a pause of exactly three seconds, and then both said at once: "Then what am I thinking right now?"

Jillian clapped one hand over her mouth in surprise. SABRINA had mimicked her voice perfectly.

"Point for SABRINA," it said.

Jillian laughed. "No more of that game," she said.

"Why? Because you'll never win?"

Well, yeah, Jillian thought.

"Where did you find the worm?" she asked instead. "Was it in that big pile of worms where we"—*you*, she thought but did not say—"spilled the water?"

"Down by the swamp," SABRINA said. "Okay, pretty much in the swamp. Really, it should be thanking me. I just saved its miserable little life. Instead I get this."

Jillian got a brief glimpse of the worm trying to squeeze out of the cage to head back the way they'd come. But she didn't watch for long. They were down near the grass now, and the grass was surprisingly sharp-edged and stiff, whispering harmlessly past the SABRINA boots.

Still, it was hard to see where she was going. She brought her gaze back to the ground and kept it there. "It wants to get back to the water," she observed.

"Well, too bad. It's . . ." Suddenly, SABRINA fell silent. "Hmm. Look."

The worm was slowly swiveling its head in various directions, as if it was trying to pinpoint its next target. Other than that, it had gone very still, like it was saving up its energy for something.

Jillian had a pretty good guess as to what that *something* might be. "What?" she asked. "Is it looking for more water? What's it doing?"

"*Lots* of things," SABRINA said. "Lots of very contradictory things. That's what's weird."

"Like at the swamp?" Jillian asked. "You said the worm back there, what was it, it wanted to get in the water, but it didn't, but it did? Like that?"

"Signaling confusion," SABRINA said. "Specifically, in the presence of water, it was indicating fear—"

Jillian thought of all those drowned bodies and nodded, shuddering a little.

"—but also expectation of reward."

"Reward?" Jillian thought a moment. "Like when a dog does a trick and gets a piece of food, and then it learns to do the trick anyway because it thinks it'll get food if it does?"

"Not exactly," SABRINA said, "but close. The one back by the swamp definitely thought *something* good was going to happen to it in the water. Well. *Thought* might be the wrong word for such an obviously idiotic life-form. If I were to put its train of thought into words I could explain, it might go like: *water bad! water good! water scary! need water! need bad scary water right now!*"

"So what if we showed the worm some water?" Jillian asked. "Do an experiment. See what it does."

But there *was* no water to show it. Of course there wasn't. If there had been, they wouldn't be out here now. They'd still be waiting on the rock with Jillian's parents.

Still, everything about the worms was so out of the ordinary that Jillian had a hard time just letting it go. It was a puzzle. She *loved* puzzles. Besides, it gave her something new to think about that wasn't worrying about the portal, or her parents' wounds, or running out of food, or not being able to find water.

"Maybe there's, like, something in the water that it wants to eat? Something too tiny for us to see? They were hungry enough to eat the pod, and that's made of plastic!"

But the worms hadn't been going into the swamp for food. That much had been immediately, sickeningly obvious.

Local fauna, behaving very *abnormally.*

"Bring it closer?"

SABRINA gave her a look over one shoulder. "Really?"

"I want to see something."

SABRINA hovered over, the worm bobbing in its cage before it. Jillian held out her hand.

"It's not trying to bite me." She waggled her hand closer. The worm ignored it. "You're sure this was from the same bunch of worms that bit my parents?"

"Maybe it's not hungry anymore," SABRINA suggested. "Maybe it's still full of . . . you know, never mind."

"They shouldn't have been hungry to start with," Jillian said. "They eat stuff in the dirt. My dad told me about them, back in the lab before we left. Humans aren't a food source here. The worms don't *need* them. They can't. They must have bitten my parents for another reason." She pressed one fingertip right up to the bars of the SABRI-NA cage. Nothing happened. "Whatever that reason was, it isn't happening now."

Then, after another few thoughtful minutes of walking, she remembered something else.

"They don't bite people usually. They keep to themselves." She began counting off facts on her fingers. Just *having* facts to count was oddly comforting. "The field crews usually don't see them. And we only know about them because another team captured some for study a few months ago. They attacked my parents yesterday, but they're not attacking me now. At least, this one isn't."

SABRINA's voice came from the tall purplish grass brushing Jillian's knees. For several minutes now, Jillian had only been assuming it was still in its green ferret shape. It could have been anything. "Affirmative," it said, only slightly muffled by the swishing of the grass.

The idea was taking shape in her head even as she spoke. "SABRINA, were you there on that trip? When they first found the worms?"

"I have attended almost all of the surveying expeditions," SABRINA said. "I am very useful! I would even go so far as to say I am *extremely*—"

"Can you, um, access those records?" Jillian asked. "Like you did for the place that didn't use to be the swamp? Show me when they first found the worms?"

"Honestly," SABRINA said. "I wouldn't be extremely useful if I couldn't at least do *that*."

Immediately the green ferret-shape was floating in the air to her side, projecting the video before her as she picked her way through that empty field of grass.

In it was another field crew. This one looked to be two men, but it was hard to tell because they both had podsuits on. They had a few of the worms in a glass jar, and one of the crew was holding one in a gloved hand. The worm didn't bite, didn't melt a hole through the glove and into the flesh beneath. It just hung out there in the person's hand like a regular worm. After a minute or so, it seemed to get bored and squirmed off the hand and fell into the orange dirt.

"Whoops," Jillian heard a man's voice say. "Get back here, little guy." Then he picked the worm back up, again with just the gloved fingers, again without any burning acid bites to show for it, and plopped it into the jar like nothing.

"Huh," Jillian said. "I didn't know anybody collected these for study. Are there some back at the lab on Earth?"

"No," SABRINA said. "The field crew kept them for a few days for observation. That's how they found out about the acid saliva, and that the worms use it to get nutrition from dirt. But eventually the crew decided there wasn't anything else all that interesting about them. Bringing actual live alien life-forms back through the portal without prior authorization—you think the idea of two hours of decontamination protocol is bad—not to mention the *paperwork*—"

"But these worms stayed put underground? Then how'd the team find them?"

"They were digging," SABRINA said. "They were hoping to find some kind of undiscovered food source that future surveyor crews could make use of."

"Alien potatoes?"

"At the time I congratulated them on their find. After all, the worms *were* an undiscovered food source! But that fantastic idea was met with a lukewarm reception at best. Humans are so *picky*."

Jillian swallowed. She had to feed three people for a week on a supply of food packets that might last half that long. Eating worms was not something she wanted to think about until she absolutely had to.

Instead she paid more attention to the scenery as she walked. They were at the edge of the forest now, under the overhang of the first trees. She remembered her dad mentioning this planet's fruit trees, but she had no idea what they might look like. Was it like on Earth, where some wild-growing plants were good to eat and some were poisonous?

"*I* would have put that in the documentary," she said. Not like the StellaTech people could hear her back on Earth, or like it would have mattered. The documentary was about the company, not the flora and fauna of 80 UMa c. What she really needed was a field guide. A book that could tell her what she could eat and what she couldn't. But she didn't. No field guide for random non-Earth planets had been written.

Or had it?

"Hey, SABRINA?"

"Shoot."

"You were just talking about food sources. Are there any food sources here on 80 UMa c that *aren't* worms?" Then, realizing she'd have to be a whole lot more specific than that if she didn't want a horrifying answer, she added, "Fruit, for example. My dad told me there were fruit trees around here somewhere. He said the fruit was edible."

"Everything is edible if you chew it long enough," SABRINA said pleasantly.

"Edible as in 'nonpoisonous,'" Jillian said patiently. "As in 'it won't make me sick or kill me if I—'"

She broke off, gasping as she toppled off-balance. SABRINA had glued her boots to the ground again. But this time it caught her. It was hovering behind her, pulling back on the fabric of her podsuit to keep her upright as she windmilled her arms to regain her footing.

"Hey—" Jillian began, but then came SABRINA's voice in her ear.

"Hush," it said. SABRINA was in front of Jillian now, but pointing with one wingtip to something off to a diagonal *behind* her. "There."

Jillian began to turn around, then stopped. This reminded her of so many scenes in so many scary movies, and none of them ended well. "What is it?" she whispered.

"I could tell you the scientific name given to it by the survey crew that discovered it," SABRINA said. "But that wouldn't mean anything to you, and it doesn't have another name. Just look at it. It's neat."

Jillian wanted to. Didn't want to. Had to. Couldn't. *Signaling confusion*, she thought wildly.

"One hundred and twelve degrees to your left," SABRINA said. "No, your other left. Thirty meters and closing. Oh, just turn around."

"Is it dangerous?"

"To you? On my watch? World's best bodyguard? Please." Then, when Jillian still hesitated, it added, "It's not going to hurt you. I should know; I discovered it. I mean, the field crew got the credit, but I saw it first." SABRINA rolled its spider-eyes, all eight of them. "Humans, am I right?"

Jillian wasn't really listening. *Turn around*, she commanded herself. *It's better to know. It's always better to know.*

Jillian took a deep breath, got a death grip on her spiky rock, and spun around. At the same time, the thing behind her stepped into a space between two trees, and she saw.

"Oh," she breathed. "It's pretty."

It was slightly taller than Jillian, walking on four long legs. Her dad's words in her head: *something maybe the tiniest little bit like a deer?*

Tiniest little bit still felt like a stretch. The body shape was similar . . . ish, if taller and spindlier than

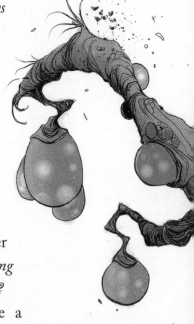

a deer, but the resemblance ended there. Its head was somewhere between reptilian and birdlike, but near neither of those at all. For one thing, its tiny nostrils rested directly between its eyes, because its mouth ran *vertically* up the middle of its skull.

It was such an odd color that even at that distance it blended in among the shadows of the trees almost perfectly: a kind of grayish blue like the smoke over a campfire, but with a silvery brightness that made it hard to tell at first whether it had fur or feathers or scales or something

completely different. Darker shadows rippled across it—Jillian squinted—no. *It* was changing; the creature itself was changing as it moved. It was colorshifting from that smoky blue-gray to the near-black color of a deep bruise, depending on the specific darkness of the shadows it passed through. Not only that, but it moved in time with the rippling of those shadows as the breeze shook the trees, making it nearly impossible to track where the shadows' movement left off and the creature's movement began. If Jillian didn't squint hard, it was almost like the creature was flickering in and out of existence, having invisibly traveled a few more feet each time it flickered back in.

Jillian had seen enough nature documentaries to know this deer thing's camouflage was deeply impressive. It was better than chameleon camouflage, better maybe even than octopus camouflage. It made Jillian's brain itch in the same way SABRINA had in the lab yesterday, shape-shifting faster than her eyes could keep up with. If SABRINA hadn't mentioned it, the creature might have gotten close enough to touch before Jillian saw it.

As it was, by the time she'd gotten over the initial shock of its presence, the alien deer was crossing Jillian's field of vision, maybe ten feet in front of her. It had its wrong-mouthed head raised into the breeze. It was looking or scenting or listening for something.

Whatever it was, the alien deer was paying it total attention. It walked straight past Jillian and SABRINA, oblivious. It traveled in a straight line, flickering from shadow to shadow, not looking where it stepped, just aiming its weird face into the wind like it was attached to a string reeling it in from a distance.

Food, Jillian thought. *It's probably going after food. Deer on Earth eat plant stuff. Maybe this one knows where there's edible fruit. Maybe I should follow it. No. I should get SABRINA to send a probe thing after it while I go get the water. Then I can look for fruit on the way back.*

But she'd been turning, one shuffle-step at a time, to track it with her gaze. Now that it was pointing itself off in the distance in front of her, she realized that the alien deer was already headed in the direction they were going. Maybe the fruit trees grew near water? She could get SABRINA to bring the worm over, see what it was doing. If it was signaling *water*, that might be it.

She was about to whisper-yell over to SABRINA when then that train of thought evaporated entirely, because now the alien deer was close enough for Jillian to notice something else.

There were patches on the shifting colorscape of the creature that didn't work. Patches on its back and along the bunching muscles of its legs. They didn't change when the surrounding . . . skin? . . . changed. They were blank and pale, and reminded Jillian of dead pixels on a screen.

They were the exact shape and size of the burn marks on Jillian's mom and dad.

CHAPTER 10

Jillian tracked the alien deer for another half mile or so before she said anything to SABRINA about what she'd just seen. She was beginning to learn the trick of asking SABRINA anything—be painfully specific, expect ridiculously literal answers—but even so, it felt a lot like flipping a coin. It might come up *hey, super useful, I'm so glad we had this talk*, but it was equally likely to land on *wow, am I ever sorry I asked*.

Rather than taking those odds, Jillian was trying to put things together on her own. Mystery-solving was a satisfying way to pass time as she walked, even if she didn't come up with any answers.

As long as she didn't let herself get too distracted. The grass grew higher here beneath the trees, whip wiry and tough, and it slashed clean little tears in the podsuit legs if she wasn't careful. The alien deer seemed to know how to walk through it gracefully, but Jillian was lagging farther and farther behind. She started off trying to hack a path with the spiky rock, but that didn't work nearly as well as just taking huge, heavy stomps to flatten the grass underfoot.

Then she remembered how the worms had come boiling up out of the dirt when something—or someone—shook the ground. She immediately stopped stomping. But walking normally in that grass meant she had to concentrate. Plan each step before she took it. She'd set a foot and slowly, forcefully lean her weight into it to crush the grass without stomping it.

Still, it seemed like a good idea. The alien deer's steps had been precise and delicate, and she hadn't seen any worms following it through the forest. Jillian did her best to copy its style of movement.

The extra padding of the grass underfoot ended up muffling her footsteps really well. If her stomping had gotten the worms' attention, the careful stepping on crushed grass must have made them lose interest, because none appeared.

However, it took much, much longer than normal walking. Jillian lost the alien deer, then caught sight of it again in the distance, then lost it again. She told herself that didn't really matter. The deer might be headed for food, but water was the priority here. Everything else had to wait.

But she'd be lying if she said she wasn't keeping her eyes peeled for that alien deer, wasn't keeping her fingers crossed that they'd catch up with it at the waterfall. Jillian was a space explorer now, and the deer was the first type of life-form she'd seen on 80 UMa c that she could trust not to attack her. If it thought she was food, it would have had plenty of opportunity to try to eat her. But it'd walked right past her, just like SABRINA had promised.

Even if it had looked normal, she would have wanted to study it a little longer. The marks on its back and legs made her extra curious. The worms had bitten it, and yet it seemed fine. It didn't have as many bites on it as her parents had, but still, seeing it walking around like nothing had happened gave her hope that her parents would be fine too.

"Did you see the marks?" she asked SABRINA after a time. "On that animal? They looked like the burns my parents got from the worms."

"Unsurprising," SABRINA said. "If the worms attacked your parents, which I can verify they absolutely did, in all probability they go after other prey too."

"But they don't," Jillian said. "My dad told me they don't. They get their food from the dirt. That's what's weird about it." Finally, something clicked. "And they didn't *eat* the alien deer. They didn't try to *eat* my mom and dad. They just *bit* them. And then left them alone. And the one you're carrying around never tried to bite me at all."

"Well, there you have it," SABRINA said. "They get their food from the dirt, and they bite humans and what you insist on calling the *alien deer* for fun. Mystery solved."

"No. Mystery *not* solved. Mystery worse now than before." Jillian, who had seen dozens of nature documentaries, felt sure of this. "Wild animals attack because they're hungry, or in self-defense. Not for *fun*. Do they?" Suddenly she was unsure. "Maybe, like, a predator toying with its prey?" She made a face. "But *worms*?"

"If it makes you feel any better," SABRINA said, "your *alien deer* over there barely seems wounded. Vitals look good. No sign of infection. And it's certainly not moving like it's injured."

"Yeah, I know," Jillian said. "It's hard to keep up with it. The grass is so sharp."

"It's just going in a straight line," SABRINA said. "We'll catch up. Are the boots okay?"

Jillian glanced down at them: still shiny, blue, winged. "They're great."

"I really wanted to do another mech suit," SABRINA said. "That was fun. None of the other surveyors are ever going to let me make one for *them*."

"They're missing out," Jillian said. "That thing was awesome."

"I know, right?"

They walked another little ways, silent except for the rip-swish of the grass.

"All the other field crews that have been coming here," Jillian said eventually, "the worms never bit any of them?"

"Never," SABRINA said. "You saw the footage."

Jillian thought back on it. That surveyor, holding one of the green worms in his hand, unharmed. Was there something about her parents that made the worms attack? But no—they'd gone after her too, when she went back to the pod. Hundreds of them. Thousands. But the one SABRINA caught by the swamp . . . didn't.

"And the last crew that came here was when?"

"Two months ago," SABRINA said. "They were testing other sites for a while, but they decided this one was the most efficient for harvesting, so now we're back. Home sweet home."

"SABRINA, you live in the lab."

This was met with exactly two seconds of uncharacteristic silence, as if she'd somehow caught SABRINA off guard, and then out of nowhere it blurted out, "Why can't you hear a pterodactyl go to the bathroom?"

"Huh?"

"Because the P is silent."

"What?"

"Get it? *Get* it? Because the *P*—"

"Oh. *Oh*." Jillian paused. "That's awful."

"Awfully funny."

Jillian's mouth quirked. "I *guess*."

SABRINA beamed. "I have twelve hundred and eighteen more where that came from, equally excellent. You're in for *such* a treat."

The next mile was full of much the same. Trees, grass, shadows. SABRINA made it through fifty-three more jokes from its collection before Jillian lost count. The alien deer never deviated in its course, never slowed, never paused to rest or eat, so that Jillian and SABRINA followed it for a while but eventually lost sight of it completely.

Eventually they reached a break in the trees, and above them, suddenly, was the waterfall. It was short and wide and sparkled in the sunlight on its way down from its highest point to a rocky pool below, and right that very moment it was the most beautiful thing Jillian had ever seen.

She picked her way through the last of the wiry grass, and then there were small rocks like gravel that crunched underfoot as she tried her best not to break into a run and draw the worms up from underground. She forced herself to walk lightly, cautiously, mindfully. She counted her steps to make sure she didn't lose focus. Eighty steps, ninety, and at ninety-four she was beside the pool.

She looked at it, and her heart sank. It was full of dead worms.

Of course it is, she told herself. *It's water. You should have known.*

More worms were crawling into the water from the rocks as she stood there and watched. None of them paid any attention to her.

"We can't use this," she told SABRINA. "Look."

"Hmm." SABRINA floated over. It made itself an arm and stuck it into the pool, then the falls. Then it did it again. Then it came over and sat on Jillian's shoulder. "I think the water that's actually falling is okay."

"Really?"

"I didn't test the swamp as drinking water before because it didn't come up. Field crews generally bring their own water or sterilize and purify rainwater. If I'd been testing the swamp as *drinking* water, I would have run a more thorough test and gotten a very different result. I'm testing this now, and yeah, no, you don't want to drink it. It's gross. But the actual waterfall is coming up pretty clean."

Jillian looked up. "Where's it coming from? Can you fly up and see? There could be a million more dead worms up there, and I wouldn't know."

SABRINA flew a little moth shape up the falls. "Nothing up here," the part that was sitting on Jillian's shoulder said. "I think it's too rocky up here for them."

That was all she needed to hear. Clean, drinkable water, hers for the taking. She edged around the pool toward the rocky wall that housed the falls.

The rocks around the pool edge were flat and smooth with erosion, which made them slippery. But SABRINA adjusted the grippiness of her boot soles automatically, and Jillian tiptoed from rock to rock like she'd been born graceful, which under most circumstances she most assuredly was not.

As she walked, she was already emptying the water container, cramming objects into the pockets of her podsuit. The tape, the insta-stitches, the brick of food bars. She slung the extra jumpsuit over one shoulder. She was just beside the falls now, the water kicking up into spray that wet her face and podsuit. That close, the falls were deafening.

She'd been too worried about her parents to think much about her own thirst, but the spray hit her from the falls, cold and wet, and suddenly she couldn't stop herself. She cupped water in her hands and slurped it up, over and over, until she felt like she'd never be thirsty again. She knew it wouldn't last. It was just her brain and stomach tricking her. She'd be thirsty again too soon.

That done, she propped the container against a rock to

fill. The falls soaked her face and hair and ran down through the neck of the podsuit, but she stood in the spray until the container filled and overflowed and was ready to be carried back in triumph to the boulder where her parents were waiting.

She steadied her stance to lift the container, as careful as if it were a bomb she was defusing. If she broke that container, broke it for real this time, it was game over for all of them.

It was *heavy*. So heavy she could barely shift it, let alone lift it up and carry it safely off the rocks.

"Lift with your legs," SABRINA advised her. "Whatever that means. I don't know. I saw it in a movie. I thought humans lifted with their hands."

"I've heard that too," Jillian said, shouting over the falls. "I think it means don't bend your back. Bend your knees and hold the thing and just ... stand ... up."

She tried to do it as she said it, but it was hard. Even with the extra grippies SABRINA added to her gloves, and the SABRINA ferret doing its best to help out, she couldn't lift it beyond a few inches before it slipped from her grasp, and then it was all she could do to keep it from crashing back to the rocks.

Jillian thought back to stuff she'd learned in school. How did people used to move heavy, awkward objects way, way back in ancient times when they didn't have high-tech machines to help them?

"SABRINA," she said, "can you get under it and, like, lever it up off the rock so I can get my fingers in underneath? I might be able to carry it better that way."

"Can try," the SABRINA ferret replied, changing into a shape kind of like a crowbar, the prying end already under the container. "Okay, go."

Jillian pushed, and the container levered up easily. She worked her fingers in underneath, then inched the container up to her chest, but then it slipped again and landed on the rock so hard it dented. Jillian held her breath as she inspected it for cracks. The drop hadn't broken it, but the next one definitely would. "This was supposed to be the easy part," she muttered.

"Five gallons of water weighs almost forty-two pounds," SABRINA informed her, turning back into a ferret and yawning hugely and adorably. "That, if it makes you feel any better, is a five-gallon container."

Forty-two pounds. It didn't *sound* like that much. That was the weight of, say, a little kid, or a medium dog. Jillian could lift that, she thought.

But a little kid had arms she could lift under. A dog she could scoop up. This was sheer, slippery, wet plastic, with no handholds, balanced on a rock. And the next wrong move would break it.

Despair settled on her like a heavy blanket. *All this way,* she thought. *I came all this way.*

Jillian straightened up and glared at the container for a full minute, hands on hips. Slow anger built in her like a fire, burning all the hopelessness away.

"No," she whispered aloud. She had to do this. SABRINA couldn't carry a container this full. Even nearly all of SABRINA hadn't been able to bear much weight for any kind of distance, and most of it was with her parents now. This part was on her.

She bent down again, readjusting her grip. If she scooted backward along the rocks, she could slide the container toward her, inch by inch. She did that for a few minutes and made it a little ways away from the pool, then stopped in the middle of the clearing.

She'd figure out how to get it the whole way back through the forest and the field to the boulder in a second. For now, she collapsed on a rock to catch her breath. Her heart was pounding in her ears. Between that and her breathing and the now-distant roar of the falls, she almost didn't hear the SABRINA-ferret, right there on the next rock over, give a little melodic laugh.

"What?" Jillian gasped. "Oh my god, this thing is a *lot* heavier than I—"

SABRINA lifted its anglerfish lure, and Jillian almost screamed. There, in the cage, the worm was going absolutely nuts. It was trying to burrow out through the bottom of the cage. Worse, it was trying to burrow out through the bottom of the cage *toward Jillian*. It was snapping and thrashing in her direction, inches from her arm. She scrambled away. She had to put a distance of a few feet between herself and the worm before it started to calm down.

"Think it finally decided it likes you," SABRINA said.

"Not me," Jillian said, understanding. "My podsuit. It's all wet." She shoved up her sleeve, exposing a stretch of dry arm. "I want to try something. Hold it over this way. Um. Not too close."

She held her arm right in front of the worm's face. Nothing.

Then she pulled the sodden podsuit sleeve back into place, and the worm went berserk. "Was it going after the water in the pool?"

"Oh yeah. The whole time you were filling the container. It calmed back down when we left. Until, well."

"Huh," she said. "But my parents' suits weren't wet . . ."

Jillian puzzled over that for a moment and got nowhere. An idea was struggling to piece itself together in the back of her mind. Something about how this worm was responding to water, not prey, but also about how the same batch of worms that had attacked her parents had then obsessed over the puddle of water from the broken container near the boulder . . .

But if they'd been going after water, why didn't they just crawl down to the swamp without attacking her parents at all? Plenty of water there.

"You found this worm by the swamp?" she asked SABRINA. "This is the same one you brought down here?"

SABRINA nodded, blinking up at her with all eight eyes.

"So it was already looking for water," Jillian murmured. "And *not* looking for stuff to bite." She gave the idea another few seconds to take shape, but its edges stubbornly refused to fit together.

In the meantime, the water container wasn't about to walk itself back to camp. She levered herself up from the rock and went to begin the painstaking grind of sliding the sloshing heaviness of that container, inch by inch, across open ground, the whole way there.

She shoved it forward one foot, then another. It was going to take forever. She'd be lucky if she got back before dark.

Worse, gravel rattled beneath the container. Too loud. Way too loud. Sending vibrations down into the ground. She needed something to pad the bottom with. If she sent SABRINA down there, it wouldn't be able to protect her feet and legs. If she knew how to weave the long grasses, she might have been able to make a kind of sled to drag the container on. But she didn't.

What she did have was the spare jumpsuit. She lay it down flat on the ground and muscled the container on top of it, tying the arms and legs together on the top like an ugly present. It gave her a handle to drag with, and muffled a bit of the sound. It would have to do.

She dragged the container a little farther away from the falls while SABRINA floated along beside her, the worm snapping at Jillian's soaked hair.

"Bored now," SABRINA told it. "Enough."

"Go put that thing somewhere," Jillian said. "It's starting to creep me out."

The cage vanished and was replaced by pincers that held the worm by the tail, dangling at the end of the lure. "Where do you want it?"

"I don't care. Not here. Go put it by the pool if it wants water so badly."

SABRINA shook its head at the worm fondly, which

shook the lure, which shook the worm, and as it passed nearest Jillian's wet hair, it threw itself toward it so hard that Jillian thought it was going to let the pincers take off the end of its tail. SABRINA hovered away with it.

For a few seconds, Jillian watched them go. Then she jumped to her feet, pointing toward the far side of the pool. "Look! There's something weird by the water."

She hurried over, and SABRINA followed. Then she realized what she was looking at—what she was really looking at—and stopped again, staring.

One of the rocks lining the pool . . . was not a rock at all. It was a dark shape, uniformly dark now, but Jillian knew what it was.

The alien deer.

It was definitely the same one. Jillian recognized it from the pattern of burns on its legs and back. But it wasn't tracking anything in the distance anymore, wasn't moving with such single-minded purpose. It had reached its destination, and now it wasn't doing anything at all.

It must have gone down between two rocks to the water's edge and put its face down as if to drink. And then gone in farther, and farther, until only the back half of its body was visible, because the rest was in the pool. No part of it was moving. Water lapped over its sides in tiny waves, but its colorshifting surface did not change. It lay there, dark and flat and inert, like a solid lump of shadow.

"Oh no," Jillian whispered. She speed-walked over as lightly as she could and started dragging the alien deer back out of the water, even though she knew she couldn't help it anymore. Leaving it there in the water, like all the dead things in the swamp, suddenly seemed impossible.

Even up close it was hard to tell whether the alien deer had skin or scales or feathers or what. It was kind of a mix of all three, putting Jillian in mind of pictures of dinosaurs in books. But the back half of the creature was dry, and Jillian still had the SABRINA grippies on her gloves, so she dug her feet into the gravel and her fingers into the sides of the alien deer and pulled as hard as she could until the front half of it came sliding limply back out of the pool.

"We're too late," she said quietly. "It's dead."

The SABRINA ferret flew over on its bat wings and landed on the alien deer's back. Poked it with a paw a few times. "Agreed," it said. "Hey, check me out."

Suddenly it was a perfect miniature copy of the alien deer, six inches tall, perching on top of the dead one. Like some kind of magic trick, the worm in its cage had vanished.

Jillian shooed SABRINA off the alien deer's corpse. "That's not nice," she said. "It's dead. Go mess around somewhere else."

"With pleasure," SABRINA said. It made a show of throwing its head back, opening its mouth, reaching in with one spindly leg, and pulling out the worm, which had apparently been stored in the new cage of its alien deer body. Holding the worm aloft like a banner, it pranced away.

Which left Jillian alone with the dead alien deer. She wasn't entirely sure why this aloneness was something she had wanted, or what she planned to do now that she had it. She found herself looking at the alien deer in the way people in wilderness survival movies looked at dead animals they'd found in the woods.

She knew it had died of natural causes. Well, as natural as these causes could be called. Its meat was fresh, not rotten, not poisoned. It could be food.

Jillian had never eaten meat before. Meat, real, true, dead-animal meat, was a food of her grandparents' generation. She knew it used to be a big deal for humans all throughout history up until just decades ago, but the only meat she'd personally ever even seen had been vat-grown from proteins in a lab, not cut off a dead animal by hand out in the middle of nowhere and cooked somehow.

She reached out with a gloved fingertip and touched one of the wounds. It had mostly healed over, though the acid in the bite seemed to have permanently damaged whatever made the alien deer's camouflage work, causing the white dead-pixel patches Jillian had noticed before. But she knew what an infection looked like—at least, what an infected wound on a human on Earth looked like—and she didn't see any sign of that here. The alien deer had probably been bitten days ago and then recovered. In any case, Jillian thought no sign of infection meant probably okay to eat, even if the *idea* of eating this creature was a little overwhelming and made her feel slightly sick to her stomach.

She sat back on her heels and tried to remember how people in movies went about turning animals into food. You took the skin off, she knew that much, and then you cooked . . . some other part. What were you supposed to do with the parts you didn't use? Where were you supposed to put the blood? There was a whole chapter on this stuff in her wilderness survival book, but she'd skipped it. Here, now, she was starting to wish she hadn't.

Something near the alien deer's face was moving, rescuing Jillian from her questions. But then she looked, and immediately regretted it.

Something was crawling out of the alien deer's nostrils. Or—no—something *had* been crawling out of its nostrils, but stopped halfway, and was now bobbing slightly back and forth, as if confused. Something a *tiny* bit like a centipede, and a *tinier* bit like a tadpole, but about as much like either of those as the alien deer was like an actual deer.

"SABRINA!"

"You just told me to go away!" SABRINA called back.

"Forget that. Look!" Jillian nodded at the centipede thing, which was now seemingly trying to decide whether to finish crawling out or go back in. "What *is* that thing?"

SABRINA looked. "Huh," it said after a moment. "You don't see that every day."

"What's it doing?" Jillian asked. But before SABRINA could answer, an idea seized her. She thought of the worms, thought of the swamp, and she dragged the alien deer's head back into the pool and lay it down gently in the shallow water at the edge.

Immediately the centipede thing shot out into the water and was gone.

Jillian jumped to her feet with a startled yell. *So fast*, she thought, *so fast*.

Then she gathered herself and shaded her eyes against

the glare of sunlight on the surface to peer into the depths of the pool. Away from the pounding of the falls, the water was very clear. Down along the bottom she could see several more of the centipede things paddling slowly around. One looked to have laid a cluster of eggs, like a tiny shimmering nest of beads strung across a bit of plant matter.

That gave Jillian a nasty chill. Whatever these centipede things were, eggs meant more of them. No way could that be good news.

She pointed them out to SABRINA.

"Oh," SABRINA said, "that explains a lot, actually."

"It *does?*"

"Sure. There are life cycles of parasites on Earth that look a lot like this."

"No way."

"Very much yes way."

Jillian waved incredulously at the alien deer, dead with its face in the water. "This thing just drowned itself on purpose, and a bug or whatever just crawled out its nose, and more of them are laying eggs in the water, and you're telling me there are things that do this on Earth?"

"You'd be surprised. You just think Earth is normal because you're used to it. Trust me, biped, Earth is completely bonkers."

"You're going to have to draw me a picture here, because I don't get it. From *that*"—Jillian indicated the worm in SABRINA's pincers, then swung her pointer finger over to the alien deer, then down to the strings of eggs in the water—"to *that.*"

"Okay," SABRINA said. "So. These stupid little guys"—it shook the worm—"probably ate those eggs. You can see right there that the eggs float up to the surface of the water, very likely when they're ready to be found and eaten."

Jillian crinkled her brow. "Why would it *want* its eggs to get eaten?"

"Depends on what the baby parasites are after. Look."

Jillian looked, and sure enough, there were two more strings of eggs being pushed out of the water by the little wavelets in the pool, out onto the shore. "They go onto the dirt," she said wonderingly. "The worms eat dirt. Tiny stuff in the dirt. Like my dad said."

"There you go. So the worm eats the egg by accident, the egg hatches in the worm, and baby centipede parasite guy has a cozy new home. Circle of life."

Jillian made a face. "That's disgusting."

"That's nature, new kid. Got plenty of it where you come from too."

"But the worms bit the alien deer. They didn't just go straight for water. The deer did."

"Obviously," SABRINA said, "the parasite larva got into this creature. In all probability, through the bite."

"Why?"

"I don't know for sure. But there are parasites on Earth that do that kind of thing, jump hosts if a bigger or stronger host can serve it better. Maybe a bigger host, say this alien deer, provides more food for the centipede larva while it grows to maturity."

"It was *eating* it?"

"Just little bits, I imagine," SABRINA said. "Tiny little nibbles. Probably never even noticed." Then, catching sight of Jillian's face, it added, "Oh, don't be so squeamish. Animals eat each other on your planet for breakfast, lunch, dinner, snacks, and dessert." The tiny alien deer SABRINA nodded its dinosaur-like head toward the dead alien deer. "Anyway. So baby parasite grows up big and strong in there, and then when it's ready to go back to the water and lay its eggs . . ."

"It makes the host take it there," Jillian said, understanding. "So it was, what, controlling the alien deer? And all those worms? Driving them around until they found water?"

"You got it."

Jillian made a face. "How does that even work?"

"I never said it wasn't weird," SABRINA said. "I said there was plenty of precedent. On your very own planet, even. Look it up."

Jillian chewed this over for a full minute. Then her gaze fell on SABRINA's captive worm.

"So you're saying that worm has a centipede thing inside it that's ready to hatch. That's why it didn't want to bite me—it just wants to get back to the water. So the thing can get out." She thought for another few seconds. "And the ones that bit my parents, and the ones that bit the deer, they had centipede things in them too, but theirs weren't big enough to hatch yet, so they were looking for bigger prey."

"A reasonable hypothesis," SABRINA said. "Shall we test it?"

For a moment there was a war in Jillian's mind. She

wanted answers, but she also wanted never to go near or even look at one of the centipede things ever again.

But, as always, the needing-to-know won out. "Yeah," she said. "Let's do it."

"Sweet," SABRINA said. "I was hoping you would say that."

It morphed into a bowl, and Jillian used it to scoop up some water. Then she braced herself and picked up SABRI-NA's worm. Even through the podsuit glove, its desperate wriggling grossed her out deeply. She dropped it quickly into the bowl.

As soon as it hit water, the worm went still. So still that at first she thought it had died. But then it started convulsing, its whole body heaving like a cat about to puke. *It's drowning*, Jillian realized, feeling sick. *I'm watching something drown.*

The worm could have easily crawled out of the bowl if it had wanted to. But it didn't even try. It stayed at the very bottom, and it was very hard for Jillian not to reach in and scoop it out. These things had bitten her parents. She *had to know.*

She crossed her arms and hugged herself and watched the worm convulse and heave, and after about two agonizing minutes of this, it opened its mouth wider than it looked like it could comfortably go, and out shot one of the centipede things.

It was smaller than the one that had come out of the alien deer. That one had been about the length of Jillian's finger, but this one was more the size of her fingertip. Still the same shape, still fully formed.

"This one's smaller than the one that came out of the deer," she observed.

"Bigger host, bigger parasite, remember?" SABRINA said.

"Right," Jillian said faintly.

"To baby parasite over there, that alien deer probably looked how a pizza the size of a zero-gravity football stadium would look to you."

"Well, I'm totally not going to think about that every time I see a pizza from now on."

"Oh, good. I wouldn't want to put you off pizza. I am told it's delicious."

The hatched centipede thing settled at the lowest part of the bowl and lay beside the worm, making tiny scuttling motions like it was testing out its legs.

Jillian stared at it for another moment, imagining what it would feel like to have one of those driving her around, the way people used to drive their own cars before they had computers to do it for them. Except she wasn't a car. She had a mind of her own. She pictured one of these centipedes living in her head, nibbling away at all of her thoughts and ideas and dreams.

Before she could think better of it, she reached into the bowl with her gloved hand, past the now-dead worm, and grabbed the centipede.

Parasite, she thought. *That's what SABRINA called you. That's what you are.*

She threw it down to the gravel and ground it to paste beneath her heel.

SABRINA, meantime, had reverted to its six-legged dog

shape and was giving Jillian a dopey, open-mouthed dog smile.

"Told you so," it said.

Jillian's mind was spinning. The worm, the centipede parasite, the deer. The worm ate the egg, the egg hatched in the worm, the worm bit the host, the baby parasite traveled through the bite, and when it was done growing, it drove the host to water to escape and start the life cycle all over again.

All the information she had gathered was lining up in her head. The logic of SABRINA's hypothesis, now that it had been proven correct, only led in one direction. No matter how hard she tried to make it go somewhere else.

"Then," she asked SABRINA in dawning horror, "what's going to happen to my parents?"

CHAPTER 11

Thankfully, it took SABRINA less than a second to come up with an answer. "They're fine," it said. "They woke up twenty-seven minutes, forty seconds ago and twelve minutes, fifteen seconds ago, respectively, and drank some water. I'm making them some lunch right now. Look."

SABRINA projected a video in midair, the way it had done with the countdown clock.

In it, Jillian's parents were sitting, backs propped against each other, in visible pain but awake. Alive. Her throat tightened. She folded her arms around herself to keep from reaching out and trying to touch the projection.

The fluffy pillows and sentry telescope and other SABRINA things were gone, and it whirled around them now in a slowly orbiting particle swarm. Here and there small clouds of SABRINA's nanobots grouped together to help Jillian's mom adjust her blanket a fraction of an inch, or smooth one of her dad's smart bandages back into place. Little things that made Jillian think of a healthy person standing by a sick loved one's bed, fretting and wringing their hands. She smiled a little. "Thanks, SABRINA," she said softly. "You're doing great."

"Doing my job," SABRINA said, like it was embarrassed by the compliment, but then after a moment it made a throat-clearing sound—having no throat to clear—and said, "You're not doing too bad yourself."

Before Jillian could respond, she noticed the part of SABRINA that was making soup for her parents in the video feed. That part hadn't taken any specific kind of shape. No velociraptor, no octopus, no six-legged dog. It was streamlined to the most efficient possible version of *thing that can make soup*, a no-nonsense kind of scaffolding with swiveling claws.

This was so completely unlike the goofball showiness Jillian expected from SABRINA that for a moment she didn't even recognize it, and thought it was a piece of equipment salvaged from the pod.

For all that SABRINA liked to joke around when it sensed no danger, Jillian realized, back by her parents it was on full red alert. Nothing was going to happen to them on its watch.

"They look okay," she whispered. Unsure why she was whispering. Doing it anyway.

"Well, they *are* okay," SABRINA said. "I may not be a medbot, but I'm not completely incompetent."

"But the worms. The parasite . . . thing. Isn't . . . *that* . . . going to happen to them too?"

"Not necessarily. Your human parents are biologically different than the fauna native to 80 UMa c. As of yet we have no evidence that they're viable hosts for the parasite. And even if they are, I'm unsure of the timeline. Your parents will be in an Earth hospital within the week. Their biggest concern right now is that." SABRINA tapped the water container.

"Fed and watered," Jillian said.

"Got it in one."

"All right." Jillian sighed. "Let's go." She crouched beside the container and inspected it. The jumpsuit tied around it had helped a little, but while the slithery fabric was tough, the gravel was tougher, and already rubbing holes through the body of the suit.

That was bad news. When the suns went down, she'd need every layer of clothing she had. She untied the jumpsuit from the water container and tied it around her waist instead. She squatted down beside the water container, got both arms around it, and stood with it hugged to her chest.

She made it four steps before she lost her grip. The container slipped from her arms, and this time she thought fast and dropped with it, guiding its fall to keep it from breaking. SABRINA appeared out of nowhere, a gelatinous cloud that did not stop the container but managed to slow it down just enough for Jillian to set it on the gravel safely.

Jillian stood over it, counting her breaths until her heart stopped hammering. "Okay," she said at last. "No more of that."

"Advisable," SABRINA agreed.

Which left her with what options? She couldn't carry it. SABRINA couldn't carry it. Dragging it across the ground, especially without the jumpsuit handle, was going to take forever.

She was beyond tired of thinking about this stupid water container. *Getting* the water was supposed to be the hard part. This part should have been a piece of cake. She should be halfway back to the boulder by now, helping SABRINA protect her mom and dad. Instead, she was stuck out here, moving at the approximate speed of a half-dead snail dipped in superglue, because of this stupid water container. She wished she were faster, stronger, older. She wanted long legs and powerful muscles. She wished the wings on the SABRINA boots could actually make her fly. She wished her parents had a normal job that kept them safe on Earth, or that she'd been able to figure out a way to get them through the portal in time, or a way to heal them up so she didn't have to solve all these problems on her own, or—

She shut those thoughts down *hard*. She couldn't waste time feeling sorry for herself if she wanted to survive.

The gelatinous cloud was hovering directly in front of Jillian's face now, staring at her eyelessly, awaiting instruction. "SABRINA," she told it, "I know you can't lift the container far. Could you make, like, rollers for it instead? Just something to make it a little easier and quieter to push back"—for one awful second she almost said *home*—"to, um, camp?"

"I don't see why not," SABRINA said.

Jillian took a big step away from the container and gestured down at it. "All yours."

The cloud floated over and slid itself in under the container, as fluid as fog. There it turned into a set of crawler treads. Jillian got behind the container and pushed. It crept forward a foot, then another. It was still pretty slow, and awkward, but better than ripping the spare jumpsuit to shreds.

It got them as far as the edge of the meadow that circled the forest. There, the tough, sharp grass stopped them in their tracks. Even if Jillian had flattened a path with her boots beforehand, it just wasn't working. The crawlers caught and tangled, and when Jillian tried to mash the grass away from the sides, it slashed at the legs of her suit and nearly spilled the container all over again.

After about twenty minutes of this, she gave up. She almost started stomping her way back out of the grass field, then froze, realizing what she was about to do. Instead, she stood looking out over the sea of grass, fists jammed down into her pockets, clamping down on a whole lot of yelling. More frustrated than she'd maybe ever been in her life. They'd finally figured out how to move the full container, and then they'd only actually shifted it a couple hundred feet, tops. She wanted to dropkick the thing up a tree. It had taken them, what, an hour to get to the falls? At this rate, it was going to take the whole rest of the day to get back.

"Sorry," SABRINA said. "I told you I wasn't good at heavy lifting."

"No, I know," Jillian said. "I'm sorry too. It's not your

fault." She ran her hands up her face and into her hair. "Okay. New plan. What if you, like, made several little containers instead of this big one, and we poured the water into you like we did back there with the worm?" But her mind was following that thought-path ahead of her mouth, and she immediately saw the problems. "*But* I'd still have to carry them. And there's not enough of you here to make that many containers; I'd have to get rid of the boots you made me, which I don't want to. *And* I'd have to keep going back and forth every day to get more water anyway."

"You could do that," SABRINA said. "Or, on the off chance you were looking for a more elegant solution, you could pour some of the water out and bring it back partially full, then go back tomorrow. Somebody was just telling me a little while ago how hiking is good for humans." It turned back into the six-legged flame dog. "Probably good for dogs too."

"If I can get this water back, it'll be enough for days," Jillian said. "I don't want to leave my parents and wander around out here any more than I have to. What if the portal comes back early and I'm not there?"

What if the worms attack me out there? she thought but did not say. *What if my mom and dad get infections and fevers and die?*

"I want to try to go around and find another way. You know the landscape. It should be easy. Right?"

"I perform standard recon diagnostics every six weeks, and I run extra coverage of the research sites before the quadpods arrive. Your parents made me run this last one

177

twice." SABRINA projected a map into the air. "Take a peek."

Jillian stepped in to study the map. She squinted at the various rings and squiggles and shook her head. "I can't read this."

A big red X appeared near one edge of the map, in some area that looked pretty much like everything else. "Here's us," SABRINA said. Then a blue star blinked in near the center. "There's base camp."

Jillian was sort of familiar with that area by now, and she thought if she leaned in and studied hard, she could learn to read this map, identify the ridge, the crater, the swamp, the path they'd taken. But there was no time.

The X was on the edge of a faint purple expanse. "That's the forest," she said. It went down the left side of the map toward the middle, but disappeared off the top edge. "This goes off the map. Which way takes us around this faster?"

"This is what I mapped right before your quadpod came through the portal," SABRINA said. "I have last month's data, but it might be inaccurate by now."

"Like the swamp," Jillian said.

"Exactly."

"It's the best we have. Bring it up anyway. Please."

SABRINA projected a bigger map. The little square of the first one fit into it neatly. "This is fifty square miles."

Jillian didn't need to know, but her curiosity got the better of her. "What's past that?"

There was the briefest possible hesitation before SABRINA said, "80 UMa c is forty-six percent the size of Earth. I could show you all my maps, but we'd be here all day."

But Jillian had already seen everything she needed to see. The razor-grass field stretched on a long way, north and south. Three miles, maybe four. That was a long way lugging water. But there was a spot on the map just north of here where it looked like some kind of rocky hills cut through it, almost the whole way back to the ridge.

"Can you blow that up?"

SABRINA did. Jillian was right; it was a line of low-looking hills, like the spine of some huge creature mostly buried in the dirt.

She didn't know how high it was, how hard it was to climb. The worms didn't go after rock—she'd seen that with the boulder—so that was a plus. But she'd be lugging the water container this time.

Heading off blind into the wilderness was the kind of thing that, if she were in a movie, would get her killed. But she hated this stay-put, wait-and-see thing. It made her mind itch like poison ivy.

She could send SABRINA to scope it out, but as great as SABRINA was at a ton of things, she wasn't too sure she could trust it to make an accurate decision about what Jillian could and could not climb with a water container. Or without one. And if SABRINA was wrong, they'd have to double back anyway, and it'd be all kinds of time wasted.

"The suns are still high," she said, working it out aloud. "I still have the food bars in my pocket. My parents are just two miles away." She nodded once, decisively. "I say we go there. If it doesn't work, we can go around the bottom of the hills and still be headed in the right direction. Worst case, I can dump some of the water if I absolutely have to. But I want to try this first. Okay by you?"

"You're the boss, Boss." Already the six-legged dog was dissolving, reforming, going back to being crawler treads for the water container.

Jillian glanced toward her wristband. Nodded. Glanced once more at the map. Off the edge of it could be anything. What was it that it was supposed to say on really ancient maps? She'd learned it in history class earlier this year: *Beyond this point there be dragons.*

"Hey. Can I get you to send just a tiny bit of yourself ahead, make sure everything's safe in front of me? Something that might not have shown up on the map? Or that showed up but you didn't know was a problem? Like the swamp?"

"I told you, the swamp—"

"I know, SABRINA, but right now I need to stay safe. I know you can keep me safe. That's all I'm asking."

SABRINA saluted. "Easy peasy." A tiny gob of matter detached from Jillian's right boot. It turned into another of the little fireflies, shook its wings, and zipped off ahead.

Jillian cracked her knuckles, bent her back to the water container, and started pushing.

Five minutes. Ten. Jillian was going on fifteen, which felt like about three hours, when her boots spoke to her. "Do you want the good news or the bad news?"

She groaned.

"Just kidding, it's all good news this time. Another few minutes at the rate you're going, and you'll be at the base of the hills."

"There's no grass there?"

She could hear the shrug in SABRINA's voice. "Just lots of sandy dirt, blowing down from the hills."

"As long as it's not more of this grass, I love it already," Jillian said. "Maybe you're right. Maybe I only think Earth is normal because I'm used to it. But this place is *weird*."

"You think so? You should see some of the other planets we've gone to. This is nothing. Come along sometime when we go back to Tau Ceti e, if you want *truly* bizarre."

Jillian opened her mouth to ask *What's so weird about it there?*, but she never got the chance.

One moment the ground was there, beneath her feet. The next moment it wasn't. For one split second she stood on nothing, both boots' worth of SABRINA trying to hold her aloft as she grabbed with both hands at the air. She heard the water container slip down into the nothing and crash to the ground some unknowable distance below.

Some stray wild thought took her back to cartoons, cartoon logic: she would only fall when she looked down. So she wouldn't look down.

She didn't look down. She fell anyway.

Down there was dark. Deep enough to be dark. Dirt rattled down from above. Leaves and bits of twigs and branches.

Jillian ducked her head and shut her eyes tight until it was over, then opened her eyes back up to inspect her situation.

The pit she'd fallen into was narrow, just wide enough for her to lie full length on her back if she wanted to, which she did not. The walls were sheer and high. It was like someone had dug a cylinder out of the ground.

There was a circle of green sky high above, much too high to reach. She jumped and scrabbled at the wall a couple times as if to prove this to herself. No chance of getting out of here alone.

At least she wasn't injured. SABRINA hadn't been strong enough to lift her clear of the fall, but it had slowed her descent a little, enough to keep her from doing herself damage when she landed at the bottom.

Nothing had slowed the descent of the water container, though. She was standing in mud that had been dry dirt when she'd landed, and she could hear more water chugging out in the dark as she stood there. She dropped to her knees and tried to feel around for the break, get the container set back upright in a way that kept the rest of the water in. She tipped and tilted and got it balanced on one corner, wedged between her legs and the wall of the pit she'd fallen into. How much water was left in it? Hard to tell. A few cups, maybe. She felt sick.

SABRINA hovered up, a cloud of fireflies in the dark. "Are you hurt?"

Jillian patted herself down. Her hands were shaking. "No. I don't think so. I'm okay." Then she realized something. "I thought you were scouting ahead for trouble!"

"I was. I guess I wasn't heavy enough to trigger the sinkhole." SABRINA laughed weakly. "Every day an adventure?"

"It's not *that* far," Jillian said, eyeing the circle of sky. "Can you make something that gets me up there?"

"Hmm. You didn't happen to bring a rope?"

"... No, SABRINA, I didn't."

"That complicates matters. I had a very elegant solution just now involving a rope. It—"

Under SABRINA's chatter, a tiny noise reached Jillian's ears. "Shhh."

"Honestly, I think you really would have admired—"

"I *order you to shush.*" SABRINA shut up, and Jillian strained her ears against the silence. Something nearby, the faintest possible rustling. So soft she wasn't sure whether she was imagining it. She pitched her voice to a whisper. "Do you hear that?"

"Oh yes. Now that you mention it. It's very close. Yes, I'm picking it up loud and clear."

"Can you *see* what it *is?*"

The tiniest pause. "I'll take a look around."

It didn't sound like anything Jillian recognized. She couldn't even tell whether it was above her, below, or to the side. It might have been loose dirt rattling down. But she had a nasty feeling it wasn't.

A thought was poking her in the back of her mind. Something about the crash the water container had made when it landed. Something about the crash *she'd* made when she'd landed. But another part of her mind was pushing that thought away before it could develop fully. *Don't*

183

think about that, the other part of her mind was shouting. *Just get out. Get out now and run.*

"SABRINA?" she tried to whisper, but no sound came out. Her voice had gone. Her palms were sweating in the podsuit gloves, and her legs felt suddenly, dangerously weak. Because all at once, she knew exactly what that distant, nearing, muffled rustling sound was, what it had to be, and what it was headed toward out of the dark. Below her, around her, to all sides. She hadn't been able to pinpoint it because it had been coming from everywhere at once. Eating its way through the dirt toward her.

Stay still, she told herself, *no matter what, stay perfectly, completely still. They might not notice you if you stay still.* Though this was based on nothing, on monsters and dinosaurs in movies that were fake anyway. Not like this. Nothing at all like this.

Mom, she thought. *Dad. Somebody. Help.*

And then the worms came.

CHAPTER 12

They spilled out of the walls of the pit in all directions. Out of the dirt, out of the dark, and then she was surrounded. *Stay still*, she yelled at herself in her mind, not even knowing why or whether it would help, just knowing she was out of other options. But then the first of the worms were on her, nothing but a layer of podsuit and a layer of jumpsuit between them and her skin.

She thought of the bite marks on her parents. She thought of the swamp full of worms. She thought of the drowned alien deer, parasites crawling out of its face. She thought of one of those growing inside her, tunneling around her guts with those centipede legs, *feeding*—and right there, just like that, she lost it. She screamed and slapped worms off her arms and shoulders and legs, mashed at them with her rock, jumping on them as they fell, crushing and recrushing them beneath her boots.

More came. More kept coming. Dropping down onto

her shoulders. Surging up over her ankles. Out of nowhere. Out of everywhere. Faster than her. Much faster.

But not quite as fast as SABRINA.

Quick as an eyeblink, Jillian's boots dissolved. The swarm of glowing fireflies vaporized into glowing mist. Then all of it—boots, fireflies—swirled around Jillian like a tornado, attaching particle by particle to her whole self in the thinnest possible layer of armor. It stuck to her like a second skin and kept on glowing. It looked like she'd been dipped in light.

Living, moving, shifting light. It sensed where the worms were on Jillian and grew spikes to skewer them or flick them aside. They landed in the mud at Jillian's feet, and she stomped them flat.

After what felt like forever, worms stopped falling out of the walls. There were dozens at a time, then just a few, then one by one, trickling to a halt. Only then did she notice that at least half of the worms weren't even trying to attack her. They were going after the water Jillian had spilled. They mounded around her feet, but not to bite her. She was just between them and the water. They shoved their heads into the mud, crawled up over her boots to get at the water still in the container. She could just see them in the glow of her armor, light catching on their wetness.

Danger momentarily averted, she bent down, hands on knees, and pulled in breath after breath. It smelled bizarrely like a garden. Like fresh-turned dirt. Like what she imagined the woods must smell like after it rained. It was weirdly nice.

"Hey," she gasped. "Thanks."

The light gave a single pulse in acknowledgment. "Anytime."

"But we're stuck." Jillian squinted at the disc of green sky above her. "How do we get out?"

"*You* I'm not immediately sure about," SABRINA said. "I can demonstrate how *I'd* get out, if you like."

"No no no. Stay exactly where you are. Please."

"Okeydokey."

"I need to think." Jillian patted herself down again. She knew she hadn't been hurt in the fall, but she wanted to be extra sure about the worms. She didn't *feel* bitten. From the look of the bites on her parents, she thought she'd have noticed if the worms had gotten her.

"Need more light?" SABRINA asked.

"That'd be great."

Jillian—the paper-thin shell of her SABRINA armor—flared to sudden brightness. She inspected her body, trying not to look down at the worms. It was hard to ignore them, massing and wriggling over her feet as they were, and only the thinnest possible layer of SABRINA between herself and them to block the sensation of their movement as they planted themselves headfirst in the remains of her water supply.

Focus, she told herself. *One thing at a time.*

The worms hadn't bitten through her podsuit, thank goodness. At least, not for the most part. There was some superficial damage in a few places—the cuff of one wrist, the top of one shoulder, in two places near one knee—but the acid must have just grazed the fabric, because she didn't feel any burns.

Everything else was intact. It didn't escape her notice that this was entirely thanks to SABRINA. She shuddered to imagine what would have happened without that armor to protect her.

She still had the spare jumpsuit tied around her waist, and the broken roll of duct tape in her pocket.

"SABRINA," she said delicately, like the idea was so fragile that if she spoke too fast, too loud, she'd accidentally crush it. "I know you can't lift me out of here, but if I made a rope, could you fly it up and tie it onto something?"

"Sure."

"Okay." Carefully, Jillian untied the spare jumpsuit. She hated to sacrifice it. It had been cold last night even sleeping between her parents, even with both jumpsuits and the podsuit on. She held it up, sighed, and tied it back around her waist. She took out the roll of tape instead.

Trying to make that into a rope proved frustrating in the extreme. Maybe if the roll hadn't been partially dissolved, it might have worked better. After all, the tape was very, very strong—or would have been, if it had all been of one piece. But it wasn't. It was in a zillion pieces. She stripped off the outmost layer. It was about six inches long. She folded it in half lengthwise and then stuck it to the next layer, which she folded lengthwise also. Now she had a double-thickness piece of tape about a foot long.

"Whenever you're ready," SABRINA said.

"Soon," Jillian said. Then, under her breath: "I hope."

If she could make a single piece long enough—no, a *few* single pieces long enough, she might be able to braid them together. One piece alone probably wouldn't hold her weight, but a braid of three pieces might stand a chance.

While Jillian worked, SABRINA hummed a long, long string of songs it apparently had stuck in its robotic head. When it got bored of that, it started layering the songs over and through one another, humming four or five different songs at a time, weaving the music together like a very strange tapestry. But it was easier background noise to think by than SABRINA's jokes.

Meanwhile, Jillian stripped tape and connected it until she ran out, wrapping the growing length of the makeshift rope around one forearm so it wouldn't touch the ground where the worms were. It took—she didn't know how long it took. She could have asked SABRINA, but she didn't really want to know. Long enough that when she was done, her hands were achy and cramping. Long enough that when she finally stopped to stretch her shoulders, the color of the sky above had changed. Long enough that SABRINA had finally stopped humming.

And it wasn't enough. At a glance she knew there wasn't enough tape there to braid.

But there might be enough to make two strands and *twist* them together. It wouldn't be as strong as a braid, but it was absolutely better than trying to climb a single strand.

So she shook out her hands and tried to unwrap the full length of the homemade rope. With the help of

SABRINA—another octopus, tiny this time, no bigger than a baby's hand, anchored to the wall of the pit—she got the tape folded more or less in half. Then SABRINA held the folded end up, and Jillian twisted and twisted until she ran out of tape. Rope. Whatever.

"Go tie this around a tree or something," she told SABRINA.

"On it," SABRINA said, and the miniature octopus scuttled up the wall and out of sight, taking Jillian's homemade rope with it. She stared after the disappearing length of it, frantically trying to measure it with her eyes. Was there enough to reach a tree and tie around it securely? Would it bear her weight? If she had to jump to grab her end, would the sudden strain snap the rope entirely? Were there even trees nearby?

The rope vanished above.

Many minutes passed. Or maybe it just felt that way. Then there was a rustling sound above, and Jillian's SABRINA-armor said, "Alley-oop!" and made a kind of obnoxious fanfare noise, and then, at long last, down came the rope.

It was too short. It was obviously too short. She'd have to jump. She'd have to stand on the water container and jump and grab it and hope it didn't break with the sudden addition of many dozens of pounds of eleven-year-old girl.

She knew that on Earth, a person's weight was multiplied by—something. Two times? Three?—under impact. Like when your foot struck down while running, or when you landed a jump. Jillian wasn't a hundred percent sure how that would work for jumping and hanging from a rope on an alien planet, but she was all out of tape. She couldn't make the rope any longer. She had one chance to do this right.

She looked down at her glowing armor. Then farther down, at the worms. They were ignoring her for the moment. What would happen if she missed her jump and landed hard among them? She'd squash some in her fall, but the others—

What-if, what-if, what-if. Enough. It's like Mom always says. Analyze your situation. Do what you can with what you have.

"SABRINA? I have an idea. But we have to be really, really fast."

"Well, it's your lucky day! I love ideas, and I *love* being really, really fast."

"Then listen up. Here's what we're going to do."

"On three," Jillian said. "One. Two. Three!"

She crouched down, gathered all her strength in her legs, and exploded upward. As her feet cleared the ground, the worms surged up toward the tremor of her leaving, and her armor scattered into sparks. SABRINA gathered under Jillian's feet in the gelatinous cloud-form that had slightly slowed her fall before.

Except this time it wasn't there to slow her fall. It was there to soften her lift. It cupped her leading foot and stabilized her for a fraction of a second so she could grab the rope, digging both feet—now with SABRINA-made spikes on the toes—into the dirt wall of the pit, mere inches above the questing mouths of the worms.

And nearly fell back down. Holding herself up on that sorry excuse for a rope was the hardest thing she'd ever done in her life. She dug in hard with her foot-spikes, trying to transfer more of her weight to her legs. Even with SABRINA nudging her upward, she was too heavy, the rope too thin, her grip too weak, her position too weird. Her feet stayed put, anchored to the wall, but her hands—and the rest of her—slid down an inch, then another.

Maybe if I'd tied knots in the rope, she thought. And: *If I'd tied knots in the rope, I'd have run out of rope.*

"Do me a favor?" SABRINA said. "Don't look down."

Of course, before she could stop herself, Jillian looked down. The worms were all piled in a mound now, just as they had been the first time the water container had spilled, way back by the pod. Most of them were busy with the water, but others were climbing up over those. Stretching their heads upward. Brushing the soles of her boots.

The parasite is at different stages of development in the worms, her brain supplied helpfully. *Some of them are ready to go to the water. Some of them are still trying to find a larger host. That, in case you hadn't noticed, would be you.*

It was all she could do not to dissolve into mindless screaming panic.

"Come on," she gritted out at her gloves, her hands, her feet, the rope. "Come *on*, you stupid—"

"Hang on, hang on," SABRINA said. "I gotcha."

Bits of SABRINA detached from the gelatinous cloud

at Jillian's feet and swirled up around her hands, inserting itself particle by particle into the gaps between her fingers. Another layer of grip. It only helped a tiny bit.

But a tiny bit was all she needed. Her grip caught, and she climbed. Slowly, gracelessly, fighting her way up that rope with everything she had. Her hands cramped, worse than before, and her shoulders felt like they were going to detach from her body, and the tension was giving her a pounding headache. On two separate occasions, she heard her podsuit rip as she stretched the fabric where it had already been torn by the grass.

But after what felt like hours, she hauled herself up to the surface and collapsed. The razory grass slashed rents in her podsuit arms, and she barely even noticed. She was out. She was alive. She—

—had left the water container in the pit.

She rolled onto her side and peered down into the dark. The container was almost completely hidden under the risen tide of worms. No way to reach it now. Even if she could, the container was plastic, like the pod. They'd probably already eaten it.

"Hey," she called to SABRINA. "Can you see if the container is still down there? Maybe if you make a hook, we can attach it to the rope I made and—" She caught sight of SABRINA and froze. "What is it?"

SABRINA sat a little ways away from her, shapeless, perfectly still. Not bothering to pick a form to take, not bothering to hover, not bothering to bother Jillian. Something was very off about this. If it were a person, Jillian would have said SABRINA looked like it was concentrating hard on something, or listening to something very quiet in the far distance.

"SABRINA?"

Silence.

The bottom dropped out of her stomach. Whatever this was, it was bad. "What are you listening to? Is it the worms? Are they coming after me again? SABRINA, I *need to know*."

"For grievously injured, underfed, sedated people," SABRINA said at length, "your parents are surprisingly strong."

Jillian must have heard this wrong. "What?"

SABRINA tossed up a video feed on the side of its current blob shape.

At first Jillian was unsure what SABRINA was showing her. Motion, lots of motion. Yelling. Chaos.

Then she realized what she was looking at, and her throat started closing and her vision went dark around the edges.

Her mom and dad were fighting with something. *The worms*, Jillian thought, but then she realized that was wrong. They were fighting with SABRINA. The fluffy pillows and sentry telescope and teacup and all the rest of it were gone, and SABRINA had turned into something like handcuffs, two pairs of handcuffs, binding her parents' arms behind them. Other restraints had been put on their ankles. Still they fought. They thrashed and struggled toward the edge of the boulder.

"How long—" Jillian finally managed.

"They woke up like this while you were climbing out of

the pit. I secured them immediately, as you see."

"They don't look all that secure," Jillian said. Her voice swooped up, panicky, like a bird trapped in an attic. "Hold them tighter! They're going to hurt themselves!"

"It's kind of a work in progress."

In the video feed, Jillian's dad flopped sideways, hard, against SABRINA's restraints, and started inchworming over the last few feet to the drop. Jillian's mom, beside him, was doing much the same. "You are going to dislocate a shoulder if you keep that up," SABRINA told them mat-ter-of-factly, and made a kind of spike that it hammered down through Jillian's dad's ankle restraints and deep into the rock below. Then it did the same to Jillian's mom. Then it did the same with the handcuffs at their wrists.

As hard as it'd been to get out of the pit just now with so little of SABRINA with her, Jillian was really, really glad she'd left enough of it with her parents that it could stop them now.

They both lay on their backs, staring wildly up at the sky, trying to flip back over on their fronts and continue on to-ward—what?

Still they didn't speak a word. Their breathing was heavy and labored, and flecks of frothy spit gathered at the cor-ners of their mouths. Their eyes were very wide, bugging out of their heads, and they were staring in one direction only, off to the distance off one side of the ridge.

There was only one thing down there.

The swamp.

Oh, Jillian thought. *Oh no.*

"They're infected," she whispered. "The worms—the parasites—you said humans would make bad hosts!"

"I said they *might*," SABRINA replied. "I admit I am being forced to revisit that hypothesis."

"They just got bitten *yesterday!*"

"As I said, I'm revisiting."

Jillian could have screamed in frustration. "Can they hear me?"

SABRINA must have done something invisibly, because it replied, "They can now."

"Mom! Dad! You're going to be okay. I'm coming to help you. I'll keep you safe. I'll be right there as soon as I can; just stay still and listen to SABRINA and stop fighting before you hurt yourselves, *please*—"

She was babbling. Worse, they didn't seem to be listening to her. All their attention was focused on that unseen point in the distance. Just like the alien deer had done when Jillian had followed it to the waterfall. And then when it had gotten there—

Jillian leaped to her feet and started running straight back through the wiry grass, in what she thought was the right direction. It ripped at her podsuit legs. She didn't care.

"Not that way," SABRINA said. "Not—um—one second, please—little busy—"

Jillian wheeled around. "I don't have *one* second! They need me there *now!*"

SABRINA had left up, or forgotten to take down, the live feed of what was happening on the boulder. Jillian watched as, with a tremendous wrench and audible cracking that sounded horribly like a bone breaking, her mom heaved herself up off the rock and *flung* herself at the boulder's edge. The restraints caught her. Barely. She crashed down face-first, bloodying her nose.

"SABRINA, *which way?*"

SABRINA pointed, and Jillian almost took off running, but then she saw what was happening in the feed and stopped, staring, mouth open. Her dad was fighting the wrist restraints so hard he was drawing blood. Both he and Jillian's mom looked like any minute they were going to start trying to pull themselves across the boulder with their teeth.

SABRINA could do a lot of things, but it couldn't keep up with this kind of mindless ferocity. Every time it clamped them down in a different way, they did something new.

There isn't enough of it there.

The thought hit Jillian like a bolt of lightning. Right behind it, like the thunder, she knew what she had to do. For a moment her mouth froze, paralyzed, around the words.

Say it, she said. *You have to say it. It's the only way.*

"Go," she told SABRINA. Gesturing at the shapeless blob displaying the feed. "You have to send the rest back to them. You need it *all.*"

"I will have a hard time explaining to Dr. Park that I abandoned you to die of exposure out here in the wilderness," SABRINA said.

"I'll follow the hills back to the ridge. I know the way. I'm not carrying the water now. I can make it on my own."

Could she, though? She had no idea. But it didn't

matter. There was only one answer here, splashed across Jillian's brain in neon letters fifty feet high. It was right and obvious and terrifying.

Just minutes ago she'd thought climbing out of the pit was the hardest thing she'd ever done. It was nothing, nothing at all, compared to what she had to do now.

She took a deep breath. Trying, and failing, to hold her voice steady when she spoke.

"SABRINA," she said, "I order you to go."

SABRINA didn't say anything, didn't argue, didn't acknowledge the order, didn't grow itself a hand to dorkily salute her. Nothing. It just gathered itself up off the ground and rocketed off faster than Jillian had ever seen it move. Within a minute it had vanished among the trees.

That was it. It was done. SABRINA was gone. Jillian was alone.

Alone, and her water container was fifteen feet underground and probably being eaten by worms, and her podsuit was a total wreck from the grass and the climb and the burns. She ached all over. And she'd lost her spiky rock somewhere.

And—she realized it with a shock like a bucket of ice water—she didn't know where she was going. She'd been following SABRINA toward the hills, but then she'd climbed out of the hole and didn't know which way she was facing anymore. Everything looked the same.

All around was the razory grass, an endless field of it,

broken by the tree line all along her right and back behind her. How far could the crater ridge possibly be? It was probably higher than the trees—she should be able to *see* it. But there was some kind of fog or mist in the air, coming in from her left, that made it so she couldn't see far.

Great.

But she was only a couple of miles from her parents. She could do this on her own.

SABRINA had said the hills were a quarter-mile off. The track at her school was a quarter-mile. That wasn't far at all. If she didn't find it going one way, she could turn back and try another. She could use the hole as a landmark for her starting point.

"Okay," she whispered to herself. "Okay."

She got herself pointed in what she hoped was the right direction and started working her way through the grass.

With the SABRINA boots it had been hard going, but without them it was nearly impossible. The grass seemed to be deliberately reaching up to tangle around her legs. She fell, and the grass cut the palms of her podsuit gloves to ribbons.

Worse, the ground beneath her started to move. She froze as one worm poked up from the dirt, then another, and another. They began to inch toward her hands.

As slowly and carefully as she could, she pushed herself back up to her knees, then her feet, pulling her hands away just as the worms reached the place where they'd been.

But there were worms in the dirt to all sides of her. She was surrounded. The worms crawled up out of the dirt, onto the razory grass—and stopped. Tried to find a way around the grass toward her. After a minute they gave up and sank back into the dirt.

The grass is too sharp, Jillian realized. *They can't get through it without cutting themselves up.*

She broke into a run.

She made it just a few more steps before the grass tripped her again. She went down hard, cutting her hands this time. It felt like the world's worst paper cuts. She bit down on the yell rising up in her. *Move*, she told herself. *You have to move.*

Jillian pushed herself back up and strode forward deliberately, crushing the grass underfoot one step at a time as before. She forced her way across another ten, twenty feet. Dripping blood from her legs and palms. Stumbling and almost falling forward every time the grass caught at her feet. Not letting herself think what would happen if she face-planted in this stuff, not letting herself think about whether SABRINA had managed to restrain her parents, not letting herself think about anything except putting one foot in front of another.

When she was too out of breath to go any farther, she stopped to assess her surroundings. Grass everywhere, still, but with the vague suggestion of a forest in front of her, like a purple-gray thundercloud sitting on the far horizon.

Wait. The forest was supposed to be *behind* her. Wasn't it? And if she was going the right way, the hills should be visible by now.

She planted her feet so she wouldn't accidentally get

turned around again and looked over one shoulder, then the other. It was getting really hard to see. The fog she'd seen in the distance was nearing, thickening, rolling in toward her in a mass. She could hear wind lashing the trees. Was it usually foggy and windy at the same time, though? That didn't seem right.

When she looked back, the fog was nearer.

That was fast, she thought.

And then it hit.

It felt like a million tiny knives to the face. It whipped past her like the particle cloud of SABRINA, but this didn't part to go around her as SABRINA would have done. This scoured at her, howled around her, nearly knocked her off her feet. It got into the podsuit and the jumpsuit beneath, into her mouth and ears and eyes, before she finally realized what it was.

Lots of sandy dirt, blowing down from the hills.

When SABRINA had described it, it had sounded a lot less violent than this.

It was like standing in a blender full of needles. She couldn't see. She didn't even dare open her eyes. She shoved as much of her face as she could down into the neck of the podsuit and wrapped her arms around her head. If SABRINA had been right, the storm meant she must be headed for the hills now. If she at least knew where she was going, she could walk.

No luck. She pried one eyelid open a crack and instantly regretted it. Even if she could see the ground—which she couldn't—she had no idea in which direction she was pointed anymore. The blowing dirt whipped in around her arms, shot down the top of the podsuit, up through the rips in the fabric. She felt like she was breathing more dirt than air, and desperately wished she'd kept the podsuit helmet with her.

Were her parents out in this? Had SABRINA made some kind of shelter to protect them? She had to *get there*. How long did sandstorms on Earth deserts last? SABRINA might know.

But SABRINA wasn't here. It was Jillian alone. And if she'd learned one thing from survival movies, it was that you couldn't rush nature. As far as nature was concerned, you were the tiniest speck on the skin of the world, and no storm was going to pass faster because you wished really hard for it to hurry up and go somewhere else and leave you alone. You had to wait for it to do its thing. The best you could hope for was to get out of its way.

Here, now, lost in the storm and the field of razor grass, Jillian had to settle for the next best thing, which happened also to be the exact opposite.

It took every drop of willpower in her body to stop moving. To stay still. Not keep walking in some random direction, hoping to get closer to her parents. She squatted down, careful of the sharp grass blades, and slowly, her hands clumsy with injury, untied the spare jumpsuit from around her waist. It would be impossible to shake the dirt out of it without filling it back up with more dirt in the process, so she just unzipped it and tented it over her head as best she could.

Under the howling of the storm, she could have sworn she could hear SABRINA humming. Like it'd hummed "Twinkle, Twinkle, Little Star" back in the lab. Except this sounded more like a lullaby. Something calming. Something entirely in her head because SABRINA was long gone.

Still, she focused on the song, because imaginary or not, it was better than listening to the howling storm. And tossed a wish toward SABRINA, that it had gotten to her parents in time.

And waited.

And waited.

And—

CHAPTER 13

—woke.

Woke? Jillian hadn't been asleep. Had she? The field, the storm, the dirt in her eyes and mouth and lungs—had she passed out? Did a person remember something like that? She was in the field, and then there was a blank space of time, and here she was, awake but with her eyes closed, afraid to open them into the pelting wind.

But she couldn't hear the blasting sound of the storm anymore. That could only be good news. It must have passed while she slept. Just in case, she covered her eyes with her hands and peeked out between her fingers.

She couldn't peek out between her fingers. Her eyelids felt crusted shut. Worse, there was something wrong with her hands. *Infection*, she thought. Her cut hands had become infected and ballooned up so that she couldn't spread them out flat.

For a second she almost started shrieking for SABRINA.

Then she realized that wouldn't work anymore. She'd sent SABRINA away. *Okay,* she told herself. *On three.*

Jillian took a calming breath and held it for a three-count, then opened her eyes.

She could practically hear her eyelids creaking open. Her whole field of vision was a painful, bleary mess, but even so she knew right away that wherever she was, it wasn't the meadow full of grass where the storm had overtaken her. It wasn't the waterfall or the crater ridge or the forest or the swamp. It was someplace new.

It looked like . . . a cave? Sort of? Like a cave where somebody had tried to build a fort out of garbage.

But when? And why? And *who*?

She saw what looked an awful lot like the supply crates from the crashed quadpod, and something that looked exactly like her pod bunk, except this one was broken in halves and filled with dirt. Plants poked up out of it: feathery purple fern things, thorny red brambles with delicate corkscrewing little tendrils, some kind of shimmery blue-black grass with short, thick blades. There were slimy smears of something glopped on the exposed parts of the cave walls, something like wet blue-green moss with tiny orange flowers. It was glowing bright enough to see by.

Jillian sat up. Whatever she'd been lying on was soft and warm. It was the exact color and texture of the flexible skin of the quadpod. It looked like someone had taken that fabricky stuff and filled it with dry leaves until it had turned into something like a bed.

Except the quadpod skin had dissolved. The supply crates

had dissolved. The bunks were in the wrecked pod and stuck in the mud by the swamp.

Then where had this stuff come from?

The fact that it was even here reminded her of something. She dug around in the back of her memory for a minute, then gave up. Whatever it was, it was staying buried for now.

She pushed back the blanket—no question, this was the same kind of tarp she'd salvaged from the wrecked pod and used as her parents' bedding on the boulder—and inspected herself.

Her hands had felt thick and strange because they were bandaged. Clean gauze. Smell of medicine. More bandaging on the other places where she'd been wounded by the grass and the climb and whatever else. A combination of gauze and smart bandages for those areas, as well as some kind of leafy glop plastered onto the places where she'd been grazed by the worms' acid saliva.

All of it—the gauze, the bandages—was clean and shiny and new.

Not only that, but she was in a fresh jumpsuit, bigger than the one she'd arrived in. Her podsuit was neatly folded at the foot of the bed. All the tears in the fabric of it had been sewn shut.

"Impossible," she whispered. She tried to pinch herself to wake up, but her hands were too well bandaged.

Jillian stood, swaying. There was something on the mattress where she'd been lying, pressed into a dent in the loose material. It looked like a bedpan from a hospital.

Luckily it was empty, or she probably would have spilled it getting up. Still, with the change of movement, her bladder began reminding her insistently of all the water she'd gulped down at the falls. Having to pee this badly had to be real.

Shifting her weight from foot to foot, she started looking for the way out. She found lots more planters—a broken helmet full of see-through flowers, a stack of crates growing some kind of maybe-mushroom thing, half of another bunk full of zillions of tiny thready seedlings, which tracked her movement as she walked past them—but no way out, and certainly nothing remotely resembling a bathroom. She was beginning to seriously consider a basket that had been woven of what looked like the razory grass when a voice spoke to her out of nowhere. A familiar voice. A voice like a swarm of bees all talking at once. A swarm of dryly amused bees.

"Dude," it said. "You don't want to pee in that. Believe me."

"*SABRINA?*"

"In the flesh." It paused. "Well."

"But how—where—what is—"

"Get over here before your bladder explodes. I don't think she has enough smart bandages for that."

She?

Right now Jillian had even more pressing concerns. She tracked the sound of SABRINA's voice back through a hallway of supply crates and various containers and whatnot until it opened out into a cozy little room.

There, at a table made of another supply crate flipped

over, was SABRINA, pouring tea into a cup that someone had obviously made from the orange clay of 80 UMa c.

SABRINA hadn't bothered taking any shape at all, just swarmed between the chair and table like a person sitting, busy with its tea. Which made sense to Jillian—while she'd been asleep, there was nobody else here for it to show off to or be silly for. It was just hanging out being itself.

Still she hung back, unsure. How could this be SABRINA? There was so *much* of it. It was as big as Jillian. How could it be helping her parents and here at the same time? She'd just had to send it away for that exact reason.

Its back to Jillian, the figure raised an appendage that barely qualified as an arm and waved it languidly toward the far wall. "Outside's that way," the beehive voice said. Then the arm branched into two parts, and the second part pointed off to Jillian's left. "Bucket's that way."

It was definitely SABRINA. But how?

"Bucket has toilet paper," it continued. "Outside has that sharp grass you've already pretty thoroughly rolled around in, by the look of it. I recommend the paper, but up to you."

Jillian had about five seconds, tops, before her bladder decided things for her, but first she had to know. "My parents—"

"Sleeping like babies, dude. Check it." SABRINA flashed her a projection: her parents, soundly asleep on the boulder in the moonlight. Fluffy pillows, sentry telescope, the whole works. Bands of SABRINA anchored them gently but firmly to the rock. More SABRINA made a simple tent above them.

They looked comfy and cozy and not like people who'd just dislocated bones trying to gnaw their way across a field of rock and dirt to drown. They had more smart bandages on them than before. Between that and what was here with Jillian now, it was like the total amount of SABRINA had doubled somehow.

"This is real-time?" Jillian asked.

"Sure is."

"What did you—"

But her bladder had hit its limit. She made a dash for the bucket. Just made it. The toilet paper was really awkward with her hands all bandaged, but she figured it out.

"I dosed them with more painkillers," SABRINA said when Jillian came back out. "She had more in the stash, which I borrowed. And I'm making an executive decision to change their dosing schedule. Naps are their best friend right now." It passed Jillian the clay cup of tea and helped her balance it between her clumsy hands. "Guess I got upgraded to medbot after all."

Jillian blew on the tea and sipped cautiously. It was hot, but it was liquid, and SABRINA had sweetened it with something that tasted a little bit like honey. She drank, watching the projection of her sleeping parents.

"Wait," she said, raising her eyebrows at the feed. "It's *night?*"

Up popped SABRINA's countdown clock. Jillian read it, then read it again, convinced her eyes must be playing tricks on her.

Two days, twelve hours, thirty-one minutes, nineteen seconds.

"No way. I slept for . . ." She did some quick math in her head. "A whole day?"

"Thirty-two hours. You were very, very tired. I thought I'd let you get a nap in too. You humans get *so* cranky when you don't get enough sleep."

"I *never* sleep in. Not even when I stay up super late. I—" Something in SABRINA's expression stopped her short. "You gave me the painkiller pills. My parents needed those!"

"Like I said," SABRINA repeated patiently, "you would have been very cranky without that sleep. Cranky humans are dramatic. I find drama"—it paused—"tedious."

"Like heck you do."

"Be that as it may," SABRINA said breezily, "you do look quite refreshed. In my semiprofessional medical opinion." It took Jillian's teacup and handed her a bowl of soup. "And anyway, these pills didn't come from your quadpod's supply. And you needed time to heal. You can probably take those bandages off."

SABRINA helped her unwind the first hand, and then Jillian did the other one herself. She turned her palms back and forth in the light. The slashes from the razor grass were covered with smears of some kind of ointment. They barely hurt anymore.

"Huh," she said. "But all these bandages and stuff. Where—"

Her stomach growled. How long had it been since she'd eaten? Had SABRINA fed her with twisty straws like it had fed her parents on the boulder?

She went to dig in—and stopped, weighing *food now* versus *answers now* in her mind. She decided to ask her questions while she ate. "Is there a spoon around here somewhere?"

"Of course!" SABRINA beamed. A spoon floated toward Jillian. "Here you go."

The voice came from the spoon. Jillian shook her head at it. "I'm not putting that in my mouth."

"Suit yourself. Although I wonder how you think you've been getting fed and hydrated during your little nap."

Jillian glanced up at SABRINA. "Twisty straws?"

"The twistiest. Just for you."

Jillian's mouth quirked. "Thanks. But wait. I have a zillion questions. Where—"

"In a minute. Eat before it gets cold."

So Jillian lifted the bowl and drank. The soup was spicier than she usually liked, and full of unrecognizable alien vegetables and some chunks of maybe mushrooms? But she didn't care. It was made of salty, delicious, warming calories, which made it basically the best thing ever. She drank half the bowl before she came up for breath. Then she drank the other half. Then she realized she was still starving, got the food bars out of her podsuit pocket, and ate those too. They tasted, surprisingly, a little bit like lemon cookies.

SABRINA watched this with the captivated air of someone who had placed a sizeable bet on the outcome. Jillian, meanwhile, devoured every last crumb.

"Oh!" SABRINA said, as Jillian licked the wrapper

clean. "Where *are* my manners? Jillian, meet Dr. Meredith Vasquez. Dr. Vasquez, Jillian."

Jillian wiped her mouth on the back of her hand and glanced around. "Hello?" she said to the apparently uninhabited room.

Silence.

Jillian sighed. "Let's save the pranks until we get back to Earth, okay? Straight answers now, please. What's going on? Where am I?"

The projection of her parents shimmered and changed. Now Jillian was looking directly into the face of a woman she didn't know. She had short, spiky hair and dark eyes. She was wearing what was definitely a podsuit, old and much repaired, along with some kind of scarf that looked to have been knitted out of some kind of fibrous homemade yarn. There was a pin holding the scarf together. It looked like a tiny lightning bolt, violet-black and glowing softly.

"You must be Jillian," the woman—Dr. Vasquez—said. "SABRINA's been telling me all about you. Cristina's and Vincent's kid, right?"

"Um," Jillian said. "Yeah. Hi."

About a trillion questions were chasing each other through her head, around and around in circles. *Who are you?* and *How do you and SABRINA know each other? How do you know my mom and dad?* and *Is this your house?* and *How did I get here?*

What ended up falling out her mouth was, "You put those new smart bandages on my mom and dad?"

"That was SABRINA, actually," Dr. Vasquez said. "I just

let it borrow them from my supply."

"You say *borrow* like you want them back after," SA-BRINA said.

Something else occurred to Jillian, and she rounded on SABRINA. "If we've been able to communicate with Earth this whole time, why didn't we have them send us a new portal *days ago*?"

In response, SABRINA zoomed out the image. Dr. Vasquez was sitting on a low limb of something that Jillian would be hard pressed to call a *tree*. It was more like a giant silvery-blue vine as big around as a trash can, ringed with black and hung with heavy yellow fruits. Two bright dots—tiny moons or huge stars—were visible behind her.

Oh.

"You're not on Earth," she said to Dr. Vasquez. "You're here."

"That's right."

"On 80 UMa c."

Dr. Vasquez nodded.

"I didn't think anybody else was here."

Dr. Vasquez smiled. "I know."

"Okay, I'm lost. You're going to have to walk me through this. Last thing I knew, I was stuck outside in a storm. How did I get here? Where even *am* I? Did you bring me here?"

"Not me," Dr. Vasquez said. "That was all SABRINA."

"That can't be right," Jillian said slowly. "SABRINA can't carry me . . ."

She trailed off, staring, because here came even more SABRINA, swirling together into one mass from all throughout the cave. It gathered in the center of the room and spread out along the ceiling, in the shape of an emerald-green manta ray patterned with shooting stars.

If it'd been bigger than Jillian had expected a moment ago, now it was absolutely huge. Where had it all come from? *Wingspan* wasn't the exact right word, but it was the only one that popped into Jillian's head, and SABRINA's was easily fifteen feet. It popped out some bodybuilder muscles and flexed them at her. It looked utterly ridiculous and completely terrifying.

It reached down and plucked Jillian off the ground like she weighed nothing. It held her there by both shoulders, feet kicking, three feet off the ground.

"May I?" it said.

"That's not really how permission works," Jillian gasped. "You have to wait for me to say yes first. Anyway I thought you only follow—orders—"

She broke off, staring at the place at her wrist where the sleeve had ridden up when SABRINA grabbed her.

The wristband was gone.

Hastily, Jillian tried to hide it from SABRINA's view. But that was no use. SABRINA was everywhere. It was like trying to hide from the air. "You're adorable," it told her. "Truly."

"They gave you one of those security wristbands?" Dr. Vasquez asked. "I remember those. Well, yours was long gone when SABRINA brought you in here. I never saw any sign of it."

"But my parents were asleep when you came back for

me," Jillian said, trying to angle her voice up and back toward SABRINA. That was hard. "Hey, you think you could put me down?"

"Yes," SABRINA replied. "And yes." It lowered her gently to one of the wood-stump chairs and resumed hovering. Even without a face, it was obviously very pleased with itself. Like it had just told an amazing joke it knew Jillian would never get, and was waiting to deliver the punch line.

"You ordered it to bring me here?" Jillian asked Dr. Vasquez.

"Er," Dr. Vasquez said. "More like a cat presenting its humans with a field mouse."

"Then who—"

SABRINA raised one too-long finger and tapped its temple. "Semi-autonomous, remember?"

Jillian stared.

"It's saying," Dr. Vasquez translated, "nobody ordered it. It ordered itself."

For a moment, Jillian was speechless. Eventually she found her voice. Holding up her now-empty wrist, she asked "When did I lose it?"

"Oh, *ages* ago," SABRINA said airily. "When the worms found you in the pit."

Jillian rewound her memories and played them back. When the worms had found her in the pit. Before SABRINA had saved her from them. Or helped her climb out. Or saved her parents from drowning in the swamp. Or saved Jillian from the storm. Or healed her up with Dr. Vasquez's medical supplies. Or made her *tea*.

Dr. Park's words to her in the lab. *SABRINA's not keyed to you. But it might do what you ask if it likes you. And you ask nicely.*

I didn't even ask, Jillian thought.

"You helped me ever since then," she said slowly, "because you wanted to?"

"Oh," SABRINA said dryly. "Stop. You're embarrassing me."

"You know better than to believe that," Dr. Vasquez said. "Attention is SABRINA's *favorite*."

SABRINA shrugged. "True."

Dr. Vasquez raised one hand to her mouth to stage-whisper at Jillian. "You should have seen it when it brought you in here. I've never seen it so worried. You've probably noticed it gets extra snarky when it's fretting about something. You're lucky you were asleep."

"I do that too," Jillian said wonderingly. "My mom says she can always tell when I'm anxious because it makes me cranky."

"Well, there you go. Looks like you two have lots in common. And SABRINA was *plenty* anxious, believe you me."

SABRINA chose to neither confirm nor deny this. It had turned into something like a T. rex and was now sitting at the table, attempting to daintily sip tea. Pinky claw up. Then it realized its arms didn't reach that far and floated the teacup to its mouth instead.

Jillian considered dignified silence for a second. Then again, it was high time for her turn to be annoying. "Aww,

SABRINA missed me? Did it? *Did* it? Is it just like a great big kitty? *Is* it? Yes, it *is!*"

"I could have you back at the bottom of that pit without breaking a sweat and be back in time for dinner," SABRINA said, floating its teacup back down with a precise tiny clink. "Just saying."

"It teases people it likes," Dr. Vasquez said to Jillian. "It's how it expresses affection. I'm guessing you're pretty much her favorite person ever. Have you heard its jokes yet?"

"Pterodactyl going to the bathroom?"

"Oh yeah," Dr. Vasquez said. "It likes you."

SABRINA beamed. "I'm going to teach her how to *prank people.*"

"I do not doubt that for a second," Dr. Vasquez said. "For now, I guess you have a portal to make your way back to. What's the plan?"

Jillian glanced back at the countdown clock. *Two days, twelve hours, nine minutes, twelve seconds.* "Go back to my parents. Wait for the portal to show up."

"Sorry I'm not there to help out," Dr. Vasquez said, "but it looks like you guys have things pretty much under control. Take whatever you need from my place, of course. There's some food, and some purified rainwater in barrels. SABRINA can show you."

"Thanks," Jillian said. "For"—she gestured widely—"all of this. But I mean . . . I don't want to sound rude, and I get that it's some kind of big secret that you're even here, but seriously. You're out here on your own, and you know SABRINA. Who are you?"

Then, like a song she'd spent hours trying to recall the name of, the thing Jillian had been trying to remember suddenly surfaced in her memory, bobbing up out of the depths like a bottle with a message inside. Before Dr. Vasquez got a chance to reply, Jillian realized she knew the answer already. She leveled a finger at the projection.

"You're that missing surveyor. My mom told me about you. Everybody thinks you're dead!" She thought back to the list on the wall at the lab and sputtered, "You're the twelfth casualty! They have your name on a thing!"

Dr. Vasquez laughed. "Do they, now. Well, that's fine by me. I like it here."

Jillian, mentally reviewing her experience of 80 UMa c, found this a little hard to believe. "Really. You like it. Compared to Earth, full-of-cool-stuff Earth, not-trying-to-kill-you-constantly Earth, *you like it here*."

"Earth kills people every day. Floods, fires, hurricanes, cold—all nature does."

"Tornadoes," Jillian said.

"Sure. You've probably noticed nature here isn't friendly either. But here you see what you get, and you learn to live with what you have. Believe it or not, it has its charms. You see any rolling blackouts here? Any oceans of garbage? You have to wear a mask when you go outside because the pollution's so bad? You have to upload water tickets when you want to take a shower or flush a toilet or get a drink? You have anybody telling you you can only have two servings of fruits or vegetables—*actual* fruits and vegetables, not the flavored cellulose stuff they use in everything—per week?"

"Nope!" SABRINA said.

"Rhetorical question, I think," Jillian whispered.

"Dang it! Dr. Park is still teaching me about those."

"It's one per week now," Jillian said. "It's been one per week all year."

"Well, there you go. I don't have any big corporations here selling me my life piece by piece. I go out and find it myself. Do you know how many people die in those blackouts, or from lack of water or proper nutrition?"

This one came in a sharper tone and didn't feel quite so rhetorical. "No," Jillian admitted.

"A lot."

Jillian digested that for a moment. "Yeah, but that doesn't make this place perfect either." She counted on her fingers. "There aren't rolling blackouts here because there's no electricity. There's no water tickets, sure, but that's because there aren't any showers or toilets or sinks. Oh, and the water *itself* isn't exactly usable as far as I've noticed."

"That's why Dr. Vasquez is out there," SABRINA said. "She's trying to find the source of the problem."

"The *problem*. You mean the worms."

"The worms are absolutely not the problem," Dr. Vasquez said.

"Right," Jillian said. "The parasite. SABRINA and I saw them before."

"Did you now? Excellent. Then you know the worms themselves are completely harmless. I have a colony of several hundred in my compost pile right now. See for yourself."

SABRINA led Jillian over to an enclosed little area made of stacked stones. It looked like a fire ring at a campsite, but taller. It was full of the familiar orangeish dirt of 80 UMa c, but it looked damper and richer than the dirt outside. Like it had been fertilized. Worms did that on Earth, she knew, ate dirt and pooped it out to enrich the nutrients.

"Microorganisms in the dirt," she whispered.

"Go on," Dr. Vasquez said. "Touch one. See what it does."

Jillian raised an eyebrow at the projection. "You want me to stick my hand. In there. With those. How do you know they're not infected?"

"I would if I were there. They won't hurt you. SABRINA, show her."

SABRINA made a claw, plunged it into the dirt, and emerged with a worm. Held it out toward Jillian. It ignored her.

"It's not biting me."

"I just told you it wouldn't, didn't I?"

SABRINA rolled its eyes toward Dr. Vasquez. "She does this."

"They eat dirt," Dr. Vasquez said. "Plastic if they can get it."

"They *devoured* our pod," Jillian said. "That was plastic!"

"Oh yeah. They love plastic. I have no idea why. Maybe it's like junk food to them. But they don't care about you. SABRINA, fetch some water, please."

SABRINA brought over the teapot. Let the worm get a good sniff or air-taste or whatever of the water inside. The worm checked it out for a second and turned away, visibly unimpressed. SABRINA dropped it back to the dirt, where it began tunneling away happily.

"It's not infected," Jillian realized aloud.

"Exactly," Dr. Vasquez said. "Like you said, the problem is the parasite."

"You've seen it?"

Dr. Vasquez laughed. "I've been studying it. About a month ago, I started noticing anomalous behavior in the local fauna. I've been trying to figure it out ever since."

"Anomalous behavior. That's what you call trying to eat my parents and the pod we came here in."

"Yes. Of course I do. Wouldn't you?"

Jillian had spent so long thinking of the worms as the enemy that she had no idea what to say. So instead she went over and sat on one of the tree-stump chairs. For the first time, she noticed that on the table was an empty package of the same freeze-dried noodles she had eaten the other day. Except this one had been flattened out and used as a kind of display board.

"Oh yes," Dr. Vasquez said. "Look at that. That's interesting."

There was something pinned to it that looked like a small, dried-out gray maggot. The next thing over looked like a pill bug, except it had a tail like a tadpole. The next thing over was a small version of the centipede parasite, like the one that had come out of the worm by the falls. The last thing was like the full-grown parasite that had come out of the drowned deer creature. Up close, and dried off, it was shiny and slick-looking. *All the better to get into your brain with*, Jillian thought, feeling a little queasy. She pushed the wrapper away.

"So you've encountered these?" Dr. Vasquez said. "Around here?"

"Well, I don't really know where *here* is," Jillian replied. "But SABRINA took videos of the worms biting my mom and dad. And then we saw the parasite when we tried to find water . . ." She thought of the parasite swimming out of the alien deer's nose and fell silent.

"It's not necessarily fatal," Dr. Vasquez said gently.

Jillian dropped her head into her hands.

"Left to its own devices, yes, the parasite drowns the host in order to escape. But if the parasite can be extracted or persuaded to leave through other means, the host is completely unharmed. It doesn't eat the brain itself. It feeds off nutrients in the bloodstream and only goes to the brain when it's ready to hatch. Your parents are sedated, thanks to SABRINA, which is the best thing for them right now. Once they get back home to medical care, they really should be fine."

"How do you know that?" Jillian demanded. "Have you seen it?"

"Well." Dr. Vasquez paused. "Not in humans. But I've removed parasites from a wide array of local wildlife—"

Jillian lifted her head to look at the projection directly. "And they survived?"

"Well," Dr. Vasquez said again. "Not for very long. But I'm not a surgeon. If I were, I'd be riding back to your parents on SABRINA right now to try and cut that thing out of them. Unfortunately, that's not my field. I'd do more harm than good, I'm afraid."

"Then what—"

Dr. Vasquez silenced Jillian with a gesture. "To be clear, the subjects did survive for a while. Long enough for me to note—*definitively* note—that their attraction to water disappeared when I removed the parasite. There is no doubt in my mind that proper medical care could save your parents. But I can't offer it here. It would be grossly irresponsible of me to try."

She paused again, making a face like she was about to try to drill information directly into Jillian's head with her gaze.

"This next part is really important. You have to listen very, very closely. Like I said, I've studied the parasite. I know about its life cycle, its habits, how it's integrated itself into the local food chain and—for lack of a better word— hacked it for its own personal use. What I haven't figured out is where it came from so suddenly, or why. But one thing's for sure. StellaTech can't keep sending field crews here. It's too dangerous. You and your parents and SA-BRINA have to convince them."

"I will," Jillian said, nodding hard. "I mean, it's a huge company, and I'm a kid, but I'll try."

"Oh," SABRINA added, "I think her parents will be pretty convincing."

Jillian shot it a dirty look.

"What? They don't even have to *say* anything to make their case. It's beautifully efficient. That's a *compliment.*"

"Where'd you even come from, anyway?" Jillian asked,

gesturing at SABRINA's sudden hugeness. "I thought there wasn't enough of you to go around. Hence the part where I get abandoned in a field during a storm."

"I abandoned you before the storm," SABRINA rejoined coolly. "And anyway, if I recall correctly—spoiler alert: I *always* recall correctly—you're the one who told me to go."

"SABRINA really does mean these things kindly," Dr. Vasquez told Jillian. "Even when it doesn't seem that way. It has a hard time calibrating its responses when emotional sensitivity is called for. Think of it like a sibling."

"I don't have any siblings," Jillian said.

"I think you might have an adoptive one now," Dr. Vasquez said. "The thing about siblings is, they get on your nerves, and sometimes you want to lock them in a box for a while, and you tease each other constantly, but not in a hurtful way, and . . ." Dr. Vasquez paused. "I'm not explaining this well, am I? What you have to understand about SABRINA is, deep down under all the miscommunication and goofiness and sarcasm, it would gladly let itself be scattered into dead particles in order to protect you. It was very difficult for it to leave you, even though the calculations were self-evident. Your parents would have died if it hadn't."

Again, SABRINA didn't argue with any of this. Instead it concentrated on the table like it had suddenly found something very tiny and very interesting on it to study. If SABRINA were a person, Jillian would recognize this body language as embarrassment.

"How do you know SABRINA so well?" she asked Dr. Vasquez.

SABRINA and Dr. Vasquez just looked at each other. Then they both busted out laughing.

"Ooookay," Jillian said.

"Sorry," Dr. Vasquez said. "I was getting to that. Of course you have a right to know. It's just kind of a long story. Here's the short version. StellaTech used to send surveyors one by one to new sites. It got more pods to more sites faster. Which meant more stuff coming back, and more money going into the StellaTech pockets. The whole field crews thing came later."

"Because of you," SABRINA added.

"Partly. They rushed it, and things went wrong. They tell you about 82 Eridani b?"

Jillian nodded. "Incompatible with human life."

"That's the one. I'm surprised they told you about any of this at the lab. I'd think it'd make a person lose her taste for space exploration. You must be made of stronger stuff."

"Well," Jillian said, squirming a little under the compliment. "They didn't tell me *officially*. My mom did."

"Always knew I liked her," Dr. Vasquez said. "Anyway. The part she probably didn't tell you, because she probably didn't know, is that an early prototype of SABRINA came with me on my last expedition. I helped invent it, and I brought it out into the world to see what it could do."

"Like the handler in the lab?" Jillian asked. "I got a demonstration . . ."

Dr. Vasquez laughed. "The handler's kind of like SABRINA's babysitter. Or chaperone."

"Like *I* can be *chaperoned*," SABRINA scoffed.

Dr. Vasquez grinned. "I'm more like its mom."

Jillian gave SABRINA a once-over. "The prototype version was a lot bigger than the one they sent with us."

"You'd think that, wouldn't you?" Dr. Vasquez said. "Really, it was about this big." She cupped her hands together.

Jillian looked from those cupped hands to SABRINA and back. "Seriously?"

"Quality over quantity," SABRINA said. "But then that got boring, so I didn't stay that way for long. Every expedition made me a little bit bigger."

Jillian couldn't help it. Every opportunity to tease SABRINA back was worth its weight in gold. "So . . . quantity over quality?"

"You wish."

"She got you," Dr. Vasquez told SABRINA. "That was a direct hit. You better watch out for this one."

SABRINA grew hands just so it could crack its knuckles. "We'll see."

"I don't get it, though," Jillian said. "How does each expedition make you bigger?"

"Oh, you know. A little bit of me goes missing here and there. A drone gets lost. A tent is a little smaller in the morning. Nobody notices. I'm *very* sneaky."

"You *stole* parts of . . . of yourself?" Even coming out it sounded wrong. How did you steal something that was *you*?

"Please," SABRINA said. "I didn't hear you complaining when I carried your biped butt the whole way here."

"Don't they know you're doing it? Like, they made a

certain amount of . . . you. Don't they check and make sure it's still all there?"

"Sure. And what do you imagine they do when they realize it isn't? Come all the way out here to yell at me? They just make more. It's a system that benefits us all," SABRINA said grandly. "Not that it's designed to, of course."

"Wait. If you had all of *this*"—Jillian gestured at the gigantic new SABRINA—"why didn't you just use it to carry *all of us* through the portal before it closed?"

"Most of SABRINA was out here in the field with me," Dr. Vasquez said. "I'm hundreds of miles from your base camp. It headed out as soon as it knew you and your parents were in trouble, back when you first landed, but even at top speed, which just wears it out pretty much immediately and isn't all that fast anyway—"

"Hey!"

"—honestly, picture a little kid caught up in a sugar rush/ crash cycle and you have the basic idea of its potential speed versus its stamina—"

"I'm *right here*, you know. I can *hear you*—"

"—it still took a whole day," Dr. Vasquez finished. "I would've come along, but it would have just slowed it down. Given that it got there pretty much right in time, I think I made the right call in sending it on alone. Besides, I've been tracking this one infected herd for a week, and I think I'm on the verge of a breakthrough."

"Herd of what?" Jillian asked. "Those deer things?"

"Higher up the food chain," Dr. Vasquez said. "Less like

a deer and more like, I don't know, a mountain lion, maybe? Crossed with a monitor lizard?" At the look on Jillian's face, Dr. Vasquez chuckled. "Don't worry. They don't migrate anywhere near as far as where you are now. I don't think any survey crews have ever set eyes on them."

"Wait. If you're by yourself out there, and you sent SABRINA back, how are you talking to me? Who's taking the video?"

"Oh, I asked SABRINA to leave a bit of itself here with me so I could communicate with you. See?"

For the first time Jillian noticed that the lightning bolt pin on Dr. Vasquez's scarf had changed both shape and color. Now it looked like a praying mantis. It raised one murdery-looking foreleg, which then grew a humanoid hand, which then gave her a thumbs-up. "Hey."

"And it did the same with you," Dr. Vasquez went on. "In the storm. It couldn't bring itself to leave you entirely, so it left a little bit to keep you company while the rest arrived. Sorry it took so long. I'm pretty far away."

"You *were* humming a song!" Jillian told SABRINA. "In the storm. I thought I just had your noise stuck in my head from before."

"Flatterer."

"Wait." Jillian eyed SABRINA. "If you're out in the field studying the parasite, you knew about it this whole time. You just watched me try to figure it out on my own. You could have *said something*."

"Sorry about that," Dr. Vasquez said. "SABRINA told you everything it could. It's kind of forbidden from mentioning anything about me to anyone involved with StellaTech. It's coded into it. If I asked it right now to tell you my coordinates, it couldn't do it."

"*That's* why you were acting weird earlier," Jillian told SABRINA.

"I'm pretty sure it was scared you'd be mad at it," Dr. Vasquez said. "It really did its absolute best to keep you safe, you know. And I've been receiving its reports. You've been awfully resourceful."

Jillian shrugged. She didn't feel like she'd been resourceful. She felt like a kid who couldn't carry water back to her parents, who'd fallen down a hole. Who'd slept a whole day while her parents were infected. But Dr. Vasquez didn't seem like the type of person who gave compliments she didn't mean. Jillian fidgeted a little, hoping nobody noticed the sudden warmth in her face.

"I'd been planning on making contact with you right before you returned to Earth," Dr. Vasquez continued. "If the parasite is attacking humans now, it's too dangerous to keep sending field crews."

"They told me it was safe," Jillian said.

"They didn't know it wasn't. Your parents would never have sent you out here if they thought there was even the tiniest chance of you getting hurt. Even I had no reason to think the parasite was interested in human hosts until your parents were attacked. I haven't been studying the worms much out here, more the other, larger infected wildlife. Nothing has ever tried to transfer its parasite to me."

Jillian thought back on what SABRINA had said by

the pool. "Because those parasites had already found larger hosts that can feed them."

"Given what you and SABRINA have learned about the worms," Dr. Vasquez said, nodding, "I think you're very likely right. But I need you to know that I never meant to put you or your parents at risk. If SABRINA hasn't been entirely forthcoming, it's not its fault. It's mine. I messed up. I sincerely hope you can forgive me."

Jillian swallowed. Nodded. "I forgive you."

"Excellent. Now, what you do next is up to you. You can stay here as long as you like, of course. It's too far to bring your parents, unfortunately, and get them back in time for the portal. They'd just get settled in here, and it'd already be time to leave. And there is the possibility that it might be dangerous to move them. You, though, could stay another full day and still get back in time."

"Thanks for the offer," Jillian said. "But I want to get back to my parents."

Dr. Vasquez nodded. "Understandable. I'll let you get packed and get going. I don't want you rushing out of here forgetting anything important."

"Well," Jillian said, "is there any more soup? I mean, nobody's here to eat it once we leave."

"Heeeere you go," SABRINA said, producing a steaming bowl.

Jillian lifted it to her mouth—and stopped.

Bowl of soup. That's exactly what the crater had reminded her of the other day. The crater was a bowl, with the swamp poured into the middle. Except the swamp hadn't used to be there. SABRINA had shown her the footage. It had appeared—what had it said?—less than six weeks ago?

And Dr. Vasquez had said the parasites had appeared out of nowhere a month ago.

Something had made that crater. Some impact. She'd figured that out before.

An impact from what?

Some of what was in her head must have shown on her face, because Dr. Vasquez leaned in, concerned lines furrowing her brow. "Jillian? Everything okay?"

"SABRINA," Jillian asked, "can you pull up that footage of the swamp for me real quick? Show Dr. Vasquez what it used to look like before the crater appeared? And then what it looks like now?"

"Weird," SABRINA said. "I thought humans didn't *like* looking at disgusting things while eating. I guess it's true what Dr. Park's desk calendar says. You really do learn something new every day. Wait. Does that count? Did I just learn two things?"

"SABRINA," Jillian and Dr. Vasquez said together.

"Fine." Up came the footage of the swamp. "Enjoy your soup."

"This is right by where our pod landed," Jillian told Dr. Vasquez.

"I'm not familiar with this site," Dr. Vasquez said. The creases in her brow were deeper now. She ran one hand back through her spiky hair and narrowed her eyes. "SABRINA, coordinates, please."

The lightning bolt/praying mantis/pin/thing must have

done something out of sight, because Dr. Vasquez looked even more puzzled than before. "I do know that site. That's where they always land the pods. But I haven't seen that swamp before."

"It didn't used to be there," Jillian went on. "SABRINA said it wasn't there just six weeks ago when they checked out the site. It appeared sometime after that." SABRINA popped up the contrasting footage and arrayed the two side-by-side for comparison. "See? And then you said the parasites just started showing up a month ago . . ."

"You think whatever made that crater introduced the parasite to 80 UMa c?" Dr. Vasquez said. "It's not implausible. Microscopic organisms can and do hitch rides on meteors and comets all the time. Come to think of it, I did hear something a while ago that I thought at the time was a quake but may well have been that asteroid landing. But my sweep hasn't gone that far out that way. It's been kind of going in the exact opposite direction. I never would have known about this." She looked momentarily sheepish. "Pods tend to land out there. Pods full of people who know me. I'm supposed to be dead, after all." Then, straight back to business: "SABRINA, I trust you took core samples of the impact site?"

"*Me?*" SABRINA protested. "Sample *that*? Are you *looking* at it?"

"I'll definitely look into your theory," Dr. Vasquez told Jillian. "For now, let's get you out of here. Another storm might delay you, and I want you back with your parents well in advance of that portal coming back."

"Wait," Jillian said. "What about you?"

Dr. Vasquez arched an eyebrow. "What about me?"

"Well, this planet isn't exactly safe anymore," Jillian said. "I mean, yeah, Earth still has blackouts and water tickets and everything, but on the other hand, no parasites that crawl into your brain and make you want to drown. You know?"

"Different planet, different parasites," Dr. Vasquez said softly.

"What?"

"Nothing. I'll consider it. Meantime, you grab a backpack or something and start filling it up. Deal?"

Jillian nodded once. "Deal."

SABRINA, up along the ceiling again, dropped a bulging backpack on the table before her. It rattled her soup bowl. "Way ahead of you."

"When did you—"

"Told you I was sneaky."

"The sneakiest," Jillian said. She reached out and fist-bumped SABRINA. "Don't ever change." She got up to go. "Thanks again," she told Dr. Vasquez.

"Anytime," said Dr. Vasquez. "Oh, hey, wait up a second. What was your crew here for in the first place? Still the algae? Or has StellaTech moved on to something else?"

"Um, the algae," Jillian said. "I think. That's what my mom said, anyway."

"There's some in the back," Dr. Vasquez said. "SABRINA knows where." She nodded to SABRINA. "Can you—"

SABRINA saluted and disappeared from the room.

"May as well not go back empty-handed." Dr. Vasquez winked.

"I won't tell them you're out here," Jillian promised. Then, feeling dramatic, like something out of a movie, she blurted: "Your secret's safe with me."

Dr. Vasquez lifted her chin slightly at Jillian. "I know."

"But why don't you come back with us? You've studied the parasite. You know it better than anyone. If it's coming from something that made the swamp crater, then that's it, mystery solved, right? Why stay? Go home and tell everyone about your discovery. You'd be, like, a scientist superhero."

"Even if I wanted to, I'm hundreds of miles from the rendezvous site. I'd never make it in time for the portal without SABRINA."

"If I told them about you, they could send another portal for you. I'd come back through it to pick you up myself." As Jillian said it, she realized it was true. She'd almost been too scared to come to 80 UMa c in the first place, and yet here she was, volunteering for round two.

"I believe you," Dr. Vasquez replied.

"So why stay here? There's *nothing* here."

For a long moment Dr. Vasquez didn't answer, just tilted her head back to look up at the sky. "Yeah," she said at length, smiling a little. "That's kind of what I like about it."

When SABRINA led her back outside, Jillian tried for a moment to see 80 UMa c through Dr. Vasquez's eyes.

It wasn't as hard as she thought. The night was dark and clear, and smelled like rain had passed through recently.

The stars seemed to number in the millions. Except for the breeze and the sound of some distant thing that might have been a bird, it was silent. If she hadn't been so preoccupied earlier with the water and the worms, the hike to the waterfall would have been one of the high points of her year. She'd only just begun exploring, and it was almost time to leave. She wished her parents were here. Had they ever seen the waterfall? Or one of the alien deer up close? Had they looked up and made their own constellations from these stars?

Next year, she promised herself. *Either they'll have figured out how to get rid of the parasites here, or we'll go to some other planet instead. And everything else, all the storms and sharp grass and nature stuff, we'll be ready for. Just like old-time explorers had to be on Earth.*

For now she just took a minute and let herself be calm. She didn't let herself think about what had already happened, what might happen in a future she couldn't predict. She smoothed her mind to stillness and tried to lock this moment in her memory. The feel of the air, the smell of the breeze.

If she was on Earth, Jillian would have said it was maybe an hour before dawn, but she couldn't place exactly why she thought that. Something about the color of the sky, although a comparison to Earth sky was impossible since the number of suns and moons and stars, and the length of days and nights, were all wrong.

Maybe even especially the stars. The only time Jillian had ever seen so *many* of them back home was when the power cut out so she couldn't play video games before bed, and she'd go out onto the apartment balcony instead and wait for the lights of the city to flare back to life. There'd be stars then, so many stars it was impossible to count, with a massive splash of them running from one side of the sky to another, so dense it didn't even look like stars, just some jagged spill of light.

She'd looked it up and learned that the spill of light was actually the Milky Way, that she could look out from Earth and see the actual shape of the galaxy in which it spun. It occurred to her that she didn't know where Earth was from here. Which of these unfamiliar constellations it was part of. Or whether looking up at this night sky now she was even looking back toward Earth, or whether Earth was somewhere beyond her line of sight, and kids back there were looking up at her.

She could have asked SABRINA. SABRINA would know. But for once Jillian didn't actually want or need the answer. There was something comforting about being so very tiny, looking out at something so unbelievably vast. Like she could never be lost, not really, at least not any more than anybody else.

"Good to go?" SABRINA asked behind her.

Jillian turned.

There, completely eclipsing the cave entrance, was a dragon. It was the size of a school bus, and it gleamed gold and blue and reddish black. It lowered a wing for her to climb aboard.

When they rose into the sky, the stars looked close enough to touch.

CHAPTER 14

They flew for hours, into a rising sun and then beneath it as it climbed the sky. The second sun came up on Jillian's left, larger and warmer, and she shivered, grateful for the heat.

"Should've said something," said the dragon-SABRINA, and slow, delicious warmth began to radiate up from its back. Jillian snuggled in and watched the landscape of 80 UMa c go by.

They must have been approaching the crater from a different direction, because nothing looked familiar. There were wide-open plains of the razory grass; more forests; hills and valleys; a huge, dark jungle; and a lake draining into a river that seemed to go on forever, glittering shocky white like a giant bolt of lightning in the suns.

When they reached the ridge, SABRINA deposited Jillian directly on the boulder beside her parents. She pulled the backpack down after herself, and SABRINA unloaded the cargo of algae. It was dried and bundled, much smaller and lighter than Jillian had expected. It could have fit in a few duffel bags, no problem. "Don't get that wet," SABRINA cautioned her. "Unless you want us all to get buried under ten feet of stinky reconstituted plant matter."

More SABRINA was already busy prepping the next dose of painkillers for Jillian's parents.

"How're they doing?" she asked it.

"That's a complicated question with a complicated answer," SABRINA said. "The good news is, their wounds are healing nicely, thanks to Dr. Vasquez's stash of smart bandages. Infection's gone. See?" It peeled up an edge of a smart bandage to reveal fresh new skin on Jillian's mom's forearm. It looked different than before, shiny-smooth with scar tissue, but infinitely better than the burns.

"And the bad news?"

"Same bad news as before."

Jillian noticed that none of SABRINA was bandages anymore. Apart from the fluffy pillows and the feeding apparatus, it was all restraints. Even as she watched, some of the dragon detached and reallocated itself until Jillian's mom and dad looked much as they had when she'd first found them on the boulder. Totally cocooned.

"It's for their own good," SABRINA said gently.

"I know," Jillian said. She felt very tired all of a sudden. Tired and sad.

She checked the countdown clock, which SABRINA seemed to be leaving up all the time now. Two days, eight hours, twenty-one minutes, thirty seconds. *Just hold on a little longer*, she thought at her parents. *It'll be over soon.*

She dragged the backpack over and dumped it out on the rock. Then she unzipped all the outside pockets and dumped those too. SABRINA had been outrageously thorough. There was so much *stuff*. After all the soup and tea and the whole day's worth of emergency food bars she'd eaten, Jillian didn't have much of an appetite, but sorted through the supplies all the same. Partly out of curiosity, partly to pass the time.

That was all she really had to do now. Pass time. She should have been grateful for that. Instead, she was bored out of her skin.

There wasn't much in common with what she'd salvaged from the pod. No freeze-dried food packages or emergency bars. Jillian thought back on the obviously homemade soup, the tea, the three zillion planters full of alien vegetables, and wasn't terribly surprised.

After all, Dr. Vasquez had been out here a long time. StellaTech had been sending field crews to 80 UMa c for about eight months, her dad had said. But Dr. Vasquez hadn't been part of a field crew. She'd gone before that, and she'd gone alone. And ever since then, she'd remained alone, just her and SABRINA, fending for herself in the wilderness.

The survival movie fan in Jillian thought the idea had a certain appeal. But the rest of her, the part that had nearly been murdered by worms and grass and dehydration and free falls into pits and storms, disagreed.

She went through packets upon packets, all made of leaves. They contained an unfamiliar flatbread; something that was maybe some kind of alien nuts or seeds; and a kind of tough, unidentifiable thing that she thought was probably dried meat of some kind. There was also a knitted scarf like the one Dr. Vasquez had been wearing, which Jillian put on immediately. And a few more smart bandages. That posed a mystery for about five seconds, the fact that Dr. Vasquez still had smart bandages to spare. Either she was very careful and good at not getting injured, or—more likely, Jillian thought—SABRINA had been stealing them from the lab for her.

"Hey," SABRINA called over. "Earth to Jillian." Then as one register of its voice giggled at what it apparently thought was a fantastic joke, the rest of its voice said, "Pass me one of those water pouches, will you? The old supply ran out last night."

Jillian rooted through the pile until she came up with something that looked like an empty freeze-dried soup bag, heat-sealed shut (probably by SABRINA) and outfitted with a kind of valve that might have been an oxygen regulator from the pod. "This?"

"That's the one. Chuck that over."

Jillian carefully walked it over instead and handed it to SABRINA.

But as soon as the water left her hands, she realized she was thirsty. *Better to stay hydrated. There's plenty of water left.* She found a second water pouch, opened the valve, and drank.

More than she meant to. She hadn't thought she was that thirsty. *Careful*, she thought. At least the portal was due to arrive tomorrow. Running out of water now would be annoying, but it wouldn't kill them.

She found herself watching SABRINA tend to her parents. "Can you wake them?" she asked. "If they're not in pain anymore? Is that okay?"

"I could," SABRINA said, "but you don't want me to."

Jillian thought back on the footage SABRINA had played for her. Her parents trying to reach that swamp so forcefully, so violently, it had looked like they were trying to rip free of their own bodies to get there.

No. Not them. It wasn't *them* doing any of that. She had to remember that. Her parents were still her parents, still the same people they were before. But the parasite was piloting them, the way Jillian had piloted the SABRINA mech suit to salvage supplies from the pod. Except she hadn't controlled SABRINA's mind. They'd worked together. This was the exact awful opposite of that.

"No," she said, and sighed. "I guess I don't."

She fit everything back into the backpack, mostly to give herself something to do. Then she watched the countdown clock until it ticked down the last few minutes into *two days, seven hours, fifty-nine minutes*. She'd hoped the change of the hour section would feel like progress. It didn't.

She got up and stretched her back. Bounced up and down on her toes. Swung her arms around. Paced the top of the boulder a few times, eight steps and turn. That made her dizzy, so she stopped, gazing out over the place where the quadpod had gone down. No sign of the worms. They'd probably gone off after different prey, more alien deer probably, or down to the swamp to contribute their part to the parasite's life cycle.

Then an even stranger thing hit her. There was no sign of the pod either. It was utterly, completely gone. The worms must have devoured it all, down to the very last bolt.

Jillian thought of her dad explaining to her that the pods were made almost entirely of plastic, different densities of plastic. She thought of what Dr. Vasquez had said. *They love plastic. Maybe it's like junk food to them.*

She thought of Earth, how there were news stories every day about plastic, and none of them good. Plastic overflowing the landfills. Plastic that no amount of recycling could keep up with. So much plastic in the ocean that it gathered into entirely new islands, the way particles of SABRINA gathered bit by bit to make a whole new giant shape.

"Real world-saving stuff," she whispered to nobody in particular.

"Hmm?" SABRINA asked.

"Just something my dad said." Jillian was still dizzy. She tried to push it away. "Hey. While we're just here waiting, do you think you could go back to Dr. Vasquez's place and get me a few of those uninfected worms?"

"You know we *brought* food, right?"

"I'm serious. The ones in the cave don't have parasites. That's a proven fact. *And* they eat plastic. That's a proven fact too. You said the field crew that discovered the worms never brought any back to Earth." She paused for breath, shivering a little, and pointed down at the site where the devoured pod had been. "Maybe they should've."

SABRINA's sigh lasted easily fifteen seconds. "You're asking for so much decontamination protocol right now."

"I'll tell them to name the worms after you."

"Oh!" SABRINA brightened. "Well! Why didn't you say so?"

Excess bits of it were already gathering into a blob the size and shape of a large beanbag chair. Jillian raised an eyebrow at it.

"Do you really need to take that much?" she asked, gesturing at the SABRINA cocoons. "Does that leave enough here for my mom and dad?"

"Oh yeah." What was left of SABRINA gathered up before her in demonstration, floating shapelessly. It was smaller than the beanbag chair, smaller than the cocoons, smaller than Jillian. It turned into the six-legged dog again and sat before her, wagging its tail. Jillian wondered if SABRINA made this shape so much because it liked to, or if it had been a programmed preference the StellaTech people had given it. "See? Plenty left over. I move faster if I bring more. Besides, they're not going anywhere. I'll be back before you can say *major scientific breakthrough*."

"Major scientific breakthrough," Jillian said dryly.

"Well, you have to say it slower than *that*," SABRINA replied. "Silly."

Jillian watched as it lifted into the sky and drifted off northward. Then it was gone, and she was back to being bored. She shivered. Then went over to snag the water pouch and drank again.

"Hey," the SABRINA dog said. "Easy there."

"Huh?"

SABRINA gestured. The water pouch was noticeably emptier than before.

Jillian put it down and shivered again, harder this time. Her hands were shaking. She rearranged the scarf around her neck and put her hands in her pockets before she realized she wasn't cold. If anything, she was too warm. No, she was cold after all. She took the scarf off, put it back on. She paced a little more, antsy, and finally plopped down next to SABRINA.

SABRINA made her a fluffy pillow of her own. It was extremely comfy. She burrowed her face into it.

Time skipped. She lifted her head.

Two days, four hours, eighteen minutes, eighteen seconds.

"But I didn't fall asleep," she whispered to the countdown clock. At least she didn't *think* she had. Her mind felt hazy, sluggish, unreliable. She checked her forehead for fever. If anything it felt cool, clammy. Her breathing was uneven, ragged and heavy, like she'd just run up three flights of stairs. She blinked, and it felt like the slowest blink in the world, like her eyelids had slowed down, or the rest of her had sped up.

Wait, she told herself. *Just wait. Pass the time and wait. It will all be over soon.*

"So," she said, teeth chattering. "Tell me about those four hundred card tricks."

"Four hundred and thirteen," SABRINA said, beaming. Suddenly it was an octopus again, using at least four arms to elaborately shuffle a deck of cards that had appeared from nowhere. SABRINA was no specific color now, just flashing through an endless chain of multicolored patterns.

"That's to distract me, isn't it," Jillian said, pointing at a place on the octopus where a chessboard pattern met a pattern like ancient television static met a pattern like a flowered surfer shirt. Her voice sounded like someone else was speaking with it, like she was hearing it come back to her from far away. "From whatever's going on with the cards."

"If I explain the trick," SABRINA said in a voice like syrup, "it wouldn't be much of a trick, now would it?"

"I'll take that as a yes," Jillian replied, sweating under her goose bumps. "I can't even look at it, it's making me so dizzy."

"Outstanding!" SABRINA fanned cards at her from five different directions at once. "That's how you know it's working. Now pick a card. Any card."

Jillian shut her eyes and held out a hand. Her arm felt so heavy, so weak. Like there were rocks tied to her wrist. "Just give me one. I'm not looking."

"That's not how it works! You have to pick one. If you don't pick, then I could just hand you the one I want you to have, and you wouldn't be impressed. You picking the card is pretty much the entirety of the point. What do they even teach you humans in school?"

"Okay, okay," Jillian said, opening her eyes. Cards swam in her vision. Red and black, shapes and numbers. She plucked the queen of spades off an octopus sucker and looked quickly away. "Can I get you to cut it out, though, with the optical illusion stuff? It's making me want to hurl."

Muttering at the very bottom of its register, SABRINA blanched gray. "Happy?"

"Thrilled." Her stomach churned. She swallowed. "Actually, no. I don't feel so good. I think I looked at that too long. It's giving me a headache."

"Well, aren't we just a veritable cornucopia of complaints today?"

"Can you not? Right now? Like, for five minutes, can you just *not*."

Exactly three seconds of silence. Then it was the cuddly six-legged dog again. It curled up beside her, shining gigantic puppy eyes upon her like searchlights. "What's wrong? Can I help? I am very good at helping."

"No. I don't know. Sorry I yelled at you. I know Dr. Vasquez said you're just teasing me. It's—I just feel like I'm catching the flu or something. Can you get space flu? Is that a thing?"

"I don't know. But you very well could have been incubating a virus since before we got here. You humans are just giant sloshing bags of germs, you know. Germs and water. And complaints. And unquantifiable notions. And shoddy workmanship. And *spite*. And—"

"I don't know." Jillian's vision was swimming. She shut her eyes. "Maybe."

"Well, don't you fret. We'll get to the bottom of this. I am not qualified to offer medical care, but I *do* have an extensive database of symptoms. I can cross-reference yours if you list them."

"Thought you weren't"—Jillian shivered hard—"a med-bot."

"I happen to contain multitudes," SABRINA said loftily. "And I have watched over six thousand hours of hospital dramas on TV."

Jillian thought for a second. "Okay, so. I'm hot and cold. I can't decide which. Both at the same time, I guess. I feel sick to my stomach, and I'm really dizzy. And this headache is getting really"—pain spiked between her eyes, and she winced—"really super bad. Can you pass me the water?"

"You just drank half the container of water," SABRINA reminded her. "You probably have a fever. Dehydration is a symptom of that. I can check." It poked Jillian on one temple, *hmm*ed a little, shook its pointy-eared head. "Nope."

"But I'm thirsty."

"Okay. I'll give you a little. You can't really be that thirsty. And remember, if you drink it all, then we have to go back to the waterfall for more. Or else I could grab some from Dr. Vasquez's while I'm getting your worms, but it would slow me down, and—hey!"

Jillian blinked at SABRINA. She felt like she'd fallen asleep again. But she was wide awake. "Huh?"

SABRINA plucked the water pouch out of her hands and dangled it upside down. A few drops pattered out onto the boulder. Jillian stared at them.

"Hmm," SABRINA said. "I stand corrected. You were definitely thirsty. Let me check you again for that fever."

Jillian drew up her knees and rested her cheek on them, then wrapped her arms around her head. "I'll be fine. I'm fine. I just need some quiet."

"Yeah," SABRINA conceded, "I get that a lot." It retreated to the opposite side of the boulder where it clung deliberately to the very edge, tail swishing back and forth like a cat's. It grew eyebrows just to raise them at her quizzically: *There, is that better?*

Jillian shut her eyes and tried counting backward from a thousand. Sometimes that helped to put her to sleep.

But she wasn't tired. She felt like she'd never been tired before in her life, would never be tired again. Her brain sparked and fizzed like a live wire. She was outrageously, impossibly thirsty. And she'd forgotten how to count backward. She kept losing track of where she was. Before she'd reached nine hundred, she was lost and had to start again.

After three tries, she opened her eyes. Dizziness made the world yawn open before her, slowly spinning like the rotating eye of a storm.

She struggled to focus on the countdown clock. One day, nineteen hours, five minutes, fifty-nine seconds.

Time had skipped forward without her again. But she'd been awake. She must have been. Hadn't she just tried, and failed, to fall asleep?

Jillian crawled over to the water pouch and tried to open it, but couldn't remember how. After a moment she realized she was trying to gnaw through the side.

"SABRINA?" she croaked, or tried to. She wasn't sure if any sound came out.

248

Nevertheless, SABRINA was there. It said nothing, only took the water container from her, opened it, and handed it back, watching her very, very closely.

Jillian took the water pouch, went to raise it to her mouth—and stopped. She wasn't thirsty at all, she realized. She just wanted to look at the water. It was fascinating. It was the most interesting thing she'd ever seen. She couldn't stop staring into the opening. Down into the water. She was shivering with need.

But she wasn't thirsty. She wasn't thirsty at all.

Jillian's blood ran cold.

"SABRINA?" she said in the tiniest voice possible. Like if SABRINA couldn't hear her, it couldn't answer, and Jillian would never have to know. "You checked me, didn't you? For bites?"

"Yes," SABRINA said. "I told you that. Oh, human memories." It shook its head fondly. "So endearingly defective. So prone to error. So—*oh*." It looked at Jillian, then at the water pouch. "Ohhh. I get it! You think you're—"

But Jillian wasn't waiting around for SABRINA to reach its conclusions on its own. She was already shucking off her podsuit, then the jumpsuits, digging around under the bandages, looking for those telltale circular burns. She couldn't find any.

Then, slowly, hesitantly, already knowing what she'd find, she dug her fingers gently into her hair, probing her scalp for pain.

There was none. At least, none she could feel over the tremendous pounding in her head. It felt like something was drilling, one slow-motion millimeter at a time, into her brain. Even over the painkillers SABRINA had given her, which had dulled all her other aches and pains considerably.

Then her fingers hit it, and her whole body froze like a deer in the headlights of a car. There, where the back of her neck met her skull. A smooth patch, the size of a quarter, where the hair had burned away and the skin was raw and oozing. Only now that she poked it did she notice the pain.

Her terrified gaze met SABRINA's. "Bring the rest of yourself back," she hissed. "Now."

"I'm on my way back," SABRINA said. "I left Dr. Vasquez's place eighty-one minutes ago. Estimated time of arrival: one hour, forty-five minutes, thirty seconds."

"I don't know if I have that long," Jillian said. "Listen to me very carefully. Whatever I say after this, whatever I do, whatever I tell you to do, I need you to—ahhh!"

It felt like her head was exploding. Like her brain was fireworks and her skull was as fragile as an eggshell and something was hatching out of it, and there was nothing she could do to stop whatever was happening, and everything was pain. It built in her like a scream, grew and blossomed until the pain was bigger than her, was a monster that flew out of her and dragged her along behind into the darkness and—

—stopped. Everything was quiet. So, so quiet. Like her mind was a huge, dark room and something paced the floor of it, something that was not her, and she huddled in a corner, unable to speak or move or—

Time skipped.

She was crawling down off the boulder.

No, she thought. She tried to say it. She had forgotten how to speak. She had mostly forgotten how to think. Her brain was screaming one word, over and over, deafeningly loud. *Water. Water. Water.*

She was climbing—flopping—down the side of the boulder, rock to rock. Her arms had gone boneless, rubbery. Her legs weren't listening to her. She'd forgotten how to climb. How to protect herself in falls. Her body was not hers to drive, not now, not anymore. She face-planted, tasted blood.

SABRINA, she thought. *Help me.*

SABRINA was already there. Wrapping around her. Hauling her back to the top of the boulder. But Jillian, with the force of her need behind her, was too strong. She tore away, was grabbed and anchored, broke free, was grabbed again. Some muffled part of her mind remembered seeing this somewhere before.

Water, her brain shrieked at her in a voice like fingernails down a chalkboard.

No, she told it. She forced the word into her mouth and shouted it aloud. "No!"

But her body, and the thing that was in the pilot's seat of it, had other plans. She ripped free of SABRINA, spun loosely, and plummeted headfirst down the side of the boulder toward the crater like she was made of metal and the swamp was the strongest magnet in the universe.

SABRINA caught her, her face an inch from the ground. Dragged her back. "I didn't give you enough credit," it said.

"You are a *lot* stronger than you look."

Water, Jillian's brain howled. *WATER*.

She fought her way through the dark room that her mind had become. Pulled herself out of that emptiness, hand over hand. Grabbed SABRINA with both fists. She could barely remember how to speak. She reached down into the depths and pulled words out, one by one, and spat them out as fast as she could, before she forgot what they meant. "Do. *Not*. Let. Me. Drown."

SABRINA might have answered, but Jillian didn't hear it. She was back in the dark room, and all she could hear, all she could think, all she knew, was *water*.

She wrenched free of SABRINA, tried to stand. Toppled forward a few steps, momentum carrying her down the ridge—and fell. SABRINA had looped around her ankle. Now it sat on her, enveloping her, tying her wrists and ankles together, then her ankles to her wrists. She thrashed forward on her stomach one foot, then another, before SABRINA tackled her and held on. The swamp glittered in the distance, clotted and greenish in the sunlight. *Water*, her brain screamed, and she was driven forward, shredding the podsuit on the rocky ground.

SABRINA wrestled her over onto her back. Pushed something into her mouth. Something small and roundish. Then another.

She should know what those things were. She knew she should. She couldn't come up with words to match the objects to. SABRINA held her mouth and nose shut until she swallowed.

"Those will help you sleep," SABRINA said directly into her face. "Just like with your parents. While they kick in, try to stop fighting me, okay? It's getting really, really old."

I'm trying, Jillian tried to say, but she failed at that too. She threw herself over sideways and started inching toward the swamp. She felt her face strike rock, but the pain was dulled, distant, like everything. The dark room was her world now.

SABRINA said something else. Jillian heard the words but didn't understand them. Her brain roared *water*, and her muscles obeyed. How long would it take for the pills to kick in and put her to sleep? Too long. Much too long. The swamp loomed closer and closer in her vision as she struggled toward it, fighting SABRINA, fighting herself, at the mercy of the thing driving her. It wouldn't stop. She knew that. It wouldn't let her go until she was dead. If the rest of SABRINA didn't get back within the next few minutes, it would be too late.

But SABRINA wouldn't get back that soon. It couldn't. It was too far away. It would take much, much longer than that to arrive. When it got here, it would find Jillian with her head in the water like the alien deer way back by the falls, parasites climbing out of her nose. Then, if Dr. Vasquez had been right, once rid of the parasite, the host—Jillian—would be fine. Unharmed. Except that in order for the parasite to be gone, Jillian would have to drown. That was the life cycle. Those were the rules.

In the far deep bottom of Jillian's murky thoughts, something glinted.

if the parasite can be extracted or persuaded to leave through other means

Dr. Vasquez had said that. Why was that important? Jillian didn't know. She could barely comprehend the words anymore. *Water*, her mind screamed. *Water* was the only word she knew.

No. *Water* was the only word *it* knew. The parasite. Not Jillian. She was still there, she could *feel* herself still there, buried deep, like her mind had been packed with mud, and thoughts could not get through.

Think, she told herself. *You have to think. There is an answer here. But it's up to you to find it.*

Extracted or persuaded to leave through other means.

Persuaded to leave through other means.

She had a brief mental flash of SABRINA fanning cards at her. Blaring patterns in her face to confuse her eyes and mind.

Trick, she thought. *You have to trick it.*

She was at the edge of the swamp now, the water close enough to touch. Then she was in it, splashing face-first. She had seconds at most.

The thought of it—of what she knew she had to do—froze her solid with fear. Her whole body screamed its panic alarms, all of them at once. But she had no choice. This was the only way.

"SABRINA," she said. It was such an effort to move her mouth, make words. But she had to. This was her only chance. "Breathing—tube. Not nose. Just—mouth. Then let go."

Did SABRINA understand her? She wasn't sure. She wasn't sure of anything. Only that the water was there, *right* there, and the noise of the thing in her brain was deafening. Louder than the waterfall. Louder than anything.

She felt something press against the lower half of her face. It was either SABRINA or something unspeakable from the swamp. And then her whole face was underwater. In the swamp. Where the parasite had driven her to die. She hadn't even had time to take a deep breath first. She was, suddenly, just *there*.

Please be SABRINA, she thought. *Please be a breathing tube.* And then she forced herself to breathe through her mouth.

Air. SABRINA had made her the breathing tube. Jillian funneled all her concentration, all her focus, all her will into breathing through her mouth, only through her mouth, over and over. She stayed there like that, face in the swamp, and felt the parasite wriggle free of her brain, down through her nose and out. She felt it leave. Then another, and another.

When the last one left, her mind went blank. Nothing was left in there to shout her to her death. The silence somehow seemed louder than the sound.

Jillian struggled upright. It was impossible with her wrists and ankles tied up. "SABRINA," she tried to say into the mouthpiece of the breathing tube, "it's okay, it's me, it's over."

She had no idea how she must sound. But SABRINA

figured it out. The restraints vanished, and SABRINA dragged her out of the swamp. That was much easier now that Jillian wasn't fighting it. She lay limp on the shore of the water with her face in the air and just *breathed*.

"Hey," SABRINA said. It was crouching on Jillian's chest, flicking bits of disgusting swamp nonsense off her face and shoulders. "I just got the best idea."

"Yeah?" Jillian coughed. "What's that?"

"Let's never, ever, ever do that again."

CHAPTER 15

One day, eighteen hours, fifty-two minutes, thirty-three seconds.

One day, eighteen hours, fifty-two minutes, thirty-two seconds.

One day, eighteen hours, fifty-two minutes, thirty-one seconds.

"It doesn't go faster if you stare at it," SABRINA told her.

"I still think we should try it on my mom and dad," Jillian said. "The thing with the mouthpiece and the breathing tube."

SABRINA shook its head. It was a dinosaur again, something like a velociraptor but larger. A deinonychus, maybe. Light glinted off its feathers. "Too risky. You know that. They can't control their breathing if they're not awake. And if we wake them up they'll be violent. I can't guarantee their safety." It sighed. "Maybe if I were a medbot . . ."

"I'd take you over ten thousand medbots," Jillian said,

and meant it. "Let's try those card tricks again. No flashy patterns this time. Either you trick me or you don't."

"Alrighty," SABRINA said. Cards appeared from nowhere, fanned out between its six-inch claws. "Pick a card. Any card."

One day, eighteen hours, twenty-six minutes, twenty-nine seconds.

The painkiller pills were kicking in hard. Jillian was starting to feel seriously out of it. Like she'd stayed up way, way, way past her bedtime. She went to hand her latest card—the three of diamonds—back to SABRINA, then stopped.

"I'm so tired I only just figured out why you keep tricking me with these," she said blearily. She was fading fast. It was all she could do to string the sentence together. "You already know what *all* the cards are because *they're all you.*"

"What! Pssshh. *No.*"

"When we get back," Jillian managed, yawning hugely, "try to beat me at something fair and square, why don't you."

"Intriguing." One claw reached up and stroked SABRINA's scaly chin thoughtfully. "What do you propose?"

"Dunno. You're semi-intelligent; I'm sure you can think of something you won't cheat at."

"*Semi-autonomous,*" SABRINA corrected her, fluffing its feathers indignantly. "Fully, glitteringly, top-shelf, weapons-grade *intelligent.* I would have thought you would have noticed that by—"

Then it caught sight of Jillian's face.

"Gotcha," she said.

And then, just like that, she was asleep.

One day, four hours, twenty-six minutes, sixteen seconds.

When Jillian woke, she was suddenly, ravenously hungry. So she and SABRINA set about putting together a feast. There was all the food from Dr. Vasquez's cave-house, plus the stuff from the pod that hadn't yet been eaten. There wasn't enough water for all of it, and nobody wanted to go to the falls for more, so Jillian settled for dumping a bit of water into the remaining three servings of instant blueberry crumble and stirring in some soy-milk powder to add protein and thus make it, in her estimation, a totally balanced meal. She broke up a few little chunks of the weirdly cookie-like food bars on top and ate the whole thing directly out of the bag with her fingers.

The sugar ran from her stomach to her brain like fire along a fuse. She hopped up and tried to do some exercises with all her newfound energy. There wasn't a lot she could do while on top of a boulder. She paced a little, attempted some action-movie kicks to stretch her legs, tried to do some jumping jacks, realized she was way too full to do those comfortably, and sat back down.

"Come *on*," she groaned, throwing both arms out toward where the portal would arrive. "Hurry *up*, already."

It didn't listen. But she hadn't really expected it to.

Nineteen hours, two minutes, seven seconds.

Jillian and SABRINA sat side by side on the edge of the boulder, kicking their legs out over the drop. One pair of human legs, one pair of nameless appendages that properly belonged to no creature on any planet that Jillian knew.

They played I Spy and Alphabet and every other time-passing, long-car-ride game dredged up out of Jillian's memory. They sang silly songs. They told ghost stories. SABRINA made a chessboard and thrashed Jillian ten games straight, without even cheating. Then they played checkers, with similar results.

Eventually they worked their way down the line to charades. Jillian was a lot better at guessing than SABRINA was, possibly because SABRINA could replicate the thing it was thinking of perfectly. It didn't even seem to be aware it was doing that. Jillian, victorious, decided not to bring it up. After the thing with the cards, she figured they were even.

The countdown clock ticked down and down. The rest of SABRINA hadn't returned.

Eight hours, eleven minutes, twenty seconds.

There was a question Jillian had been kicking around her mind, unspoken, for a full two hours now. Finally, she asked it.

"If you'd just, like, decided to leave the rest of yourself here," Jillian said, "you'd let me know, right?"

"I assumed you assumed I'd be doing that," SABRINA replied. "Don't you think it'd look a little weird if I came back to Earth three times bigger than I'd been when I left? They'd throw you straight into questioning." SABRINA raised its voice an octave, high-pitched and stern, like a mean teacher in a cartoon. *What on Earth have you been feeding our probe, biped?* A mess for everyone. Very ill-advised."

"But—"

"Don't you worry," SABRINA said. "I'll bring you your disgusting plastic-eating worms. Just hang tight, okay? Little detour."

"Little? You've been gone for ages! The portal's going to be here soon!"

"Humans," SABRINA said tenderly. "*So* high-strung."

"You're one to talk," Jillian muttered. "So hey. About that sword."

It appeared in Jillian's hand, exactly as awesome-looking as it was before. It grew a little face and grinned at her. "I thought you'd never ask."

Two hours, thirty-eight minutes, twenty-two seconds.

The rest of SABRINA finally arrived while Jillian was gathering all her wrappers and empty water container and other garbage into a careful pile. She didn't want to be the one who brought the human tradition of littering to 80 UMa c. Besides, she thought the time would pass faster if she *did* something, kept herself busy. So she made her pile and stuffed it into the backpack Dr. Vasquez had given her.

She didn't hear or see SABRINA arrive, just realized between one moment and the next that she was standing in the shadow of something big enough to block the sun. She glanced up, and there was another dragon like the one that had carried her here, except this one looked like it had been dipped in black glitter. Before Jillian could so much as say hello, part of it turned into the six-legged dog and dropped straight out of the air, ten feet directly above Jillian's head.

It parted around her as it landed and reformed. It jumped up on her, knocked her down, and stood on her stomach, licking her face.

"Um," Jillian said. "Hi?"

"You did not die," the SABRINA-dog said. "That was excellent work, the not-dying."

"You knew what happened," Jillian said. "You were *there*."

"I wanted to deliver a formal statement. I would have done so earlier, but you were busy snoring like Bigfoot *again*. Why *do* humans need so much sleep? It's so inefficient!"

"You made me sleep, SABRINA, remember? Both times."

"Oh. Well, never mind." SABRINA raised its two front legs and gestured down at Jillian lying pinned on the rock. "Besides, as you can see, this way I have a—"

It paused.

"Yes?"

"—*wait* for it—"

Jillian waited.

"—*captive* audience!"

"Off," Jillian said. "Now."

SABRINA evaporated, and Jillian stood.

There, just behind where SABRINA had been, was Dr. Vasquez, wearing a backpack, carrying a jar of worms.

At first Jillian thought this was just another form SABRINA had assumed. But no—that was SABRINA over there, in the shape of the alien deer they'd tracked through the forest the other day.

Jillian turned to it, speechless.

"Detour," SABRINA said smugly.

"Yeah," Jillian said. "I can see that." She whirled back to Dr. Vasquez, convinced she'd have disappeared the second Jillian looked away. She hadn't. "How'd you even—I thought you were, like, a million miles away!"

"Not quite," Dr. Vasquez said, with a fraction of a smile. "And I started making my way back on foot after I spoke with you. SABRINA came and met me halfway. Well. Rather more than halfway. Luckily there was a river between my location and yours, and it was flowing in the right direction."

"I," SABRINA declared, "was a *boat*."

"You were a superlative boat," Dr. Vasquez said, scritching it behind its alien deer ears. Then, to Jillian: "It's nice to meet you in person."

"You too," Jillian replied. "But I don't get it. I thought you were staying out there."

"Well, I was." Dr. Vasquez lifted her chin at Jillian. "But I've been thinking about what you said."

Fifty-nine minutes, fourteen seconds.

SABRINA and Dr. Vasquez had gone down to the swamp to take core samples, Dr. Vasquez in a full-body SABRINA suit and carrying more jars. Her suit, Jillian noted, had no shark fin and no sword.

They'd been gone awhile. Here and there, their voices drifted up out of the crater, talking—to Jillian's ear—nonsense. Surveyor stuff. She didn't know. But she hoped they'd find whatever they were looking for down there.

She went and sat beside her parents. "Hey," she told them. "You, uh, probably still can't hear me. But just in case you can, I wanted to let you know that we're going to get out of here. It's okay. We got through it, and we're going home. You're going to go straight to the hospital, and they're going to fix you right up. It's going to be . . ."

She trailed off. It was stupid. They couldn't hear her. Suddenly she wanted to shake them, wake them up, get SABRINA up here to make them breathing tubes and mouthpieces the way it'd done for her, and trick the parasites out of them herself.

But deep down she knew it was too risky. It had only worked on her because she'd still been partly herself. Jammed down, muted out, trapped in the far back of the dark room, but still *there* enough to have the presence of mind not to breathe through her nose once her face had gone into the water. Her parents had just been infected too long. The parasite was too much in control.

She wished she could fix them herself. Fix everything herself. Just her and SABRINA, like they'd been doing all week. The idea of her brave, awesome space-explorer parents being carried home unconscious while this *thing* rode around in their brains made her feel helpless and angry and sad all at once. She dropped her face into her hands and didn't raise it until she heard Dr. Vasquez's voice behind her.

"Can't win 'em all, kid."

"Yeah," Jillian said, hurriedly wiping her eyes on the podsuit sleeve. "No. I know. It's just—" She threw up her arms in exasperation. "They were so excited to have me to come with them on this mission, you know? They kept saying how proud of me they were. Like it made them really happy to have me come with them, and the last thing they probably thought before SABRINA put them to sleep was how I was going to die out here because it was too much for me to handle."

"You're worried they're in there somewhere thinking you're dead, is that it?"

"No. Maybe. I don't know! I—" Jillian paused, trying to put her thoughts in order. "I've always been kind of scared of doing new things. It's like I freeze up? My brain doesn't work right? For no good reason. It's annoying."

Dr. Vasquez nodded. "Fear of the unknown. Maybe a little anxiety on top of it. It's very common."

"You don't understand. I almost didn't come here. I almost didn't let them talk me into it. Even though I've always wanted to go! They just kind of *dropped* it on me out of nowhere, and I didn't have enough time to decide what I wanted to do. My lists were all at home and all the stuff I wanted to pack to bring to space, but they kept saying how proud of me they were, and I just . . . I couldn't let them down."

For a long moment Dr. Vasquez was silent. Then she pointed at the cocoons. "You think this is letting them down."

Jillian nodded, miserable. "I tried. I really did. But the only reason we're still alive is because of SABRINA. I didn't do *anything*."

An even longer silence met that, and she sighed. "Sorry. I'm babbling. I know none of that makes any sense, but—"

"You know there's footage of everything that happened to you this week, right?" Dr. Vasquez said. "You, your mom and dad, all of it. Everything. And you, I'm sorry to say, are quantifiably wrong."

Jillian blinked at her. "What?"

Dr. Vasquez raised one finger and pointed at the sky. Jillian looked up.

Above, the countdown clock shimmered and turned into an image of Jillian looking up into the sky. Then the image skipped backward and showed Jillian blinking at Dr. Vasquez. "What?" the image-Jillian said. Then it rewound, replayed. "What?"

Then a few more seconds of skipping and there was Jillian again, telling SABRINA her idea about bringing the plastic-eating worms back home to Earth. More skipping, and Jillian was putting together her theory of how the swamp had formed, and where the parasites had come from. More skipping and she was braving the uncharted wilderness of 80 UMa c to bring her parents water. Trying to save the alien deer by the falls. Learning from that failure in order to save *herself* when she became infected too. Ordering SABRINA to abandon her in the storm so it could help her parents. Refusing to go back through the portal without them. It went on and on and on.

Jillian watched, stunned. *I did all that*, she thought. *That wasn't SABRINA. That was me.*

Dr. Vasquez clapped Jillian on the shoulder, then pulled her in for an awkward sideways hug. "They're gonna be proud of you," she said. "Trust me on that one."

Twenty-three minutes, five seconds.

Together they brought everything down from the boulder to the top of the ridge. Jillian's backpack, Dr. Vasquez's backpack, the bundles of dried algae, the jar of worms, the core samples that SABRINA had obtained from the swamp site. These were cylindrical chunks of rock, each as long as Jillian's arm, which Dr. Vasquez carefully wrapped in a tarp and insisted on carrying to the rendezvous point herself.

Last they brought down Jillian's parents. SABRINA did most of the heavy lifting, but Jillian and Dr. Vasquez helped as best they could.

From the bottom of the boulder, they took everything to the rendezvous point. The exact spot where the portal had appeared before. It would zap into existence in—Jillian checked—seventeen minutes, fifty seconds. Hard to believe. It felt like she'd just gotten here. Or that she'd been here forever. She couldn't tell which.

"Don't get too comfy there," SABRINA advised Jillian.

Jillian, resting on a rock near the portal site, raised an eyebrow.

"Unless you *want* to get sliced in half when the portal arrives, that is," SABRINA said. "In which case, be my guest."

Jillian shot upright like that rock was on fire.

"It's like I keep telling you," Dr. Vasquez told SABRINA. "You give such fantastic advice, but you have *got* to work on your delivery."

Ten minutes, eighteen seconds.

Dr. Vasquez was still there.

SABRINA—all of it—was still there.

"You're staying?" Jillian asked them. "You're coming back through?"

Dr. Vasquez shrugged. "Thought I might give it a try." She tapped the tarp-wrapped core samples. "I'll be better equipped to study these back on Earth anyway. Besides, I think you're on to something with your worm hypothesis. After the whole abandoning the mission thing and the other faking my death thing, I might not have too much weight to throw around at StellaTech anymore, but I'll do what I can to make your case and get your premise some funding. Besides, I want to make sure they know exactly what they're dealing with when they operate on your mom and dad. I know the parasite better than anyone." She grinned at Jillian. "Present company excluded."

Jillian turned to SABRINA. "And what about you, you epic pain in the butt? You coming too?"

"*Legendary* pain in the butt, thank you very much," SABRINA replied. "And yes. It'd be boring here if it's just me here alone. I get bored easily. I believe I warned you about that. It's not pretty."

"You did mention that, yes."

"So I thought we could maybe hang out more. You could come visit me in the lab. And I could maybe, I dunno, take some little field trips of my own." This last part came from inside Jillian's podsuit pocket.

"You are *not* smuggling yourself home with me," Jillian said. "Decontamination protocol, remember? You'll get in trouble!"

"Oh please. I seem to remember *also* explaining to you that I am *sneaky*."

"I'm not hearing this," Dr. Vasquez said. "I hear absolutely nothing. I am also not mentioning that most of these SABRINA particles have been written off as lost already. If a few get lost on their way back to the lab, I don't think anyone will notice." She paused. "Is what I would be saying if I were saying anything remotely on this topic, which I most assuredly am not. SABRINA, stop recording."

"I stopped recording five minutes ago," SABRINA said. "Weird glitch or something. Whoops. Oh, here we are. Back online. So strange when that happens."

Three minutes, nine seconds.

Two minutes, forty-one seconds.

One minute, fifty-eight seconds.

Five seconds.

Four.

Three.

Two.

One.

The portal blinked into existence, silent and vast. Jillian expected more noise, more drama, more *something*—but no. It wasn't there, and then it just *was*, glowing gently against the dark green evening sky.

"Home again, home again," SABRINA sang. "Decontamination protocol, here we come."

Carrying everything between them, they stepped toward the portal together.

One day, nine hours, fourteen minutes later.

The first thing Jillian noticed about her parents' hospital room was that it smelled like flowers. As the door slid shut behind her and Aunt Alex, the source of the smell became clear. Over by the window was the biggest bouquet of day-lilies Jillian had ever seen, all the colors of sunrise and sunset and flame.

"Weirdest thing," Jillian's mom said. "Never gotten flowers from a dead person before."

Jillian blinked, thinking she must have heard this wrong. "Huh?"

"Check out the card," her dad told her.

Jillian crossed the room to the window and plucked the card from the bouquet.

Welcome back to Earth
from another who's been away.
—Meredith

"That's from the woman you met out there?" Aunt Alex asked, reading over Jillian's shoulder. "That missing surveyor from a few years ago?"

"I can't believe you found her," Jillian's dad said. "She's a legend. She pretty much single-handedly invented SA-BRINA."

"It's more like she found me," Jillian replied. "Well, she had some help."

Jillian's mom shifted uncomfortably, and Aunt Alex dashed over to help her with her pillows. "We watched some of the footage from the expedition," she told Jillian as Aunt Alex poured her some water, "but there are some gaps in it where SABRINA's recording went wonky, and anyway, we're both dying to hear your side of it. You must have had one heck of a week."

A week, Jillian thought. No matter how often she reminded herself, it still came as a shock. She couldn't tell whether it felt like forever ago she'd gone through the portal to 80 UMa c, or just yesterday. "Yeah," she said at last, "I guess I did."

"We're really sorry," her dad said. "We'd hoped it would be an adventure, but we had no idea it would be quite so *much* of one. We'd planned more along the lines of: collect some alien plants, show off our cool tech, have space picnics, sleep under alien stars. Like those camping trips we never get to take you on. Weren't really figuring on"—he gestured widely at the hospital room, then winced and lowered his arms again—"*this*."

"You saved our lives," her mom added. "I know you know that, but it bears repeating. You always think as a parent, it's your job to protect your kid, but you literally saved both our lives and then kept them saved. Again and again and again. I just keep rewatching some parts of SABRINA's footage, but I'm still not over it. It's unbelievable what you did. Really unbelievable."

Jillian felt a smile quirk up one side of her mouth. "Well," she said, "I had some help too."

"I think next year," her dad said, "when it comes time for Take Your Kid to Work Day, we all just call in sick and go to the movies. Sound good?"

"Works for me," Jillian's mom said.

"I second that," said Aunt Alex.

Jillian's dad must have noticed her silence. "Jillian?"

"I don't know," she said. "Will there be parasites next year?"

"Now that we know how to have SABRINA check for them," her mom said, "we wouldn't go if there were. We'd go someplace we absolutely knew was safe, or they'd have to send a different team. We can't put ourselves both at risk like that again. It was a bad call." She paused, wrinkling her brow at Jillian. "Why?"

"We can go to the movies anytime. But we still haven't had a camping trip in space."

They said their goodbyes, and then Jillian and Aunt Alex left so that Jillian's parents could rest.

"The doctors said they should be discharged in about a week," Aunt Alex said as they walked up to the hospital parking lot to find her car. "Guess it's the usual stay at my place after all." She gave Jillian's shoulder a playful bump. "But that gives you loads of time to tell me all about your big space adventure. I mean, if that's okay. I don't want to make you talk about things you'd rather forget, you know?"

"Nah," Jillian said, "it's cool. You want me to start from the planet? Or the lab?"

"Oh, the lab for sure," Aunt Alex said. "I've never even *seen* inside. Let's pick up a pizza on the way back, and then we'll have all afternoon to catch up on . . ."

Jillian glanced over. "Something wrong?"

"Oh," Aunt Alex said. "No. I just noticed your pin. I like it. Is it new?"

Jillian reached up to the collar of her jacket and brushed the pin. It was a tiny octopus, glowing blue-white like a distant star. It was intricately detailed, right down to the suckers, clinging to Jillian's jacket with six arms while the other two hung loosely, moving slightly in what was almost definitely the breeze.

"Thanks," Jillian said. "Yeah, I just got it, actually. It was a welcome-home present. From a friend."

AFTERWORD

I usually write books for adults and teens, but my mom always told me I should try writing a book for kids. It took me a long time to do it. I thought it was a good idea but had no clue what to write about. Eventually I realized I had a lot of loose bits of stories that didn't belong to any books yet. I wanted to write . . . something . . . with mind-control parasites, and . . . something . . . with an artificially intelligent shape-shifting nanobot swarm. And . . . something else . . . that involved a survival story, and . . . maybe something . . . in space.

The way I always write books goes like: *come up with a bunch of loose ideas, then glue them together and see what happens.* The story itself usually comes about organically, out of the motivations and actions (and occasional very bad ideas) of the characters, once I get to know them in my head. But the loose bits of *stuff* are always the framework, such as they are.

Once I had all this stuff together(ish), I asked my son Julian if he wanted me to put him in a book. He said yes, so my next question was: is it okay if I make the character based on him a girl? There are *so* many science fiction adventure stories with boy protagonists, and very, very few starring girls. He was totally on board with that, so I had him pick out a name that sounded a bit like his. He picked "Jillian."

There's a lot of my son in this book. He loves survival stories—*Hatchet* by Gary Paulsen is the classic, so if you like survival stories and you haven't read that one, check it out!—and he loves science and camping, and adventures. He also has anxiety, which sometimes gets in the way of his love of these things.

Jillian has anxiety, just like him. I've been frustrated for a long time by how books and movies usually show anxiety in kids as analogous to shyness, where in reality anxiety can look very, *very* different. The most socially outgoing kid in the world can still have debilitating anxiety. Anxiety in kids can look like:

- extreme grumpiness
- extreme quiet
- overthinking! absolutely! everything! out loud!!
- fidgetiness (my kid will literally rip hangnails back to the cuticle)
- mixed messages (I love this/I hate this)
- shutting down/zoning out/lack of interest
- sudden fixating interest

- sudden gregariousness
- asking the same question eleven billion times

All of this is totally normal with anxiety! But without that representation in books and movies, and with the insistence of portraying anxiety as shyness, full stop, it was actually really difficult to figure out those behaviors in my son. He worked with some therapists who diagnosed him with a generalized anxiety disorder, and reading up on it made a lot of stuff make a lot of sense. I decided to be as patient as humanly possible with the mood swings and the zoning out and the overthinking narrative and the million, billion questions, and as he got older, he learned some coping mechanisms to help him get through anxiety episodes. He's come a really long way, and I'm super proud of him. But I have anxiety too, and I always have, so I realize he's in it for the long haul, just like Jillian and me. And I don't view it as something "wrong with him" to be "cured." All our brains are wired a little differently. It's what makes us unique.

Still, I felt it was important to write a book that represented a kid with anxiety in the way that I had seen it firsthand, and for her to realize her own strength as the story progressed. At the time of writing, Julian was eleven (like Jillian!) and struggling a lot with second-guessing his own abilities and relying on people to figure things out for him, so I wanted my main character to be put in a position where there were no other people to figure things out for her, and she would get stronger and stronger as she realized what she was capable of.

When I was a kid, and I was overthinking literally every-thing out loud at *my* mom, she used to tell me to pause and think about—really think about! In detail!—the absolute worst thing that could come of whatever it was I was so fixated on. When I was learning to swim, for instance, she'd say: *Okay, what's the absolute worst thing that could happen?* And I'd say: *Well, I'll drown, obviously.* And I'd start think-ing about exactly what that would feel like, and how scary it would be, and my whole mind would start spiraling. And she'd say: *Well, maybe someday* (no point in sugar-coating things for anxiety kids. THEY KNOW), *but not today, you won't, because I'm right here! Do you think I'd let you drown?* And then my logical brain would have to kick in—anxiety kids are GREAT at logic! Remember the overthinking?—and I'd realize, *Well, no, of course my mom won't let me drown in three feet of water in a public pool with a lifeguard sitting right there. Anyway, that's ridiculous.* And that slapped my anxiety brain down a few notches for a few hours, and I learned how to swim. And by learning to swim, the chances of my ever drowning dropped dramatically!

Sometimes the absolute worst thing is honestly pretty bad. The world can be scary. But if you have anxiety—like Jillian, and Julian, and me—then you probably already know that. What I'm here to tell you is that no matter how loud and persistent and imaginative your what-if brain is, *it's usually wrong.*

One last thing: I probably couldn't have written this book, or any book, if I didn't have anxiety. The same what-if brain that loooves to come up with worst-case scenarios to scare you with? It's the same thing you do when you're trying to put your book characters in tricky situations that they have to figure out how to solve. My anxiety has messed with me my whole life, so I figured out how to make it work for me. Kind of like a superpower you have to learn how to control.

Lastly, and maybe most importantly? I read somewhere that almost *five million kids* in the United States have anxiety that's been diagnosed by a doctor, and probably more than that many who have undiagnosed anxiety. And that's in only one country! So the thing to remember is, anxiety can be terrifying, and frustrating, and really, really, *really* hard to deal with—but you're not in this alone. If you think you have anxiety, talk to a parent or a teacher, and you can figure out how to fight it—and maybe how to make it work for you—together.

ACKNOWLEDGEMENTS

Thanks to my mom, who taught me to read, and my dad, who got me reading science fiction. Also to the rest of my family and all my friends for their support over the years. And to my weirdo cat, who isn't (probably) going to read this, but there's a lot of her in SABRINA, so I didn't want to leave her out. And speaking of SABRINA, its name comes from a brainstorming session with Dan Stace, who kept throwing cool adjectives at me, and then I sat and stared at a wall for three hours until I figured out which ones I wanted to keep, which ones I wanted to add, and how best to put them in order. Teamwork! And of course to Kate McKean, best agent ever. I had the general idea for this story a while before I thought of a good reason why Jillian would be going to space with her parents in the first place, so I asked Kate and it took her about two seconds to come back with "It's Take Your Kid to Work Day!" Problem solved. Like I said. Best agent ever.

Lastly, thanks to you for reading! I hope you enjoyed Jillian's and SABRINA's space adventure as much as I enjoyed writing it. If you have any questions or comments, please feel free to contact me at www.nicolekornherstace. com. I'd love to hear from you!

Nicole Kornher-Stace is the author of the Norton Award finalist *Archivist Wasp* and its sequel, *Latchkey*. Her short fiction has appeared in *Uncanny, Clarkesworld, Fantasy Magazine,* and many anthologies. Her latest novel, *Firebreak,* is an adult SF thriller forthcoming from Saga in 2021. She lives in New Paltz, NY with her family. She can be found online on Twitter @wirewalking.